THE LAST APPRENTICE

NIGHT *of* THE SOUL STEALER

·BOOK THREE·

THE LAST APPRENTICE

NIGHT OF THE SOUL STEALER

Illustrations by
PATRICK ARRASMITH

JOSEPH DELANEY

GREENWILLOW BOOKS
An Imprint of HarperCollinsPublishers

The Last Apprentice: Night of the Soul Stealer
Copyright © 2006 by Joseph Delaney

First published in 2006 in Great Britain by The Bodley Head, an imprint of Random House Children's Books, under the title *The Spook's Secret*. First published in 2007 in the United States by Greenwillow Books.

Illustrations copyright © 2007 by Patrick Arrasmith

The text of this book is set in Cochin.
Book design by Chad W. Beckerman and Paul Zakris.

Library of Congress Cataloging-in-Publication Data
Delaney, Joseph, (date).
Night of the soul stealer / Joseph Delaney ; illustrations by Patrick Arrasmith
p.cm. — (The last apprentice; bk. 3.)
"Greenwillow Books."
Summary: Tom is dismayed when his master the Spook decrees that they will be spending the winter on gloomy and forbidding Anglezarke Moor but soon discovers the reason for his master's decision, as they tangle with two dangerous witches and struggle to keep a dark mage from resurrecting an ancient evil
ISBN-13: 978-0-06-076624-5 (trade bdg.) ISBN-10: 0-06-076624-7 (trade bdg.)
ISBN-13: 978-0-06-076625-2 (lib. bdg.) ISBN-10: 0-06-076625-5 (lib. bdg.)
[1. Apprentices—Fiction. 2. Supernatural—Fiction. 3. Witches—Fiction.] I. Title.
PZ7.D373183 Nig 2007 [Fic] 22 2006051423

First American Edition 10 9 8 7 6 5 4 3 2 1

Greenwillow Books

FOR MARIE

NIGHT *of* THE SOUL STEALER

CHAPTER I
An Unexpected Visitor

IT was a cold, dark November
night, and Alice and I were sitting by
the kitchen fire with my master, the
Spook. The weather had been getting
steadily colder, and I knew that any day
now the Spook would decide it was
time to set off for his "winter house" on
the bleak moor of Anglezarke.

I was in no rush to go. I'd only been

the Spook's apprentice since the spring and had never seen the Anglezarke house, but my curiosity certainly wasn't getting the better of me. I was warm and comfortable here in Chipenden, and that's where I'd rather have spent the winter.

I glanced up from the book of Latin verbs I was trying to learn, and Alice caught my eye. She was sitting on a low stool close to the hearth, her face bathed in the warm glow of the fire. She smiled and I smiled back. Alice was the other reason I didn't want to leave Chipenden. She was the closest I'd ever had to a friend, and she'd saved my life on a number of occasions over the last few months. I'd really enjoyed having her living here with us. She made the loneliness of a spook's life more bearable. But my master had told me in confidence that she would be leaving us soon. He'd never really trusted her because she came from a family of witches. He also thought she would start to distract me from my lessons, so when the Spook and I went to Anglezarke, she wouldn't be coming with us. Poor Alice didn't know this, and I hadn't the heart to tell her, so for now I was just enjoying another of our last precious evenings together in Chipenden.

But as it turned out, that was to be our last one of the year: as Alice and I sat reading by the glow of the fire and the Spook nodded off in his chair, the tolling of the summoning bell shattered our peace. At that unwelcome sound, my heart sank right down into my boots. It meant only one thing: spooks' business.

You see, nobody ever came up to the Spook's house. For one thing, they'd have been ripped to pieces by the pet boggart that guarded the perimeter of the gardens. So, despite the failing light and the cold wind, it was my job to go down to the bell in the circle of willow trees to see who needed help.

I was feeling warm and comfortable after my early supper, and the Spook must have sensed my reluctance to leave. He shook his head as if disappointed in me, his green eyes glittering fiercely.

"Get yourself down there, lad," he growled. "It's a bad night and whoever it is won't want to be kept waiting!"

As I stood up and reached for my cloak, Alice gave me a small, sympathetic smile. She felt sorry for me, but I could also see that she was happy to sit there warming her hands while I had to go out into the bitter wind.

I closed the back door firmly behind me and, carrying a lantern in my left hand, strode through the western garden and down the hill, the wind trying its very best to tear the cloak from my back. At last I came to the withy trees, where two lanes crossed. It was dark, and my lantern cast disturbing shadows, the trunks and branches twisting into limbs, claws and goblin faces. Above my head the bare branches were dancing and shaking, the wind whining and wailing like a banshee, a female spirit that warned of a death to come.

But these things didn't worry me much. I'd been to this spot before in the dark, and on my travels with the Spook I'd faced such things that would make your hair stand on end. So I wasn't going to be bothered by a few shadows; I expected to be met by someone far more nervous than I was. Probably some farmer's lad sent by his ghost-plagued dad and desperate for help; a lad who'd be scared just to come within half a mile of the Spook's house.

But it wasn't a lad waiting in the withy trees, and I halted in amazement. There, beneath the bell rope, stood a tall figure dressed in a dark cloak and hood, a staff in his left hand. It was another spook!

The man didn't move so I walked toward him, halting just a couple of paces away. He was broad-shouldered and slightly taller than my master, but of his face I could see little as the hood kept his features in shadow. He spoke before I could introduce myself.

"No doubt he's warming himself by the fire while you're out in the cold," the stranger said, the sarcasm heavy in his voice. "Nothing changes!"

"Are you Mr. Arkwright?" I asked. "I'm Tom Ward, Mr. Gregory's apprentice. . . ."

It was a reasonable enough guess. My master, John Gregory, was the only spook I'd ever met but I knew there were others, the nearest being Bill Arkwright, who plied his trade beyond Caster, covering the northern border regions of the County. So it was very likely that this man was him—although I couldn't guess why he'd come calling.

The stranger pulled the hood back from his face to reveal a black beard dappled with flecks of gray and an unruly thatch of black hair silvered at the temples. He smiled with his mouth, but his eyes were cold and hard.

"Who I am is none of your business, boy. But your master knows me well enough!"

With those words he reached inside his cloak, pulled out an envelope, and handed it to me. I turned it over, examining it quickly. It had been sealed with wax and was addressed *To John Gregory*.

"Well, get on your way, boy. Give him the letter and warn him that we'll be meeting again soon. I'll be waiting for him up on Anglezarke!"

I did as I was told, pushing the envelope into my breeches pocket, only too pleased to get away, for I didn't feel comfortable in this stranger's presence. But when I'd turned and taken a few paces, curiosity made me glance back. To my surprise, there was no sign of him at all. Although there hadn't been time for him to take more than a few steps himself, he'd already vanished into the trees.

Puzzled, I walked quickly, anxious to get back to the house and out of the cold, biting wind. I wondered what was in the letter. There'd been a threatening tone in the stranger's voice, and from what he'd said it didn't sound like the stranger and my master would have a friendly meeting!

With these thoughts whirling through my head, I passed the bench where the Spook gave me lessons when the weather was warm enough and reached the first trees of the western garden. But then I heard something that made me catch my breath with fear.

An earsplitting roar of anger bellowed out of the darkness beneath the trees. It was so fierce and terrifying that it halted me in my tracks. It was a throbbing growl that could be heard for miles, and I'd heard it before. I knew it was the Spook's pet boggart about to defend the garden. But from what? Was I being followed?

I turned around and held up the lantern, peering anxiously into the darkness. Maybe the stranger was behind me! I could see nothing so I strained my ears, listening for the slightest sound. But all I could hear was the wind sighing through the trees and the distant barking of a farm dog. At last, satisfied that I wasn't being followed after all, I continued on my way.

I'd hardly taken another step when the roar of anger came again, this time much closer. The hair on the back of my neck began to rise, and now I felt even more afraid as I sensed that the boggart's fury was being directed at me. But why should it be angry with me? I'd done nothing wrong.

I kept perfectly still, not daring to take another step, fearing that my slightest movement might cause it to attack. It was a cold night, but sweat was forming on my brow and I felt in real danger.

"It's only Tom!" I called out into the trees at last. "There's nothing to fear. I'm just bringing a letter for my master. . . ."

There came an answering growl, this time much softer

and farther away, so after a few hesitant steps I walked on quickly. When I reached the house, the Spook was standing framed in the back door, staff in hand. He'd heard the boggart and come to investigate.

"You all right, lad?" he called.

"Yes," I shouted back. "The boggart was angry, but I don't know why. It's calmed down now though."

With a nod of his head the Spook went back into the house, leaning his staff behind the door.

By the time I'd followed him into the kitchen, he was standing with his back to the fire, warming his legs. I pulled the envelope from my pocket.

"There was a stranger down there, dressed like a spook," I told him, holding out the letter. "He wouldn't tell me his name but asked me to give you this. . . ."

My master stepped forward and snatched the letter from my hand. Immediately the candle on the table began to flicker, the fire died low in the grate, and a sudden coldness filled the kitchen, all signs that the boggart still wasn't best pleased. Alice looked alarmed and almost fell off her stool. But the Spook, with widening eyes, tore open the envelope and began to read.

When he'd finished, he frowned, his brow creased with annoyance. Muttering something under his breath, he threw the letter into the fire, where it burst into flames, curling up and blackening before falling into the back of the grate. I stared at him in astonishment. His face was filled with fury, and he seemed to tremble from head to foot.

"We'll be setting off for my house at Anglezarke early tomorrow morning, before the weather takes a turn for the worse," he snapped, glaring directly at Alice, "but you'll only be coming part of the way, girl. I'll be leaving you near Adlington."

"Adlington?" I said. "That's where your brother Andrew lives now, isn't it?"

"Aye, lad, it is, but she'll not be staying there. There's a farmer and his wife on the outskirts of the village who I reckon owe me a few favors. They had many sons, but sadly only one lived. Then, to add to that tragedy, there was a daughter who was drowned. The lad mostly works away now—the mother's health is beginning to fail and she could do with some help. So that will be your new home."

Alice looked at the Spook, her eyes widening in astonishment. "My new home? That ain't fair!" she exclaimed. "Why can't I stay with you? Ain't I done everything you asked?"

Alice hadn't put a foot wrong since the autumn, when the Spook had allowed her to live with us at Chipenden. She'd earned her keep by making copies of some of the books from the Spook's library, and she'd told me lots of the things that her aunt, the witch Bony Lizzie, had taught her so that I could write them down and increase my knowledge of witch lore.

"Aye, girl, you've done what I asked, so I've no complaints there," the Spook said. "But that's not the problem. Training to be a spook is a hard business: the last thing Tom needs is to be distracted by a girl like you. There's no place for a woman in a spook's life. In fact it's the only real thing we have in common with priests."

"But where's this come from all of a sudden? I've helped Tom, not distracted him!" Alice protested. "And I couldn't have worked harder. Has someone written to tell you otherwise?" she demanded angrily, gesturing toward the back of the grate, where the burned letter had fallen.

"What?" asked the Spook, raising his eyebrows in puzzlement but then quickly realizing what she meant. "No, of course not. But what's in private correspondence is none of your business. Anyway, I've made up my mind," he said, fixing her with a hard stare. "So we won't debate it any further. You'll get a fresh start. It's as good a chance as any to find your proper place in this world, girl. And it'll be your last chance, too!"

Without a word or even a glance at me, Alice turned away and stamped up the stairs to bed. I stood up to follow her and offer some words of comfort, but the Spook called me back.

"You wait here, lad! We need to talk before you go up

those stairs, so sit yourself down!"

I did as I was told and sat back down by the fire.

"Nothing you say is going to change my mind! Accept that now and things will be a lot easier," the Spook told me.

"That's as may be," I said, "but there were better ways of telling her. Surely you could have broken it to her a bit more gently?"

"I've got more things to worry about than the girl's feelings," said the Spook.

There was no arguing with him when he was like this, so I didn't waste my breath. I wasn't happy, but there was nothing I could do about it. I knew my master had made up his mind to do this weeks ago and wasn't about to change it now. Personally, I didn't understand why we had to go to Anglezarke anyway. And why were we going now, so suddenly? Was it something to do with the stranger and what he'd written in the letter? The boggart had reacted oddly, too. Was it because it knew that I was carrying that letter?

"The stranger said he'd be seeing you up on Anglezarke,"

I blurted out. "He didn't seem too friendly. Who was he?"

The Spook glared at me, and for a moment I thought he wasn't going to answer. Then he shook his head again and muttered something under his breath before speaking.

"His name is Morgan, and he was once an apprentice of mine. A failed apprentice, I might add, even though he studied under me for almost three years. As you know, not all my apprentices make the grade. He just wasn't up to the job, so he holds a grudge, that's all. Hopefully you'll see nothing of him when we're up there, but if you do, keep well clear. He's nothing but trouble, lad. Now, get yourself upstairs: as I said, we've an early start tomorrow."

"Why do we need to go to Anglezarke for the winter?" I asked. "Couldn't we just stay here? Wouldn't it be more comfortable in *this* house?" It was something that just didn't make any sense.

"You've asked enough questions for one day!" the Spook said, his voice filled with irritation. "But I will say this. We don't always do things because we want to do them. And if it's comfort you want, then this isn't the trade for you. Like it or lump it, folk need us up there — especially when the nights draw in. We're needed, so that's why we go. Now off to bed. Not another word!"

It wasn't the full answer that I'd hoped for, but the Spook had a good reason for everything he did and I was just the apprentice with a lot to learn. So, with an obedient nod, I went off to bed.

CHAPTER II
FAREWELL TO CHIPENDEN

ALICE was sitting on the stairs outside my room, waiting for me. A candle beside her flickered shadows onto the door.

"Don't want to leave here, Tom," she said, coming to her feet. "Been happy here, I have. His winter house would be the next best thing. Old Gregory ain't being right with me!"

"I'm sorry, Alice. I agree, but he's made up his mind. There's nothing I can do."

I could see that she'd been crying, but I didn't know what else to say. Suddenly she seized my left hand and squeezed it hard. "Why does he always have to be like that?" she asked. "Why does he hate women and girls so much?"

"I think he's been hurt in the past," I said gently. I'd recently learned some things about my master, but so far I'd kept them to myself. "Look, I'm going to tell you something now, Alice, but you have to promise not to tell anybody else and never let the Spook know I told you!"

"I promise," she whispered, her eyes very wide.

"Well, do you remember when he almost put you in the pit when we came back from Priestown?"

Alice nodded. My master dealt with malevolent witches by keeping them trapped alive in pits. He'd been about to put Alice in one a while ago, even though she hadn't really deserved it.

"Do you remember what I shouted?" I asked.

"I couldn't hear properly, Tom. I was struggling and

terrified, but whatever you said did the trick because he changed his mind. I'll always be grateful to you for that."

"I just reminded him that he hadn't put Meg in the pit, so he shouldn't do it to you!"

"Meg?" Alice asked. "Who's she? Never heard her mentioned before."

"Meg's a witch. I read all about her in one of the Spook's diaries. As a young man he fell in love with her. I think she broke his heart. And what's more, she's still living somewhere up on Anglezarke."

"Meg who?"

"Meg Skelton."

"No! That can't be right. Came from foreign parts, Meg Skelton did. Went back home years ago. Everybody knows that. She was a lamia witch and wanted to be with her own kind again."

I knew a lot about lamia witches from a book in the Spook's library. Most of them came from Greece, where my mam once lived, and in their wild state they fed upon the blood of humans.

"Well, Alice, you're right about her not being born in the County, but the Spook says she's still here and I'll get to meet her this winter. For all I know she could be living in his house."

"Don't be daft, Tom. That ain't likely, is it? What woman in her right mind would live with him?"

"He's not that bad, Alice," I reminded her. "We've both been sharing a house with him for weeks, and we've been happy enough!"

"If Meg is living in his house up there," Alice said, a wicked smile on her face, "don't be surprised if he has her buried in a pit."

I smiled in return. "Well, we'll find out when we get there," I said.

"No, Tom. *You'll* find out. I'll be living somewhere else. Remember? But it's not all bad because Adlington's close to Anglezarke," she said. "Ain't much of a walk, so you could visit me, Tom. Would you? Would you do that? That way I wouldn't be so lonely. . . ."

Although I wasn't sure that the Spook would let

me visit, I wanted to make her feel better. Suddenly I remembered Andrew.

"What about Andrew?" I said. "He's the only brother the Spook has left, and he's living and working in Adlington now. My master's bound to want to see him from time to time, what with living so close. And he'll probably take me with him. We'll be popping into the village all the time, I'm sure, so there'll be lots of chances for me to see you."

Alice smiled then and let go of my hand. "Then make sure you do, Tom. I'll be expecting you. Don't let me down. And thank you for telling me all that stuff about Old Gregory. In love with a witch, eh? Who'd have thought he had it in him?"

With that, she snatched up her candle and went up the stairs. I really was going to miss Alice, but finding an excuse to see her might be harder than I'd suggested. The Spook certainly wouldn't approve. He didn't have much time for girls and had warned me on many occasions to beware of them. I'd told Alice enough for now about my master, too much perhaps, but there was more to the Spook's past than just Meg. He'd also got himself involved with another woman, Emily Burns, who had already been betrothed to another of his brothers. The brother was dead now, but the scandal had divided his family, causing a deal of trouble. Emily was also supposed to be living somewhere near Anglezarke. There are two sides to every story, and I wasn't about to judge the Spook until I knew more; still, it was twice as many women as most County men ever have in their lifetimes: the Spook had certainly lived a bit!

I went into my room and put my candle on the table beside the bed. Written on the wall close to its foot were lots of names, scrawled there by former apprentices. Some had completed their training with the Spook successfully: Bill Arkwright's name was there in the top left-hand corner. A lot had failed and hadn't completed their time. Some had even died. Billy Bradley's name was there in the other corner. He'd been the apprentice before me, but he'd made a mistake and had his fingers bitten off by a boggart. Billy had died of shock and loss of blood.

I searched the wall carefully that night. As far as I knew, anyone who'd ever stayed in this room had written his name there, including me. My own name was very small because there wasn't much space left, but it was there all the same. Yet as far as I could see there was one name missing. I searched the wall carefully just to be sure, but I was right: there was no "Morgan" written on the wall. So why was that? The Spook said he'd been his apprentice, so why hadn't he added his name?

What was so different about Morgan?

The following morning, after a quick breakfast, we packed and got ready to go. Just before we left, I sneaked back into the kitchen to say good-bye to the Spook's pet boggart.

"Thanks for all the meals you've cooked," I said aloud to the empty air.

I wasn't sure if the Spook would have been too happy about me making a special trip to the kitchen to say thanks: he was always going on about not getting too close to "the hired help."

Anyway, I know the boggart appreciated the praise, because no sooner had I spoken than a deep purring began under the kitchen table, and it was so loud that the pots and pans began to rattle. The boggart was mostly invisible, but occasionally it took the shape of a big ginger tomcat.

I hesitated, gathered my courage, and spoke again. I wasn't sure how the boggart would react to what I had to say.

"I'm sorry if I made you angry last night," I said. "I was just doing my job. Was it the letter that upset you?"

The boggart wasn't able to speak, so I wasn't going to get a reply in words. Instinct had made me ask the question. A feeling that it was the right thing to do.

Suddenly there was a whoosh of air down the chimney, a faint smell of soot. Then a fragment of paper flew up from the grate and landed on the hearth rug. I stepped forward and picked it up. It was burned around the edges and part of it crumbled away in my fingers, but I knew that it was all that remained of the letter I'd delivered for Morgan.

There were just a few words on that scorched scrap of paper, and I stared at them for a while before I could make them out.

Give me what belongs to me or
I'll make you sorry you were ever born.
You can start by

That was all there was, but it was enough to tell me that Morgan was threatening my master. What was it all about? Had the Spook taken something from Morgan? Something that rightfully belonged to him? I couldn't imagine the Spook stealing anything. He just wasn't like that. It didn't make any sense at all.

My thoughts were disturbed by the Spook shouting from the front door. "Come on, lad! What are you up to? Don't dawdle! We haven't got all day!"

I screwed up the paper and threw it back into the grate,

picked up my staff, and ran to the door. Alice was already standing outside, but the Spook was in the doorway, eyeing me suspiciously, two bags at his feet. We hadn't packed much, but I still had to carry both of them.

By now the Spook had given me a bag of my own, although so far I hadn't got much to put inside it. All it contained was a silver chain given to me by my mam, a tinderbox, which was a leaving present from my dad, my notebooks, and a few clothes. Some of my socks had been darned so much that they were almost new, but the Spook had bought me a winter sheepskin coat, which was very warm, and I was wearing it under my cloak. I had a staff of my own, too—a new one my master had cut himself from rowan wood, which was very effective against most witches.

The Spook, for all his disapproval of Alice, had been generous regarding her clothing. She too had a new winter coat, a black woolen one that came down almost to her ankles; it had an attached hood to keep her ears warm.

The cold didn't seem to bother the Spook much, and he wore his cloak and hood just as he had in spring and summer. His health had been poor in the last few months, but now he seemed to have recovered and appeared as strong as ever.

The Spook locked the front door behind us, squinted up into the winter sun, and set off at a furious pace. I picked up both bags and followed as best I could, with Alice close at my heels.

"Oh, by the way, lad," the Spook called back over his shoulder, "we'll be calling in at your dad's farm on our way south. He still owes me ten guineas as the final payment for your training!"

I'd been sad to leave Chipenden. I'd grown fond of the house and gardens, and I was sorry to think that Alice and I would be apart from now on. But at least I'd have a chance to see my mam and dad. So my heart leaped with happiness, and there was a new energy in my step. I was on my way home!

CHAPTER III
HOME

AS we traveled south, I kept glancing back at the fells. I'd spent so much time walking up there close to the clouds that some fells were like old friends, particularly Parlick Pike, which was the nearest one to the Spook's summer house. But by the end of the second day of walking, those big familiar hills were no more

than a low purple line on the horizon and I was very glad of my new coat. We'd already spent an uncomfortable night freezing in a roofless barn, and although the wind had dropped and the sun was shining weakly, it now seemed to be getting colder by the hour.

At last we approached home, and my eagerness to see my family again grew with every stride. I was desperate to see my dad. On my last visit he'd just been getting over a serious illness, with little chance that he'd ever fully recover his health. He'd intended to retire and hand the farm over to my eldest brother, Jack, at the beginning of the winter anyway. But his illness had brought things forward. The Spook had called it my dad's farm, but that wasn't really true anymore.

Suddenly, below us, I could see the barn and the familiar farmhouse with a plume of smoke rising from the chimney. The patchwork of surrounding fields and the bare trees looked bleak and wintry, and I longed to warm my hands by the kitchen fire.

◎ ◎ ◎

My master stopped at the end of the lane. "Well, lad, I don't think your brother and his wife will be too pleased to see us. Spooks' business upsets most people, so we shouldn't hold it against them. Off you go and fetch my money; the girl and I will wait here. No doubt you'll be looking forward to seeing your family again, but don't be longer than an hour. While you're sitting by a warm fire, we'll be freezing our socks off here!"

He was right: my brother Jack and his wife didn't like spooks' business and had warned me in the past not to bring it to their door. So I left Alice and the Spook and ran up the lane toward the farm. When I opened the gate, the dogs began to bark and Jack came around the side of the barn. We hadn't got on too well together since I'd become the Spook's apprentice, but for once he looked happy to see me, and his face split into a broad grin.

"Good to see you, Tom," he said, putting his arm across my shoulders.

"And you, too, Jack. But how's Dad?" I asked.

The smile slipped from my brother's face as quickly as

it had come. "The truth is, Tom, I don't think he's that much better than the last time you were here. Some days are an improvement on others, but first thing in the morning he coughs and splutters so much he can hardly get his breath. It's painful to listen to. We want to help him, but there's nothing we can do."

I shook my head sadly. "Poor Dad. I'm on my way down south for the winter," I told Jack, "and I've just called in for the rest of the money Dad owes the Spook. I wish I could stay, but I can't. My master's waiting at the end of the lane. We're to set off again in an hour."

I didn't mention Alice. Jack knew she was the niece of a witch and had little time for her. They'd crossed swords before, and I didn't want a repeat performance.

My brother turned and gazed back toward the lane before looking me up and down. "You certainly dress the part anyway," he said with a grin.

He was right. I'd left the bags with Alice, but wearing my black cloak and carrying my staff, I looked like a smaller version of my master.

"Like the jacket?" I asked, pulling back my cloak to let him see it properly.

"Looks warm."

"Mr. Gregory bought it for me. Says I'll need it. He has a house up on Anglezarke Moor, not far from Adlington. That's where we're spending the winter, and it's bitterly cold over there."

"Aye, it'll be cold up there all right—you can be sure of that! Rather you than me. Anyway, I'd best get back to my chores," Jack said. "Don't keep Mam waiting. She's been really bright and cheerful today. Must have known you were coming."

With that, Jack set off back across the yard, pausing to wave from the corner of the barn. I waved back and then walked toward the kitchen door. Most likely Mam had known I was on my way. She has a way of sensing things like that. As a midwife and healer, she often knows when someone is coming to seek her help.

As I pushed open the back door, I found Mam sitting in her rocking chair by the fire. The curtains were closed because she is sensitive to sunlight. She smiled as I walked into the kitchen.

"Good to see you, son," she said. "Come here and give me a hug, and then you can tell me all your news!"

I went across and she held me close. Then I drew up a chair next to her. A lot had happened since I'd last seen Mam in the autumn, but I'd sent her a long letter telling her all about the dangers I'd faced with my master during the final stages of a job in Priestown.

"Did you get my letter, Mam?"

"Yes, Tom, I did, and I'm really sorry for not writing back, but things have been busy here and I knew you'd be calling in on your way down south. How's Alice getting on now?"

"She's definitely turned out all right in the end, Mam, and she's been happy living with us in Chipenden, but the trouble is, the Spook still doesn't trust her. We're going to his winter house, but Alice is going to stay on a farm with people she's never even met."

"It might seem harsh," Mam replied, "but I'm sure Mr. Gregory knows what he's doing. It'll all be for the best. As for Anglezarke, you take care there, son. It's a grim, bleak moor. Reckon Alice has been let off lightly."

"Jack told me about Dad. Is it as bad as you expected, Mam?" I asked. Last time I'd seen her she'd kept the worst of her fears from Jack but had hinted to me that Dad's life was drawing to a close.

"I'd hoped he'd gain a little more strength. He'll take careful nursing to get him through the winter, which I suspect is going to be as bad as any I've witnessed since coming to the County. He's upstairs sleeping now. I'll take you up to see him in a few minutes."

"Jack seems more cheerful, though," I said, trying to lighten the mood. "Perhaps he's come round to the idea of having a spook in the family."

Mam smiled broadly. "And so he should, but I suspect it's got rather more to do with the fact that Ellie's expecting again and it's going to be a boy this time—I'm certain of it. Jack's always wanted a son. Someone to inherit the farm one day."

I was pleased for Jack. Mam was never wrong about

things like that. Then I realized that the house seemed quiet. Almost too quiet.

"Where *is* Ellie?" I asked.

"Sorry, Tom, but you've chosen the wrong day to call. Most Wednesdays she goes to visit her own mam and dad, taking little Mary with her. You should see that child now! She's a big girl for eight months, and she crawls so fast, you need eyes in the back of your head! Anyway, I know your master's waiting for you and it's cold out there, so let's go up and see your dad."

Dad was fast asleep, but there were four pillows at his back so that he was almost sitting up.

"Makes it easier for him to breathe in that position," said Mam. "He's still got some congestion in his lungs."

Dad was breathing noisily; his face was gray and there was a line of sweat on his brow. Truth was, he looked really ill—a mere shadow of the strong, healthy man who'd once run the farm single-handed while being a good loving father to seven sons.

"Look, Tom, I know you'd like a word or two with him, but he didn't sleep at all last night. It's better if we don't wake him now. What do you say?"

"Of course, Mam," I agreed, but I felt sad I couldn't talk to my dad. He was so ill, I knew I might never see him again.

"Well, just give him a kiss, son, and we'll leave him to his slumber. . . ."

I looked at my mam in astonishment. I couldn't remember the last time I'd kissed Dad. A pat on the shoulder or a quick handshake was more like it.

"Go on, Tom, just kiss him on the forehead," Mam insisted. "And wish him well. He may be asleep, but part of him will hear what you say and it'll make him feel better."

I looked at Mam and her eyes met mine. There was iron in her gaze and I felt the force of her will. So I did exactly what she asked. I leaned over the bed and kissed Dad lightly on his warm, damp forehead. There was a strange smell that I couldn't quite identify. A smell of flowers. A type of flower that I couldn't put a name to.

"Get well soon, Dad," I whispered very softly. "I'll call back in the spring and see you then."

My mouth was suddenly dry, and when I licked my lips, I tasted the salt from his brow. Mam smiled sadly and pointed to the bedroom door.

As I followed her out, Dad started to cough and splutter behind me. I turned back in concern, and at that moment he opened his eyes and looked at me.

"Tom! Tom! Is that you?" he called before starting another bout of coughing.

Mam brushed past me in the doorway and bent over Dad anxiously, stroking his forehead gently until the coughing finally subsided.

"Tom *is* here," she told him, "but don't you go tiring yourself out with too much talking."

"Are you working hard, lad? Is your master pleased with you?" Dad asked, but his voice was weak and croaky, as if there was something caught in his throat.

"Aye, Dad, it's going well. In fact that's one of the reasons I'm here," I said, approaching the bed. "My master's definitely keeping me on, and he wants the last ten guineas you owe him to pay for my apprenticeship."

"That's good news, son. I'm very pleased for you. So you've enjoyed working up at Chipenden?"

"I have that, Dad," I said with a smile, "but now we're off to spend the winter at his house on Anglezarke Moor."

Suddenly Dad looked alarmed. "Oh, I wish you weren't going there, son," he said, glancing at Mam. "There are strange tales about that place, and none of them good. You'll need eyes in the back of your head up there. Make sure you stay close to your master and listen carefully to everything he says."

"I'll be all right, Dad. Don't you worry. I'm learning more each day."

"I'm sure you are, son. I must confess that I had my doubts about apprenticing you to a spook, but your mam was right. It's a hard job, but somebody has to do it. She's told me about the things you've achieved so far, and I'm really proud to have such a brave son. I don't have favorites, mind. Seven sons I've had, all good lads. I love all my boys and I'm proud of every one, but I have a feeling that you might turn out to be the best of the whole crop."

I just smiled, not knowing what to say. Dad smiled back, then closed his eyes, and within moments the rhythm of his breathing changed and he drifted back off to sleep. Mam gestured toward the door and we left the room.

When we were back in the kitchen, I asked Mam about the strange smell.

"You've asked, so I won't try to hide it from you, Tom," she said. "As well as being the seventh son of a seventh son, you've inherited some things from me. We're both sensitive to what are called 'intimations of death.' So what you smell is death's approach. . . ."

A lump filled my throat and the tears began to prick behind my eyes. Immediately Mam came forward and put her arm around me.

"Oh, Tom, try not to get upset. It doesn't mean that your dad is necessarily going to die a week, a month, or even a year from now. But the stronger the smell, the closer death is. If someone recovers fully, the smell goes away. And it's the same with your dad. Some days the smell is hardly there at all. I'm doing my very best for him, and there is still some hope. Anyway, there it is, I've told you, and it's something else you've learned."

"Thanks, Mam," I said sadly, preparing to go.

"Now don't go rushing off in that state," Mam said, her voice soft and kind. "Just sit yourself down near the fire and I'll make you some sandwiches for the journey."

I did as I was told while she quickly made up a parcel of ham and chicken sandwiches for the Spook, Alice, and me.

"Aren't we forgetting something?" she asked as she handed me the parcel.

"Mr. Gregory's money!" I replied. I'd forgotten all about it.

"Wait there, Tom," she said. "I'll just have to go up to my room and get it."

By "my room" she didn't mean the bedroom that she shared with Dad. She meant the locked room near the top of the house where she kept her possessions. I'd only been in it once since I was a toddler, and that was when she'd given me her silver chain. Nobody else went in that room. Not even Dad.

There were lots of boxes and chests in there, but I hadn't a clue what they contained. From what Mam had just said, there was money in there, too. Mam's money had bought our farm in the first place. She'd brought it with her from her own country, Greece.

Before I left, Mam handed me the pack of sandwiches and counted ten guineas into my hand. When she looked into my eyes, I could see the concern there.

"It's going to be a long, hard, cruel winter, son. All the signs are there. The swallows flew south almost a month earlier than usual and the first frost came while the last of my roses were still in bloom—something I've never seen before. It's going to be harsh, and I don't think any of us will come through it unchanged. And there couldn't be a worse place to spend it than up on Anglezarke. Your dad was worried about you, son, and I am, too. And what he said was right. So I won't mince my words.

"There's no doubt that the dark's growing in power, and there's a particularly baleful influence up on that moor. It's where some of the old gods were worshipped long ago, and in winter some of them start to stir from their sleep. The worst of them was Golgoth, whom some call the Lord of Winter. So stay close to your master. He's the only real friend you've got. You must help each other."

"But what about Alice?"

Mam shook her head. "Maybe she'll be all right and maybe not. You see, up on that cold moor you're closer to the dark than most other places in the County, so being near there will put her to the test again. I hope she comes through it, but I can't see the outcome. Just do as I say. Work closely with your master. That's what counts."

We hugged each other one more time, then I said good-bye and set off down the lane again.

CHAPTER IV
The Winter House

THE nearer to Anglezarke we got, the worse the weather became.

It had begun to rain, and the cold southeasterly wind increased until it was driving hard into our faces, the gray cloud low and oppressive like a leaden weight hanging above our heads. Later the wind blew even harsher and the rain turned to sleet and hail. The ground became mud underfoot, and our progress was very slow. To make matters worse, we kept stumbling into areas of moss land and treacherous soggy marsh, and it took all the Spook's knowledge to get us across safely.

But on the morning of the third day the rain eased and the clouds lifted so that we could see a grim line of hills directly ahead.

"There it is!" the Spook said, pointing at the skyline with his staff. "Anglezarke Moor. And there, about four miles or so to the south"—he gestured again—"is Blackrod."

It was too far away to see the village. I thought I could just make out a few wisps of smoke, but it might have been cloud.

"What's Blackrod like?" I asked. My master had mentioned it from time to time, so I imagined it would be the place where I'd be collecting our weekly provisions.

"It's not as friendly a place as Chipenden, so it's best to keep away," said the Spook. "Awkward people live there, and a lot of them are family. I was born there, so I should know. No, Adlington's a far nicer place, and it's not too far ahead now. About a mile to the north of it is the place where we'll be leaving you, girl," he said to Alice. "Moor View Farm, it's called. You'll be staying with Mr. and Mrs. Hurst, who own it."

About an hour later we reached an isolated farmhouse close to a big lake. As the Spook went ahead, the dogs started barking; soon he was standing in the yard, talking to an old farmer who didn't exactly look pleased to see him. After about five minutes the farmer's wife joined them. They hadn't one smile to share among the three of them.

"Ain't going to be welcome here, that's for sure!" Alice said, twisting the corners of her mouth downward.

"It may not be all that bad," I said, trying to make excuses. "Don't forget, they lost a daughter. Some people never get over a tragedy like that."

While we waited, I looked at the farm more carefully. It didn't look very prosperous, and most of the buildings were in a state of disrepair. The barn was leaning over, and it looked like the next storm would flatten it. Everything in sight looked dismal. I couldn't help wondering about the nearby lake, too. It was a bleak expanse of gray water edged with marsh on the far side, with just a few stunted willows on its near shore. Was that where their daughter had drowned? Whenever they looked out of their front windows, the Hursts would be reminded of what had happened.

After a few minutes the Spook turned and beckoned us forward, and we trudged through the mud toward the yard.

"This is my apprentice, Tom," the Spook said, introducing me to the old farmer and his wife.

I smiled and said hello. They both nodded at me but didn't return my smile.

"And this is young Alice," continued the Spook. "She's a hard worker and will be a great help around the house. Be firm but kind, and she'll give you no trouble."

They looked Alice up and down but said nothing; after a brief nod in their direction and a flicker of a smile she just stared down at her pointy shoes. I could tell that she was unhappy; her stay with the Hursts wasn't getting off to a very good start. I didn't really blame her. They both looked miserable and defeated, as if they'd been beaten down by life. Mr. Hurst's face and forehead were deeply lined in a way that suggested he'd had more practice frowning than laughing.

"Seen much of Morgan lately?" asked the Spook.

At the sudden use of the name Morgan, I looked up sharply to see Mr. Hurst's left eyelid twitch and go into a spasm. He looked nervous. Maybe even scared. Was it the same Morgan who'd given me the letter for the Spook?

"Not much at all," Mrs. Hurst answered morosely, without meeting the Spook's gaze. "He stays the odd night but comes and goes as he pleases. At the moment he mostly keeps away."

"When was he here last?"

"Two weeks. Maybe more. . ."

"Well, when he comes visiting again, let him know that I'd like a word or two with him. Tell him to come up to the house."

"Aye, I'll tell him."

"See that you do. Well, we'll be on our way."

The Spook turned to leave, and I picked up my staff and the two bags and followed. Alice came running after me and caught hold of my arm, bringing me to a halt.

"Don't forget what you promised," she whispered into my left ear. "Come and visit me and don't leave it longer than a week. Counting on you, I am!"

"I'll come and see you, don't worry," I said, giving her a smile.

With that, she walked back to join the Hursts, and I watched as all three went into the farmhouse. I felt really sad for Alice, but there was nothing I could do.

As we left Moor View Farm behind, I told the Spook what had started to worry me.

"They didn't seem that happy to take Alice in," I said, expecting that the Spook would contradict me. To my shock and surprise, he agreed with what I'd said.

"Aye, that's true enough, they weren't too happy at all. But they hadn't much say in the matter. You see, the

Hursts owe me quite a tidy sum. Twice I've rid their place of troublesome boggarts. And I still haven't received even a penny for my hard work. I agreed to cancel their debt if they took Alice in."

I couldn't believe what I was hearing. "But that's not fair on Alice!" I said. "They might treat her badly."

"That girl can take care of herself, as you well know," he said with a grim smile. "Besides, no doubt you won't be able to keep away and will be calling in from time to time to see if she's all right."

When I opened my mouth to protest, the Spook's grin became even wider so that he looked like a hungry wolf, widening its jaws to snap the head off its prey.

"Well, am I right?" he asked.

I nodded.

"Thought so, lad. I know you well enough by now. So don't go worrying too much about the girl. Worry about yourself. It's likely to be a hard winter. One that'll test the both of us to the limits of our strength. Anglezarke is no place for the weak and fainthearted!"

Something else had been puzzling me, so I decided to get it off my chest. "I heard you ask the Hursts about somebody called Morgan," I said. "Is that the same Morgan who sent you the letter?"

"Well, I certainly hope there aren't two of them, lad! One's trouble enough."

"So he sometimes stays with the Hursts?"

"He does that, lad, which is to be expected seeing as he's their son."

"You've sent Alice to stay with Morgan's parents!" I uttered in amazement.

"Aye. And I know what I'm doing, so that's enough questions for now. Let's get on our way. We need to be there long before nightfall."

From the very first moment I saw them up close, I'd liked the look of the fells around Chipenden, but somehow Anglezarke Moor was different. I couldn't quite put my finger on what it was, but the nearer we got the lower my spirits sank.

Maybe it was the fact that I was seeing it at the tail end of the year, when it was gloomy and winter was drawing in. Or perhaps it was the dark moor itself rising up before me like a gigantic slumbering beast, clouds shrouding its somber heights. Most likely it was that everyone had been warning me against it and telling me how severe the winter was going to be. Whatever it was, I felt even worse when I saw the Spook's house, the grim place where we'd be staying for the next few months.

We approached it by following a stream toward its source, climbing up into what the Spook called a clough, which was a cleft in the moor, a deep narrow valley with steep slopes rising up on either side. At first the slopes were just scree, but those loose stones soon gave way to tussocks of grass and bare rock, and the dark cliffs of the clough seemed to close in on either side.

After about twenty minutes the clough curved away to the left, and suddenly there was the Spook's house directly ahead, built right back against the cliff face to our right. My dad always said that your first impression of something is almost always correct, so my spirits dropped right down into my boots. It was late afternoon and the light was already past its best, so that didn't help. The house was bigger and more imposing than the one at Chipenden, but was constructed from much darker stone, which gave it a distinctly sinister appearance. Additionally the windows were small, which, combined with the fact that the house was built in a clough, would surely make the rooms inside very dark. It was one of the most uninviting houses I'd ever seen.

The worst thing, though, was that it had no garden. As I said, the house was built right against the sheer rocky crag behind it; in front, five or six paces brought you to the edge of the stream, which wasn't very wide but looked deep and very cold. Another thirty paces, crunching across the pebbles, and you'd be stubbing your big toe against the opposite rock face. That's if you managed to get across the slippery stepping stones without falling in.

There was no smoke rising from the chimney, which suggested there would be no welcoming fire. Back in

Chipenden, the Spook's pet boggart had always known when we were returning, and not only was the house already warm, but a piping-hot meal would be waiting on the kitchen table.

Far above, the sides of the clough almost seemed to meet over the house and there was just a narrow strip of sky. I shivered because it was even colder down in the clough than it had been on the lower slopes of the moor, and I realized that even in the summer, the sun wouldn't be visible for more than an hour or so each day. It made me appreciate what I'd had back in Chipenden, with woods, fields, the high fells and the wide sky above. There we'd looked down on the world; here we were trapped in a long, deep, narrow pit.

I glanced up nervously at the dark edges of the clough where it met the sky. Anybody or anything could be up there peering down at us, and we wouldn't know it.

"Well, lad, here we are. This is my winter house. We have a lot to do: tired or not, we'll have to get busy!"

Rather than walking up to the front door, the Spook

led the way around to a small flagged area at the back of the house. Three paces from the back door brought us to the rock face, which was dripping with water and hung with ice stalactites, like the teeth of the dragon in a tall story that one of my uncles used to tell me.

Of course, in a hot mouth like that those "teeth" would have turned to steam in an instant; in this cold spot behind the house they'd last most of the year, and once it snowed, there'd be no getting rid of them at all until late spring.

"We always use the back door here, lad," the Spook said, taking from his pocket the key that his brother Andrew, the locksmith, had made for him. It would open any door as long as the lock wasn't too complicated. I had a similar key myself, and it had come in useful more than once.

The key was stiff in the lock, and the door seemed reluctant to open. Once inside, I was depressed by how dark the room was, but the Spook leaned his staff against the wall, pulled a candle from his bag, and lit it.

"Put the bags there," he said, pointing to a low shelf next to the back door.

I did as I was told and then placed my staff next to the Spook's in the corner before following him farther into the house.

My mam would have been shocked by the state of the kitchen. I was pretty sure by now that there was no boggart to do the work. It was clear that nobody had looked after the place since the Spook left at the end of last winter. There was dust on every surface and cobwebs hung from the ceiling. The sink was piled high with unwashed pots, and there was half a loaf of bread on the table, green with mold. There was also a faint, sweet, unpleasant smell, as if something were slowly rotting away in a dark corner. Next to the fire was a rocking chair similar to Mam's back at the farm. Draped over the back was a brown shawl that looked in need of a good wash. I wondered who it belonged to.

"Well, lad," the Spook said, "we'd better get to work. We'll start by warming the old house up. That done, we'll set about cleaning."

At the side of the house was a big wooden shed heaped

with coal. I didn't like to think how so much coal had been brought up the clough. At Chipenden I'd been sent for the weekly provisions, and I just hoped that fetching sacks of coal wouldn't be one of my jobs here.

There were two big coal scuttles, and we filled these and brought them back into the kitchen.

"Know how to get a good coal fire burning?" asked the Spook.

I nodded. In winter, back home at the farm, my first chore each morning had been to light the kitchen fire.

"Right, then," said the Spook. "You attend to this one and I'll see to the one in the parlor. There are thirteen fireplaces in this old house, but lighting six should start to warm things up for now."

After about an hour we managed to get the six fires alight: one in the kitchen, one in the parlor, one in what the Spook called his study, which was on the ground floor, and one in each of the three upstairs bedrooms. There were seven other bedrooms, including an attic, but we didn't bother with those.

"Right, lad, that's a good start," the Spook said. "Now we'll go and fetch some water."

Carrying a big jug each, we went out through the back door again and around to the front, where the Spook led the way to the stream. The water was as deep as it had looked, so it was easy to fill our jugs, and clean, cold, and clear enough to see the rocks at the bottom. It was a quiet stream and hardly did more than murmur its way down the clough.

But just as I'd finished filling my jug, I sensed a movement somewhere far above. I couldn't actually see anything; it was more a feeling of being watched really, and when I glanced up to where the rock formed a dark edge against the gray sky, there was nothing there.

"Don't look up, lad," snapped the Spook, an edge of irritation in his voice. "Don't give him the satisfaction. Pretend you haven't noticed."

"Who is he?" I asked, feeling very nervous as I followed the Spook back toward the house.

"Hard to say. I didn't look so I can't be sure," said the

Spook, suddenly coming to a halt and putting his jug down. Then he quickly changed the subject. "What do you think of the house?" he asked.

My dad had taught me to tell the truth whenever possible, and I knew the Spook wasn't a man whose feelings were easily hurt. "I'd rather live on top of a hill than like an ant in a deep crack between paving stones," I told him. "So far, I prefer your house at Chipenden."

"So do I, lad," said the Spook. "So do I. We've only come here because it has to be done. We're right on the edge here, on the edge of the dark, and it's a bad place to be in winter. There are things up on the moor that don't bear too much thinking about, but if we can't face them, then who can?"

"What sort of things?" I asked, remembering what Mam had told me but interested to see what the Spook would say.

"Oh, there are boggarts, witches, ghosts, and ghasts aplenty and other things even worse. . . ."

"Like Golgoth?" I suggested.

"Aye, Golgoth. No doubt your mam's told you all about him. Am I right?"

"She mentioned him when I told her we were heading for Anglezarke, but she didn't say that much. Just that he sometimes stirs in winter."

"That he does, lad, and I'll be adding to your knowledge about him at a more appropriate time. Now look at that," he said, pointing up at the big chimney stack to where thick brown smoke was rising high into the air from the two rows of cylindrical pots. He jabbed toward the smoke with his forefinger. "We're here to show the flag, lad."

I looked for a flag. All I could see was the smoke.

"I mean that just by being here we're saying this land belongs to us and not to the dark," the Spook explained. "Standing up to the dark, especially up on Anglezarke, is a hard thing to do, but it's our duty and well worth it. Anyway," he said, picking up his jug, "let's get inside and start cleaning."

For the next two hours I was really busy scrubbing, sweeping, polishing, and going outside to beat clouds of dust from the rugs. Finally, after washing and drying the dirty dishes, the Spook told me to make up the beds in the three second-floor rooms.

"*Three* beds?" I asked, wondering if I'd misheard him.

"Aye, three it is, and when you've finished you'd better go and wash your ears out! Go on! Don't stand there gawping. We haven't got all day."

So, with a shrug, I did as I was told. The linen was damp, but I turned the sheets down so that the fires would dry them out. That done, exhausted with my efforts, I went downstairs. It was as I passed the cellar steps that I heard something that made the hair on the back of my neck start to rise.

From below, I heard what sounded like a long shuddering sigh, followed almost immediately by a faint cry. I waited at the top of the steps on the edge of the darkness, listening carefully, but it wasn't repeated. Had I imagined it?

I went into the kitchen to find the Spook washing his hands in the sink.

"I heard something cry out from the cellar," I told him. "Is it a ghost?"

"Nay, lad, there are no ghosts in this house now — I sorted them all out years ago. No, that'll be Meg. No doubt she's just woken up."

I wasn't sure if I'd misheard him. I'd been told I'd meet Meg and knew that she was a lamia witch living somewhere up on Anglezarke. I'd also half expected to find her staying in the Spook's house. But seeing it abandoned and cold had driven that prospect from my head. Why would she be sleeping down there in a bitterly cold cellar? I was curious, but knew better than to ask questions at the wrong time.

Sometimes the Spook was in the mood for answering, and he'd sit me down and tell me to get out my notebook and fill my pen with ink, ready to write. At other times he just wanted to get on with the business in hand, and now I could see the determined expression glinting in his green eyes, so I just kept quiet while he lit a candle.

I followed him down the stone cellar steps. I wasn't

exactly scared, because he knew what he was doing, but I was certainly very nervous. I'd never met a lamia witch before, and although I'd read a bit about them, I didn't know what to expect. And how had she managed to survive down there in the cold and dark all through the spring, summer, and autumn? What had she been eating? Slugs, worms, insects, and snails, like the witches the Spook bound in pits?

When the steps turned the first corner, there was an iron trellis gate blocking our way. Beyond it, the steps suddenly became much wider, so that four people could have walked down side by side. I'd never seen such wide cellar steps before. Not far beyond the gate I could see a door set into the wall, and I wondered what was behind it. The Spook took a key from his pocket and inserted it into the lock. It wasn't his usual key.

"Is it a complicated lock?" I asked.

"That it is, lad," he said. "More complicated than most. If you ever need it, I usually keep this key on top of the bookcase in the study closest to the door."

When he opened the gate, it made a clanging noise so loud that it seemed to ring right through the stones both upward and downward, so that the whole house acted like a huge bell.

"The iron would stop most of 'em getting past this point, but even if it didn't, we'd hear what was going on from upstairs. This door's better than a guard dog."

"Most of who? And why are the steps so wide?" I asked.

"First things first," snapped the Spook. "Questions and answers can come later. First we need to see to Meg."

As we carried on down the steps, I started to hear faint noises from below. There was a groan and what sounded like a faint scratching, which made me even more nervous. It didn't take me long to realize that there must be at least as much of the house belowground as there was above it: each time the steps turned a corner, there was a wooden door set into the wall, and on the third turning, a small landing with three doors.

The Spook paused directly in front of the middle door

of the three, then turned to me. "You wait here, lad," he said. "Meg's always a bit nervous when she first wakes up. We need to give her time to get used to you."

With those words he handed me the candle, turned his key in the lock, and went into the darkness, closing the door behind him.

I was left waiting outside for about ten minutes, and I don't mind telling you it was very creepy on those stairs. For one thing, the farther down the steps we'd gone, the colder it had seemed to get. For another, I could hear more disturbing noises coming from below, around the next corner, out of sight. They were mostly very faint whisperings, but once I thought I heard a distant groan, as if someone or something was having a very bad time of it.

Then there were muffled noises from inside the room the Spook had entered. My master seemed to be talking quietly but firmly, and at one point I heard a woman crying. That didn't last long, and there were more whisperings, as though neither of them wanted me to hear what they were saying.

At last the door creaked open. The Spook appeared, and someone followed him out onto the landing.

"This is Meg," said my master, stepping to one side so that I could see her properly. "You'll like her, lad. She's just about the best cook in the whole County."

As Meg looked me up and down, she looked puzzled. I stared back at her in sheer astonishment. You see, she was just about the prettiest woman I'd ever seen, and she was wearing pointy shoes. When I'd first gone to Chipenden, in my very first lesson, the Spook had warned me about the dangers of talking to girls who wore pointy shoes. Whether they realized it or not, he'd told me, some of them would be witches.

I'd paid no heed to his warning and talked to Alice, who'd got me into all sorts of trouble before eventually helping me to get out of it. But here was my master, ignoring his own advice! Only Meg wasn't a girl; she was a woman, and everything about her face was so perfect that you couldn't help just staring at it: her eyes, her high cheekbones, her complexion.

It was her hair that gave her away, though. It was silver, the color you'd expect in someone much older. Meg was no taller than me and only came up to the Spook's shoulder. Looking at her more closely, you could tell that she'd been sleeping for months in the cold and damp: there were bits of cobweb in her hair and patches of mold on her faded purple dress.

There are several different types of witches, and I'd filled pages of my notebooks with lessons the Spook had taught me about them. But I'd discovered what I knew about lamia witches by sneaking a look at books in the Spook's library that I wasn't supposed to be studying.

Lamia witches come from overseas, and in their own lands they feed upon the blood of men. Their natural condition is known as the "feral," and in that state they aren't like humans at all and have scales covering their bodies and long thick claws on their fingers. But they are slow shape-shifters, and the more contact they have with humans, the more human their appearance gradually becomes. After a while they turn into what's known as domestic lamias, who look like human females but for a line of green and yellow scales that runs the length of their spine. Some even become benign rather than malevolent. So had Meg become good? Was that another reason why the Spook hadn't dealt with her, by putting her in a pit as he had with Bony Lizzie?

"Well, Meg," said the Spook, "This is Tom, my apprentice. He's a good lad, so you two should get along just fine."

Meg held out her hand toward me. I thought she wanted to shake mine, but just before our fingers touched, she dropped her arm suddenly, as if she'd been burned, and a worried expression came into her eyes.

"Where's Billy?" she asked, her voice silky smooth but edged with uncertainty. "I liked Billy."

I knew she was talking about Billy Bradley, the Spook's apprentice before me who'd died.

"Billy's gone, Meg," the Spook explained gently. "I've told you that already. Don't worry about it. Life goes on. You'll have to get used to Tom now."

"But it's *another* name to remember," Meg complained sadly. "Is it worth the effort when none of them last very long?"

Meg didn't start on our supper right away.

I was sent to get more water from the stream, and it took me a dozen trips back and forth before Meg was finally satisfied. Then, using two of the fireplaces, she began to heat the water, but to my disappointment I realized that it wasn't for cooking purposes.

I helped the Spook to drag a big iron bath into the kitchen and fill it with hot water. It was for Meg.

"We'll retire to the parlor," said the Spook, "so that Meg can have a little privacy. She's been down in that cellar for months and wants to freshen up."

I grumbled silently to myself that if my master hadn't locked her down there she could have kept the house clean and tidy for his return each winter. And, of course, that led to another question—why didn't the Spook take Meg with him to his summer house at Chipenden?

"This is the parlor," said my master, opening the door and inviting me in. "This is where we do our talking. This is where we meet people who need our help."

Having a parlor is an old County tradition. It's the best room, as posh as you can make it, and it's rarely used because it's always kept nice and tidy to receive guests. The Spook didn't have a parlor back in Chipenden because he liked to keep people away from the house. That's why they had to go to the crossroads under the withy trees and ring the bell and wait. It seemed that the rules were going to be different here.

Back home on the farm we didn't bother with a parlor either, because seven brothers made us a big family, and when we all lived at home, we needed all the rooms just to live in. Anyway, Mam, who wasn't born in the County, thinks that keeping a parlor is a really daft idea.

"What's the use of a best room that's hardly ever used?" she always says. "People can take us as they find us."

The Spook's parlor wasn't really that posh, but the battered old settee was as comfortable as the two armchairs looked and the room had warmed up nicely, so no sooner had I sat down than I began to feel sleepy. It had been a long day, and we'd walked for miles and miles.

I stifled a yawn, but I couldn't fool the Spook. "I was going to give you another Latin lesson, but you need a bright sharp mind for that," he said. "Straight after supper you'd better take yourself off to bed, but get up early and revise your verbs."

I nodded.

"Just one more thing," my master said, opening the cupboard next to the fireplace. He pulled out a big brown glass bottle and held it up high so I could see it. "Know what this is?" he asked, raising his eyebrows.

I shrugged, then I saw the label on the bottle and read it out to him. "Herb tea," I said.

"Never trust the label on a bottle," said the Spook. "I want you to pour half an inch of this into a cup first thing each morning, fill it up with very hot water, stir it thoroughly, and give it to Meg. Then I want you to wait around until she's finished every last drop. It'll take a while because she likes to sip it. That'll be your most important job of the day. Always tell her it's her usual cup of herb tea to keep her joints supple and her bones strong. That'll keep her happy."

"What is it?" I asked.

The Spook didn't answer for a moment.

"As you know, Meg's a lamia witch," he said eventually, "but the drink makes her forget who she is. It's a dangerous and upsetting thing for anyone to remember who they *really* are, so hope that it never happens to you, lad. It'll be an especially dangerous thing for all of us if Meg remembers who she is and what she can do."

"Is that why you keep her in the cellar and away from Chipenden?"

"Aye, best to be safe. And I can't have folks knowing she's here. No one would understand. There's a few in these parts who remember what she's capable of—even if she can't herself."

"But how does she survive without food all summer?"

"In their feral state, lamia witches can sometimes go without food for years, apart from insects, grubs, or the odd rat or two. Even when they're domestic like Meg, going hungry for months is no problem. And as well as making her sleep, a large dose of the potion has lots of nutrients, so Meg comes to no real harm.

"Anyway, lad, I'm sure you're going to like her. She's an excellent cook, as you'll find out soon enough," said the Spook, "as well as being a really methodical and tidy person. She always keeps her pots and pans as clean and shiny as new and sets them out in the cupboard exactly as she likes them. Her cutlery is the same. Always tidy in the drawer, knives on the left, forks on the right."

I wondered what she'd have thought of the mess we'd found. Maybe that's why the Spook had been so anxious to make sure that everything was made clean and tidy.

"Well, lad, we've talked enough. Let's go and see how she's doing. . . ."

◌ ◌ ◌

After her bath, Meg's face had scrubbed up to a nice healthy pink so that she looked younger and prettier than ever, and even with her silver hair you'd have thought her half the Spook's age. She was now wearing a clean frock, which was brown, the color of her eyes, and fastened at the back with white buttons. It was hard to be sure, but they looked like they'd been made from bone! I didn't like to think about that. If it *was* bone, where had it come from?

To my disappointment, she didn't make the supper. How could she when there wasn't any food in the house apart from half a moldy loaf?

So we had to make do with the last of the cheese that the Spook had brought with him for the journey. It was good County cheese, a nice crumbly pale yellow, but there wasn't anywhere near enough of it to satisfy three people.

We sat around the kitchen table nibbling at it slowly to make it last. There wasn't much conversation. All I could think about was breakfast.

"As soon as it's light, I'll go and get the week's provisions," I suggested to the Spook. "Should I go to Adlington or Blackrod?"

"You just keep away from both villages, lad," said the Spook. "Especially Blackrod. Bringing provisions is one job you won't have to do while we're staying here. Stop worrying. What you need is an early night, so get off to bed now. Yours is the room at the front of the house—go and get a good night's sleep. Meg and I have a few things to say to each other."

I did as I was told and went straight to bed. My room was a lot bigger than the one I'd been given back in Chipenden, but it still only contained a bed, a chair, and a very small chest of drawers. Had it faced the rear, I'd have been able to see nothing but the sheer wall of rock at the back of the house. Luckily it was at the front, and the moment I raised the sash window, I could hear a very faint murmur from the stream below and the whine of the wind gusting past the house. The cloud had cleared and a full moon was shining, casting its silvery light down into the clough to be reflected back by the stream. It was going to be a cold, frosty night.

I stuck my head out of the window for a better look. The moon was sitting right on top of the cliff directly ahead, looking impossibly large. Against it, in silhouette, I could see someone kneeling on the facing cliff, looking down. In an instant the figure was gone, but not before I'd seen that it was wearing a hood!

I stared up at the cliff for a few moments, but the figure didn't reappear. Cold air was beginning to fill the room, so I closed the window. Was it Morgan? And if so, why was he spying on us? Had it been Morgan watching us, too, when we were getting water from the stream?

I got undressed and climbed into bed. I was tired but still found it hard to get to sleep. The old house creaked and groaned a lot, and at one point there were patterings near the foot of the bed. It was probably just mice under the floorboards, but being a seventh son of a seventh son, I might well have been hearing something very different.

Despite that, I finally managed to drift off to sleep—

only to awake suddenly in the middle of the night. I lay there feeling uneasy, wondering why I'd woken up so abruptly. It was pitch dark and I couldn't see a thing, but I just felt that something was wrong. There'd been a noise of some sort. I felt sure of it.

I didn't have to wait long before hearing it again. Two different sounds that began gradually, becoming louder and louder as the seconds passed. One was a sort of high-pitched humming noise and the other a much lower, deep rumble, as if someone were rolling huge boulders down a stony mountainside.

Only it seemed to be happening somewhere beneath the house, and it was so bad that the windowpanes were rattling and even the walls seemed to be shaking and vibrating. I began to feel afraid. If it got any worse, then the whole house seemed sure to collapse. I didn't know what it could be, but a thought crashed through my mind. Was an earthquake causing the clough to collapse onto the house?

CHAPTER V
WHAT LAY BENEATH

EARTHQUAKES did happen, but they were very rare in the County. There hadn't been a serious one in living memory. Yet the house was shaking so much, I really was worried. So I dressed quickly, pulled on my boots, and went downstairs.

The first thing I noticed was that the cellar door was open. Faint sounds were coming from below, so, feeling curious, I went down a couple of steps. The rumbling sounded even worse down there, and I distinctly heard a shrill scream, more animal than human.

But immediately following that, I heard the gate clang and a key turn in the lock. A candle flickered in the darkness below, and footsteps drew nearer. For a second I was afraid, wondering who it could be, but I soon saw that it was the Spook.

"What is it?" I asked, thinking that he'd been dealing with something down there.

The Spook looked at me, a startled expression on his face. "What are you doing up at this hour?" he demanded. "Get off with you, back to bed at once!"

"I thought I heard somebody cry out," I told him. "And what's causing all that noise? Is it an earthquake?"

"Nay, lad, it's not an earthquake. And it's nothing to bother yourself about! I've more on my mind at the moment than answering your questions. It'll be over in a few moments, so just get yourself back to your room and

I'll tell you all about it in the morning," he said, ushering me from the steps and locking the door behind him.

His tone of voice told me that it was no use arguing, so I went back upstairs, still concerned about the way the house continued to shake and vibrate.

Well, the house didn't fall down, and as the Spook had promised, everything became quiet again. I managed to get back to sleep but woke up about an hour before dawn and went down to the kitchen. Meg was asleep in her rocking chair, and I wasn't sure if she'd been there all night or had crept down from her room when the noises began. She wasn't exactly snoring, but each time she breathed out, there was a faint whistling sound.

Taking care not to make too much noise and wake her, I added a bit more coal to the fire and soon had it blazing away. That done, I settled down on a stool by the hearth and began to revise my Latin verbs. I had two notebooks with me: one to write down everything the Spook taught me about boggarts and other spook business: the second for my Latin lessons.

Mam had taught me Greek, which saved me from having to study that language as well, but I was still hard pressed to keep up with Latin, and the verbs in particular gave me a lot of trouble. Many of the Spook's books were written in Latin, so I had to work hard to learn it.

I started at the beginning with the first verb the Spook had ever drummed into me. He'd taught me to learn Latin verbs in a sort of pattern. That's important because the ending of each word is different according to what you're trying to say. It's also useful to recite them aloud because, as the Spook explained, it helps to fix them into your memory. I didn't want to wake Meg so I kept my voice to hardly more than a whisper.

"*Amo, amas, amat,*" I said, without glancing at my notebook, reciting three words that mean "I love, you love, he, she, or it loves."

"I used to love someone once," said a voice from the rocking chair, "but now I can't even remember who it was."

It startled me so much that I almost dropped my notebook and fell off my stool. Meg was looking into the fire rather than at me, with an expression on her face that was a mixture of puzzlement and sadness.

"Good morning, Meg," I said, managing a smile. "I hope you've had a good night's sleep."

"It's nice of you to ask, Billy," Meg replied, "but I didn't sleep well at all. There were a lot of loud noises and I've been trying to remember something all night but it just keeps whirling round in my head. It's something very fast and slippery and I just can't manage to catch hold of it. I don't give up easily though, and I'm just going to sit here by the fire until it comes back to me."

At that I became alarmed. What if Meg remembered who she was? What if she realized that she was a lamia witch! I had to do something quickly, before it was too late.

"Don't worry about it, Meg," I said, putting down my notebook and leaping to my feet. "I'll make you a nice hot drink."

Quickly I filled the copper kettle with water and hung

it from the hook in the chimney so that, as my dad says, the fire could warm its bottom. Then I picked up a clean cup and took it with me into the parlor. There I took the brown bottle from the cupboard and poured half an inch of the mixture into the cup. That done, I went back into the kitchen and waited for the kettle to boil before topping up the cup almost to the brim and stirring it thoroughly as the Spook had instructed.

"Here, Meg, here's your herb tea. It'll help to keep your joints supple and your bones strong."

"Thank you, Billy," she said with a smile. She accepted the cup and began to blow into it, then sipped very slowly, still staring into the flames.

"This is delicious," she said after a while. "You really are a kind boy. It's just what I need to get my old bones started in the morning. . . ."

I felt sad when she said that. Part of me wasn't happy about what I'd done. She'd been awake most of the night, trying to remember something, and now the drink would make her memory even worse. While she was busy leaning forward and sipping her drink, I moved behind her to get a better look at something that had bothered me the previous evening.

I stared hard at the thirteen white buttons that did up her brown dress from neck to hem. Of course, I couldn't be absolutely certain, but I was sure enough.

Each button was made out of bone. She wasn't a witch who practiced bone magic; she was a lamia witch, a type that wasn't native to the County. But I wondered about the bone buttons. Had they come from victims she'd killed in the past? And underneath those buttons, inside the dress, I knew that as a domestic lamia witch she'd have a line of green and yellow scales running the length of her spine.

Soon afterward there was a knock at the back door. I went to answer it as my master was still sleeping after his disturbed night.

A man stood outside, wearing a strange leather cap with flaps that came down over his ears. He was holding a lantern in his right hand; with his left he led a little pony that was loaded up with so many brown sacks that it was a wonder its legs weren't buckling.

"Hello, young man, I've brought Mr. Gregory's order," he said, giving me a tight-lipped smile. "You must be the new apprentice. He was a nice lad, that Billy, and I was sorry to hear what happened."

"My name's Tom," I said, introducing myself.

"Well, Tom, how d'you do? My name's Shanks. Could you please tell your master I've brought up extra provisions and that I'll double up each week until the weather turns nasty. Looks like being a harsh winter, and when the snow comes, it might be a long time before I can get up here again."

I nodded at him, smiled, then looked up. It was still dark, but it was just beginning to lighten and the crack of sky was mostly full of gray clouds blowing in from the west. Just then, Meg joined me in the doorway. She was loitering slightly behind me, but Shanks saw her all right, because his eyes nearly bulged out of their sockets and he took two quick reverse steps, almost backing into the little pony.

I could tell that he was scared, but after Meg had turned and gone back inside, he calmed down a bit and I helped him to unload the sacks. While we were doing that, the Spook came out and paid the man.

When Shanks turned to go, the Spook followed him down the clough about thirty paces or so. They started talking but were too far away for me to catch every word of their conversation. It was about Meg, though, I was sure of it, because I heard her name twice.

I distinctly heard Shanks say, "You told us she'd been dealt with!" to which the Spook replied, "I have her safe enough, don't you worry yourself. I know my business all right, so it's no concern of yours. And you'll keep it to yourself, if you know what's good for you!"

My master didn't look too happy when he walked back toward me. "Did you give Meg her herb tea?" he asked suspiciously.

"I did it just as you said," I told him, "as soon as she woke up."

"Did she go outside?" he asked.

"No, but she came to the door and stood behind me. Shanks saw her, and it seemed to scare him."

"It's a pity he saw her at all," said the Spook. "She doesn't usually show herself like that. Not in recent years, anyway. Maybe we need to increase the dose. As I told you last night, lad, Meg used to cause a lot of trouble in the County. Folk were afraid of her and still are. And until now the locals didn't know she had the freedom of the house. If it were to get out, I would never hear the last of it. People round here are stubborn: once they get their teeth into something they don't easily let it go. But Shanks'll keep his mouth closed. I pay him well enough."

"Is Shanks the grocer?" I asked.

"No, lad, he's the local carpenter and undertaker. The only person in Adlington who's got the courage to venture up here. I pay him to collect and deliver."

After that we got the sacks safely inside, and the Spook opened the largest one and gave Meg what she needed to start cooking the breakfast.

○ ○ ○

The bacon was better than the Spook's pet boggart had managed, even on the best of mornings, and Meg had fried potato cakes and scrambled fresh eggs with cheese. The Spook hadn't been exaggerating when he'd said that Meg was a good cook. While we wolfed down our breakfast, I asked him about the strange noises in the night.

"It's nothing much to worry about for now," he told me, swallowing another big mouthful of potato cake. "This house is built on a ley line, so we can expect problems occasionally. Sometimes an earthquake thousands of miles away can cause disturbances to a whole series of leys. Boggarts can be forced to move from places where they've been happily settled for years. Last night a boggart passed under us. I had to go down to the cellar just to see that everything was safe and secure."

The Spook had told me all about leys when we were back in Chipenden. They were lines of power beneath the earth, like roads that some types of boggart could use to travel quickly from place to place.

"Mind you, it sometimes means trouble ahead," he continued. "When they set up home in a new location, they often begin by playing tricks—sometimes dangerous tricks—and that means work for us. You mark my words, lad, we could well have a boggart to deal with locally before the week's out."

After breakfast we went to the Spook's study for my Latin lesson. It was a small room with a couple of straight-backed wooden chairs, a large table, a solitary wooden stool with three legs, bare boards, and lots of tall, dark-stained bookcases. It was a bit chilly, too: yesterday's fire was now just gray ashes in the grate.

"Sit yourself down, lad. The chairs are hard, but it doesn't do to get too comfortable when you're studying. Wouldn't want you to fall asleep," said the Spook, giving me a sharp look.

I looked around at the bookcases. The room was gloomy, lit only by the gray light from the window and a couple of candles, so I hadn't noticed until then that the shelves were empty.

"Where are all the books?" I asked.

"Back in Chipenden—where do you think, lad? Not much point in keeping books here in the cold and damp. Books don't like those conditions. No, we'll just have to manage with what we've brought with us and maybe write some of our own while we're here. You can't just be reading books all the time and leaving the writing of them to others."

I knew the Spook had brought quite a few books with him and it had made his bag very heavy, whereas I'd just brought my notebooks. For the next hour I struggled with Latin verbs. It was hard work, and I was pleased when the Spook suggested that we have a rest, but not by what he did next.

He dragged the wooden stool close to the bookcase nearest the door. Then he climbed up onto it and searched the top shelf with his fingers.

"Well, lad," he said, holding up the key, his face very grim. "We can't put it off any longer. Let's go down and look at the cellar itself. But first we'll go and see that Meg is all right. I don't want her to know we're going down there. It might make her nervous. She doesn't like the thought of those steps one little bit!"

Those words made me excited and scared at the same time. I'd been bursting with curiosity to find out what was farther down the cellar steps, but at the same time I knew that to go down there would be anything but a pleasant experience.

We found Meg still in the kitchen. She'd done the washing-up and was now sitting in front of the fire, dozing again.

"She's happy enough for now," said the Spook. "As well as affecting her memory, the potion makes her sleep a lot."

We each lit a candle before going down the stone steps, the Spook leading the way. This time I took more notice of my surroundings, trying to fix the underground part of the house in my memory. I'd been down in quite a

94

few cellars, but I had a feeling that this was likely to be the most scary and unusual one yet.

After the Spook had unlocked the iron gate, he turned and tapped me on the shoulder. "Meg rarely goes into my study," he said, "but whatever happens, don't ever let her get hold of this key."

I nodded, watching the Spook lock the gate behind us. I looked down.

"Why are the steps below so wide?" I asked again.

"They need to be, lad. Things are fetched and carried down these steps. Workmen need good access—"

"Workmen?"

"Blacksmiths and stonemasons, of course—the trades we depend on in our line of work!"

As we descended, the Spook leading the way, my candle flickered his shadow up onto the wall, and despite the echo of our boots on the stone steps, I heard the first faint noises from far below. There was a sigh and a distant choking cough. There was definitely something or someone down there!

There were four levels underground. The first two both had just one door, set into the stone, but at last we came to the third, which had the three doors I'd seen the day before.

"The middle one, as you know, is where Meg usually sleeps when I'm away," the Spook said.

Now she'd been given a room upstairs, next to the Spook's, probably so that he could keep an eye on her — though based on the evidence from last night, she preferred to sleep in her rocking chair by the fire.

"I don't use the others much," continued the Spook, "but they can be very useful for keeping a witch locked up safely while all the arrangements are made — "

"You mean while a pit is prepared?"

"Aye, I do that, lad. As you'll have noticed, it's not like Chipenden here. I don't have the luxury of a garden, so I have to make use of the cellar."

The fourth and lowest level was, of course, the cellar itself. Even before we turned the final corner and it came into full view, I could hear things that made the candle tremble in my hand, sending the Spook's shadow dancing wildly.

There were whisperings and groans and, worst of all, a faint sound of scratching. Being the seventh son of a seventh son I can hear things that most people can't, but I never really get used to it. On some days I'm braver than others, that's all I can say. The Spook seemed calm enough, but he'd been doing this for a lifetime.

The cellar was big, even bigger than I'd expected, so big, in fact, that it must have been larger in area than the actual ground floor of the house. One wall was dripping with water, and the low ceiling directly above it was oozing with damp, so I wondered if it was on the edge of the stream or actually underneath it.

The dry part of the ceiling was covered in cobwebs, so thick and tangled that an army of spiders must have been at work. If just one or two had spun all that, I didn't want to meet them.

I spent a lot of time looking at the ceiling and walls because I was delaying the moment when I had to look at the ground. But after a few seconds I could feel the

Spook's eyes on me, so I had no choice and finally forced myself to look down.

I'd seen what the Spook kept in two of the gardens back at Chipenden. I suppose this was just more of the same, but whereas the graves and pits back there had been scattered among the trees where the sun occasionally shone to dapple the ground with shadows, here there were lots more, and I felt trapped, closed in by the four walls and the low cobwebbed ceiling.

There were nine witch graves in all, each one marked with a gravestone, and in front of this six feet of soil edged with smaller stones. Fastened to those stones by bolts, and covering each patch of earth, were thirteen thick iron bars. They'd been placed there to stop the dead witches under them from clawing and scratching their way to the surface.

Then, along one wall of the cellar, there were much heavier, larger stones. There were three of those, and each one had been carved by the mason in exactly the same way:

I
Gregory

The Greek letter beta told anyone who could read the signs that boggarts were safely bound beneath them, and the Latin numeral "I" in the bottom right-hand corner said that they were of the first rank, deadly creatures capable of killing a man quicker than you could blink your eyes. Nothing new there, I thought, and as the Spook was good at his job there was nothing to fear from the boggarts who were trapped there.

"There are two live witches down here as well," said the Spook, "and here's the first one," he continued, pointing to a dark, square pit with a boundary of small stones crossed by thirteen iron bars to stop her from climbing out. "Look at the cornerstone," he said, pointing downward.

I saw something then that I hadn't noticed before, even back in Chipenden. The Spook held his candle closer so that I could see it better. There was a sign, *much smaller* than that on the boggart stones, followed by the witch's name.

Gregory

Bessy Hill

"The sign is the Greek letter sigma because we classify all witches under S for sorceress. There are so many types that, being female and subtle, they're often difficult to categorize precisely," said the Spook. "Even more so than a boggart, a witch has a personality that can change over time. So you have to refer to their history—the full history of each, bound or unbound, is recorded in the library back at Chipenden."

I knew that wasn't true of Meg. There was very little

written about her in the Spook's library, but I didn't say anything. Suddenly I heard a faint stirring from the darkness of the pit and took a quick step backward.

"Is Bessy a first-rank witch?" I asked the Spook nervously, because they were the most dangerous and could kill. "It isn't marked on the stone. . . ."

"*All* the witches and boggarts in this cellar are first rank," the Spook told me, "and I bound 'em all, so it's not always worth putting the mason to extra trouble with the carving, but there's nothing to fear here, lad. Old Bessy's been in there a long time. We've disturbed her and she's just turning over in her sleep, that's all. Now come over here and look at this. . . ."

It was another witch pit, exactly like the first one, but I suddenly shivered with cold. Something told me that whatever was in that pit was much more dangerous than Bessy, who was asleep and just trying to get herself comfortable on the cold, damp ground.

"You might as well take a closer look, lad," said the Spook, "so that you can see what we're dealing with.

Hold up your candle and look down, but be sure to keep your feet well back!"

I didn't want to do it, but the Spook's voice was firm. It was a command. To look down into the pit was part of my training, so I had no choice.

I leaned my body forward, keeping my toes well back from the bars, and held the candle up so that it cast a flickering yellow light down into the pit. At that very moment I heard a noise from below, and something big scuttled across the floor and into the dark shadows in the near corner. It sounded wick with life, as if it could scamper up the wall of the pit faster than you could blink!

"Hold your candle right over the bars and take a proper look!" commanded the Spook.

I obeyed, holding it out at arm's length. At first all I could see were two large, cruel eyes staring up at me, two points of fire reflecting the candle flame. As I looked more carefully, I saw a gaunt face framed by a tangle of thick, greasy hair, and a squat, scaly body below it. There were four limbs, and they were more like arms than legs, with huge, elongated hands that ended in long, sharp claws.

I shuddered, and my hand trembled so much that I almost dropped the candle through the bars. I stepped back too quickly and nearly fell over, but the Spook caught hold of my shoulder and steadied me.

"Not a pretty sight, is it, lad," he muttered, shaking his head. "What we've got down there is a lamia witch. She looked human enough over twenty years ago when I first put her there. Now she's become feral again. That's what happens when you put a lamia witch in a pit. Deprived of human companionship, she slowly reverts to type. And even after all these years, she's still strong. That's why I have the iron gate on the stairs. If she ever managed to get out of here, that would slow her up for a while.

"And that's not all, lad. You see, a normal witch pit isn't good enough for her. There are iron bars on the sides and bottom of the pit, too, buried under the soil. So she's really in a cage. That, and a layer of salt and iron beyond that. She can dig fast and deep with those four clawed hands as well, so it's the only way we can stop her from getting out! Anyway, do you know who she is?"

It was a strange sort of question. I looked down and read her name from the stone.

Gregory

MARCIA SKELTON

The Spook must have seen the expression on my face as the penny dropped, because he smiled grimly. "Aye, lad. That's Meg's sister."

"Does Meg know she's down here?" I asked.

"She did once, lad, but now she can't remember; so it's best to keep it that way. Now come over here—I've got something else to show you."

He led the way between the stones to the far corner, which seemed to be the driest place in the cellar; the ceiling above seemed mostly clear of cobwebs. It was an open pit, ready for use, and the cover lay next to it on the ground, waiting to be dragged into position.

I saw then, for the first time, how the cover for a witch pit was made. The outer stones were cemented together in a square, and long bolts went through them from end to end to make sure they stayed in place. The thirteen steel bars were also really long bolts, too, which were tightened by nuts recessed into the stones. It was all quite clever, and a stonemason and a smith, working together, would have needed a lot of skill to make it.

Suddenly my mouth dropped open and stayed that way just long enough for the Spook to notice. This time there was no sign, but a name had already been carved on the nearest cornerstone:

MEG SKELTON

"Which do you think's the better way, lad?" the Spook asked. "Herb tea or this? Because it's got to be one or the other."

"Herb tea," I said, my voice hardly more than a whisper.

"Right, so now you know why you can't afford to forget to give it to her each morning. If you forget, she'll remember, and I don't want to have to bring her down here."

I had a question I wanted to ask then, but I didn't, because I knew the Spook wouldn't like it. I wanted to know why what was good enough for one witch wasn't good enough for them all. Still, I knew I couldn't complain that much: I would never forget how close to the dark Alice had once got. So close that the Spook had thought it best to put *her* in a pit. He'd only relented because I'd reminded him of how he'd let Meg off.

That night I found it difficult to get to sleep. My head whirled with what I'd seen and the realization of where I was living. I've seen some scary things, but living in a house with witch graves, bound boggarts, and live witches in the cellar didn't make me rest easy. In the end I decided to tiptoe downstairs. I'd left my notebooks in the kitchen and I wanted my Latin one: I knew that half an hour staring at boring lists of nouns and verbs would be sure to send me off to sleep.

Even before I reached the foot of the stairs, I heard noises that I didn't expect. Someone was crying softly in the kitchen, and I could hear the Spook talking in a low voice. When I reached the kitchen door, I didn't go in; it was slightly open and I saw something through the crack that halted me in my tracks.

Meg was sitting in her rocking chair close to the fire. She had her head in her hands, and her shoulders were heaving with sobs. The Spook was leaning over her, speaking softly and stroking her hair. His face, lit by candlelight, was half turned toward me and wore an expression on it that I'd never seen before. It was similar to the way my brother Jack's big, craggy face sometimes softens when he looks at his wife, Ellie.

Then, as I watched, to my astonishment, a tear leaked from my master's left eye and ran all the way down his cheek to reach his mouth.

I knew not to pry any longer, so I went back up to bed.

CHAPTER VI
A NASTY PIECE OF WORK

THE days soon began to settle into a steady routine.

In the mornings my chores were to light the downstairs fires and bring fresh water from the stream. Every second day I had to light all the fires in the house to keep the place from getting too damp. As I made the bedroom fires, my instructions were to open each window for about ten minutes to air the room. I had to clean out all the grates first, and I went up and down stairs so much that I was glad when it was over. The one in the attic was the worst, of course, and I always used to do that first, before my legs got too tired.

The attic was a really big room, the biggest in the house, with a lot of floor space. It only had one window, and that was a huge skylight in the roof. The room was empty except for a large mahogany writing desk, which was locked. On the brass plate around its keyhole was an embossed pentacle, a five-pointed star within three concentric circles. I knew that pentacles were used to protect magicians when they summoned daemons, and I wondered why the plate had that design.

The desk looked very expensive, and I also wondered what was in it and why the Spook didn't bring it down to his study, which would have been a much more suitable and useful place. I never did get around to asking him about that desk. And when we finally talked about it, it was already too late.

After airing the attic, I would work my way down, a floor at a time. The three bedrooms directly below the attic weren't furnished. There were two at the front of the house and one at the back. The back room was the worst and darkest room in the whole house, because it only had one window, which faced back toward the cliff. As I raised the sash and peered out, the damp rock was so close that I could almost reach out and touch it. There was a ledge on the cliff with a path running upward. It seemed to me that it might be possible to climb out of the window and up onto the ledge. Not that I was daft enough to try it! One slip and I'd dash out my brains on the flags below.

After lighting the fires, I gave Meg her herb tea, then practiced my Latin verbs until breakfast, which was a lot later in the morning than it had been at Chipenden. Following that, it was lessons for most of the day, but late in the afternoon I usually went for a short walk with the Spook, no more than twenty minutes downhill to the foot of the clough, where it opened out onto the lower slopes of the moor. Despite the hard work seeing to the fires, I'd got a lot more exercise back in Chipenden and was starting to feel restless. Each morning the air seemed colder, and the Spook told me that the first of the snow would be with us soon.

One morning my master went off to Adlington to see his brother Andrew, the locksmith. When I asked if I could go with him, he refused.

"Nay, lad, somebody needs to keep a careful eye on Meg. Besides, I've got things to talk to Andrew about. Family things that are private. And I need to bring him up to date on what's been happening."

By that I guessed the Spook was going to tell his brother the full story of what had happened to us in Priestown, when my master had almost been burned to death by the Quisitor. Once we were back in Chipenden, the Spook had sent a letter to Adlington, telling his brother that he was safe, but now he probably wanted to fill in the details.

I was disappointed to be left behind—I was desperate to find out how Alice was getting on—but I had no choice, and despite the herb tea Meg really did need watching carefully. The Spook was particularly concerned that she might leave the house and wander off, so I had to make sure that both front and back doors were kept locked. As it happened, what she did was completely unexpected.

It was getting late in the afternoon, and I'd been in the Spook's study writing up a lesson in my notebook. Every fifteen minutes or so, I'd go and see if Meg was all right. Usually I'd find her dozing in front of the fire; either that or preparing the vegetables for supper. But when I checked this time she wasn't there.

I ran to the doors first, just in case, but they were both locked. After looking in the parlor, I went upstairs. I expected to find her in her room, but after knocking and receiving no reply, I tried the door. The room was empty.

The farther upstairs I went, the worse I began to feel. When the attic was empty, too, I started to panic. But then I took a deep breath. *Think!* I told myself. Where else could Meg be?

There *was* only one other place, and that was on the steps that led down to the cellar. It didn't seem likely, because the Spook had told me even the thought of the steps made her nervous. First I checked in his study, standing on the stool to search the top of the bookcase. There was no way she could have got the key without me noticing, but I confirmed that anyway. It was still there. With a sigh of relief, I lit a candle and went down the steps.

I heard the gate long before I reached it. It kept clanging loudly, sending that din reverberating right up through the house. If it hadn't been for the fact that I expected to find Meg there, I would have assumed something had come up from the cellar and was trying to get out.

But it was Meg, all right. She was gripping the bars tightly, and tears were streaming down her face. By the light of the candle I saw her shake the gate. From the force she put into it, I could tell that she was still very strong.

"Come on, Meg," I said gently, "Let's go back upstairs.

It's cold and drafty down here. If you're not careful, you'll catch a chill."

"But there's someone down there, Billy. Someone down there who needs help."

"There's nobody down there," I told her, aware that I was lying. Her sister Marcia, the feral lamia, was down there, trapped in her pit. Was Meg starting to remember?

"But I'm sure there is, Billy. I can't remember her name, but she's down there and she needs me. Please open the gate and help me. Let me go down and look. Why don't you come with me and bring your candle?"

"I can't, Meg. You see, I don't have the key to open the gate. Come on, please. Just come back up to the kitchen. . . ."

"Will John know where the key is?" Meg asked.

"Probably. Why don't we ask him when he gets back?"

"Yes, Billy, that's a good idea. We'll do that!"

Meg smiled at me through her tears and walked back up the steps. I led her into the kitchen and sat her down in her rocking chair by the fire.

"You sit here and warm yourself, Meg. I'll go and make you another cup of herb tea. You'll need it after being down those cold, damp stairs. . . ."

Meg had already drunk her usual dose for the day and I didn't want to risk making her ill, so I just put a very small amount in her cup and added hot water. She thanked me and soon gulped it down. By the time the Spook returned, she was already asleep.

When I told him what had happened, he shook his head. "I don't like the sound of this, lad! From now on, her morning dose needs to be three-quarters of an inch in the bottom of a cup. I don't want to do it, but we've no choice."

He looked really down in the mouth. I'd rarely seen him look so dejected. But I soon found out that it wasn't just because of Meg.

"I've had some bad news, lad," he told me, sinking wearily into a chair by the kitchen fire. "Emily Burns has passed away. She's been cold in her grave for over a month."

I didn't know what to say. Long years had passed since

he'd been with Emily. Since then, Meg had been the woman in his life. Why should he be so sad?

"I'm sorry," I said lamely.

"But not half as sorry as me, lad," the Spook said gruffly. "She was a good woman, Emily. She had a hard life but always did her best. The world will be a poorer place now that she's gone! When the good die, it sometimes unshackles evil that would otherwise have been kept in check!"

I was going to ask him what he meant by those mysterious words, but at that point Meg started to stir and opened her eyes, so we lapsed into silence, and he didn't mention Emily again.

At breakfast on the eighth morning after we'd arrived, the Spook pushed back his plate, complimented Meg on her cooking, and then turned to me.

"Well, lad, I think it's about time you went to see how the girl's coping. Think you can find your way?"

I nodded, trying not to grin too widely, and within ten

minutes I was striding down the clough to emerge onto the hillside with the open sky above. I headed north of Adlington, toward Moor View Farm, where Alice was staying.

When the Spook had decided to travel to his winter house, I'd assumed that the weather would break soon afterward, and indeed it had been getting steadily colder. But today things seemed to have changed for the better. Although it was a cold, frosty morning, the sun was shining, the air was clear, and I could see for miles. It was the kind of morning when it feels good to be alive.

Alice must have seen me approaching down the hill, because she came out of the farmyard and walked up to meet me. There was a small wood just outside the boundary of the farm, and she waited there in the shadow of the trees. She looked really gloomy, so I knew, even before we spoke, that she wasn't happy in her new home.

"It ain't fair, Tom. Old Gregory couldn't have found me a worse place to stay! Ain't much fun staying with the Hursts."

"Is it really that bad, Alice?" I asked.

"Be better off at Pendle, and that's saying something."

Pendle was where most of Alice's family of witches lived. She hated it there because they treated her badly.

"Are they cruel to you, Alice?" I asked, becoming alarmed.

Alice shook her head. "Ain't laid a hand on me yet. But they don't talk to me much either. And it didn't take me long to work out why they're so quiet and unhappy. It's that son of theirs—the one called Morgan, who Old Gregory asked about. Cruel and mean, he is. A really nasty piece of work. What kind of son would hit his own father and shout at his mother till she cries? He don't even call 'em Mam and Dad. 'Old Man' and 'Old Woman' is the best they get from him. Scared of him, they are, and they lied to Old Gregory because Morgan visits a lot. Dread his visits, they do. Nothing to do with me, but I can't stand much more of it. If need be, one way or another, I'll sort him out."

"Don't do anything yet," I told her. "Let me talk to the Spook first."

"Don't think he'll exactly be rushing to help. Reckon Old Gregory's done it on purpose. That son of theirs is one of his own kind. Wears a cloak and hood and carries a staff, too! Probably asked him to keep an eye on me."

"Well, he's not a spook, Alice."

"What else could he be?"

"He's one of the Spook's failed apprentices, and they don't get on. Remember the last night at Chipenden when I brought that letter and the Spook got really angry? Didn't get a chance to tell you, but that letter was from Morgan. He's been threatening the Spook. He said my master's got something that belongs to him."

"Well, he's a nasty piece of work all right," continued Alice. "Don't only visit the house. Some nights he walks down the hill and goes to the lake. Watched him last night. He stands right on the edge of the shore and stares at the water. Sometimes his mouth moves like he's talking to someone. His sister drowned in the lake, didn't she? Reckon he's talking to her ghost. Wouldn't be surprised if he drowned her!"

"And he hits his dad?" I asked. That had shocked me more than anything. It made me think of my own dad, and a lump came to my throat at the memory. How could anyone raise a fist to their own dad?

Alice nodded. "They've rowed twice since I've been here. Big rows. First time, old Mr. Hurst tried to push him out of the house and they struggled. Morgan's much younger and stronger, and you can guess who came off worst. Second time he dragged his dad upstairs and locked him in his room. The old man started crying. I didn't like that. It made me remember what it was like living with my own family back in Pendle. Maybe if you tell Old Gregory how bad it is, he'll let me come and stay with you."

"I don't think you'd like it much up on Anglezarke. The cellar's full of pits and he has two live witches down there, and one of them is Meg's sister and she's a feral lamia. Watching her scuttle about her pit is really scary. But I feel most sorry for Meg herself. You were right about her. She does live in the house with the Spook, but he's got her dosed up with a potion so that she can't remember who she is. She spends more than half the year locked in a room downstairs near the cellar. It's very sad to watch. But the Spook hasn't any choice. It's either that or put her in a pit like her sister."

"It ain't right to keep a witch in a pit. Never did hold with that. But I'd still rather be there with you than here having to see Morgan most days. I feel lonely, Tom. I miss you!"

"I miss you, too, Alice, but there's nothing I can do about it at the moment. I *will* tell the Spook what you've said, though, and ask him again. I'll do my best, I promise. Anyway, is Morgan down there now?" I asked, nodding toward the farm.

Alice shook her head. "Not seen him since yesterday. No doubt he'll be back soon."

We didn't talk much longer after that because Mrs. Hurst, the farmer's wife, came to the back door and started yelling Alice's name, so she had to go.

Alice pulled a face and raised her eyes to heaven.

"I'll come back and see you soon!" I said as she turned to go.

"Do that, Tom. But ask Old Gregory, please!"

I didn't go straight back to the Spook's house, though. I climbed right up onto the moor, to where the wind could blow the cobwebs from my mind. My first impression was that the moortop was pretty flat, and the scenery was nowhere near as good as on the fells above Chipenden. Neither was the view of the countryside below as dramatic.

Still, there were higher hills to the south and east, and beyond Anglezarke, even more moors. There was Winter Hill and Rivington directly south, Smithhills beyond that and, to the east, Turton Moor and Darwen Moor. I knew that because I'd studied the Spook's maps before we left, taking care to fold them properly afterward. So I already had a good idea of the layout of the area in my head. There was lots to explore, and I decided I'd ask the Spook if I could have a day off to do just that before the winter weather really closed in. I thought he'd probably agree, because part of a spook's job is to know the geography of the County, in order to get quickly from place to place and find the way when someone sends for help.

I walked farther until I saw a small, domed hill in the distance, right on top of the moor. It looked artificial and I guessed that it was a barrow, a burial mound for some ancient chieftain. Just as I was about to turn away, a figure appeared on its summit. He carried a staff in his left hand and wore a cloak with its hood pulled forward. It had to be Morgan!

His appearance on the barrow was so sudden that it almost seemed as if he'd materialized out of thin air. However, common sense told me that he'd simply walked up the slope on the far side of the hill.

But what was he doing? I couldn't work it out. It looked like some sort of dance! He was throwing himself about and waving his arms in the air. Then, very suddenly, he gave a roar of rage and hurled his staff to the ground. He was in a fury. But at what?

A moment later, and a patch of mist drifted in from the east to hide him, so I walked on. I certainly didn't fancy meeting him face-to-face. Especially with the mood he was in!

After that I didn't stay too long up on the moors. Anyway, if I returned in reasonable time, the Spook would be more likely to let me go and see Alice again soon. And I wanted to get back and tell him what I had learned.

So after our midday meal, I told my master about seeing Morgan up on the moor and all that Alice had said about him.

The Spook scratched his beard and sighed. "The girl's right. Morgan's a nasty piece of work, that's for sure. He dresses like a spook, and that's what some gullible folk now think he is. But he lacked the discipline to master our trade. He was lazy, too, and liked to cut corners. It's almost eighteen years since he left me, and since then he's mostly been up to no good. He fancies himself as a mage and takes money from good honest folk who are at their most vulnerable. I tried to stop him from falling into bad ways, but some people, it seems, just refuse to be helped."

"A mage?" I asked, not familiar with the word.

"It's another word for a magician or wizard, lad. Someone who practices so-called magic. He does a bit of healing, too, but his speciality is necromancy."

"Necromancy? What's that?" I asked. I'd never heard the Spook use that term before, either, and I realized I'd have a lot of notes to write up in my book after our chat.

"Think, lad. It comes from the Greek, so you should be able to work out what it means!"

"Well, *nekros* means corpse," I said, after a bit of careful thinking. "So I suppose it's something to do with the dead."

"Good lad! He's a mage who uses the dead to help him and give him power."

"How?" I asked.

"Well, as you know, ghosts and ghasts are both part of the job. But whereas we give 'em a good talking-to and send 'em on their way, he does the opposite. He uses the dead. He uses them as spies. Encourages them to stay trapped on earth—to serve his purposes and help him line his pockets with silver. Sometimes by tricking vulnerable, grieving folk."

"Is he just a fraud, then?" I asked.

"No, he talks to the dead, all right. So remember this and remember it well: Morgan is a dangerous man, and his meddlings with the dark have given him some very real and dangerous powers that we should fear. He's ruthless, too, and would seriously hurt anyone who got in his way. So stay well clear, lad."

"Why haven't you stopped him before now?" I asked. "Shouldn't you have sorted him out years ago?"

"It's a long story," said my master. "Happens I should have, but the time wasn't right then. We'll deal with him soon. Try to steer clear of him till we're ready—and stop telling me how to do my job!"

I hung my head, and my master tapped me lightly on the arm. "Come on, lad, no harm done. Your point's a good one. I'm glad to see you're thinking with your head.

And the girl did well to spot him talking to his sister's ghost. That's exactly why I placed her there, to look out for things like that!"

"But that's not fair!" I protested. "You knew that Alice would have a hard time of it there."

"I knew it wouldn't be a bed of roses, lad. But the girl has to make up for what she's done in the past, and she's more than capable of looking after herself. Still, once we've dealt with Morgan, it'll be a far happier household. But first we've got to find him."

"Alice says the Hursts lied. Morgan visits the farm a lot."

"Does he now!"

"She said he isn't there at the moment but he could come back at any time."

"Well, perhaps that's where we should start our search tomorrow," the Spook said, looking thoughtful.

When the silence lengthened, I kept my promise to Alice, even though I knew it was a waste of time asking.

"Couldn't Alice stay with us again?" I asked. "She's

really having a terrible time. It's cruel to leave her when there's room enough for her here."

"Why ask a question when you already know the answer?" said the Spook, glaring at me angrily. "Don't talk soft. If you let your heart rule your head, then the dark will beat you every time. Remember that, lad—it may just save your life one day. And we've enough witches living here already."

So that was the end of that. But we didn't visit the Hursts' farm the following day. Something happened that changed everything.

CHAPTER VII
THE STONE-CHUCKER

STRAIGHT after breakfast, a big, burly farmer's lad hammered on the back door with both fists, as if his very life depended on it.

"What are you trying to do, you big lummox?" cried the Spook, opening the door wide. "Break the blooming thing?"

The lad stopped banging at the door,

and his face turned a bright red. "I asked for you down in the village," he said, pointing back toward Adlington. "A carpenter came out of his yard and pointed the way up here. He told me to knock hard at the back door."

"Aye, but he said knock, not thump it back into a tree," said the Spook angrily. "Anyway, what's your business with me?"

"Dad sent me. He said to come right away. It's a bad business. A man's dead."

"Who's your dad?" asked the Spook.

"Henry Luddock. We're at Stone Farm near Owshaw Clough."

"I've met your dad and I've worked for him before. Are you William, by any chance?"

"That's right."

"Well, William, the last time I visited Stone Farm, you were just a tiny babe in arms. Now, I can see you're upset, so come inside and take the weight off your feet. Then take a deep breath, calm yourself, and start right at the beginning. I want all the details, so leave nothing out," ordered the Spook.

As we walked through the kitchen to reach the parlor, I saw no sign at all of Meg. When she wasn't working, it was usual for her to sit in her rocking chair, warming her hands at the kitchen fire. I wondered if she was keeping out of the way now that we had visitors—something she should have done when the groceries were delivered by Shanks.

Once in the parlor, William began his tale of events that had begun badly and then got a whole lot worse. It seemed that a boggart, probably the one my master and I had heard passing along the ley line nights before, had settled itself at Stone Farm, starting its mischief by making a few noises during the night. It had rattled the pots and pans in the kitchen, banged on the front door, and thumped the walls a few times. That was enough for me to identify it right away from the notes I had made about boggarts.

It was a hall-knocker, so I'd already guessed what was

coming next in William's story. The next morning it had started throwing stones. At first they were just small pebbles that it pinged against the windows, rolled down the slates, or dropped down the chimney. Then the stones got bigger. Much bigger.

The Spook had taught me that hall-knockers sometimes developed into stone-chuckers. These were bad-tempered boggarts and very dangerous to deal with. The dead man was a shepherd employed by Henry Luddock. His body was found on the lower slope of the moor.

"He'd been brained," William told us. "The stone that did it was bigger than his head."

"Can you be sure it wasn't an accident?" the Spook asked. "He might just have tripped up, fallen, and bashed himself."

"We're sure, all right: he was lying on his back and the stone was on top of him. Then, while we were bringing the body down, other stones started falling around us. It was terrible. I thought I was going to die. So will you come and help? Please. My dad's going mad with worry.

There's work to be done, but it's not safe to go out-doors."

"Aye, go back and tell your dad I'm on my way. As for the work, milk the cows and do only what's necessary. The sheep can take care of themselves, at least until the snows come, so stay off the hillside."

When William had left, the Spook turned to me and shook his head gravely. "It's a bad business, lad," he said. "Stone-chuckers cause mischief but rarely kill, so this one's a rogue that could well do the same again. I've sorted out one or two like this before and usually ended up with at least a bad headache for my trouble. It's dif-ferent to dealing with a ripper, but sometimes it can be just as dangerous. Spooks have been killed by stone-chuckers."

I'd dealt with a ripper in the autumn. The Spook had been ill, and I'd had to do it without him, helped by a rigger and his mate. It had been pretty scary, because rippers kill their prey. This was scary too, but in a different way. There wasn't much you could do to defend yourself against boulders falling from the sky!

"Well, someone has to do it!" I said with a smile, putting a brave face on it.

The Spook nodded gravely. "They certainly do, lad, so let's get on with it."

There was something that had to be done before we left. The Spook led me back into the parlor and told me to take down the brown bottle labeled HERB TEA.

"Make Meg up another drink, lad," said the Spook. "Only this time make it stronger. Pour out a good couple of inches. That'll do the trick, because we should be back within the week."

I did as I was told, using at least two inches of the dark mixture. Then I boiled the kettle and filled the cup almost to the brim with hot water.

"Drink this, Meg," the Spook told her as I handed her the steaming cup. "You'll need this because the weather's turning colder and it might make your bones ache."

Meg smiled at him, and within ten minutes she'd drained the cup and her head was already beginning to nod. The Spook handed me the key to the gate on the stairs and told me to lead the way. Then he picked Meg up as if she were a baby and followed hard on my heels.

I unlocked the gate, then went down the steps and waited at the middle door of the three while my master carried Meg into the darkness inside. He left the door open, and I could hear every word he said to her.

"Good night, my love," he said. "Dream about our garden."

I'm sure I shouldn't have heard that, but I had, and I did feel a little embarrassed to hear my master of all people talk like that.

And what garden was the Spook talking about? Did he mean the gardens at Chipenden? If so, I hoped he meant the western garden with its view of the fells. The other two, with their boggart pits and graves for witches, didn't bear thinking about.

Meg said nothing in reply, but the Spook must have woken her up when he came out and locked the door behind him, because she suddenly started to cry like a child afraid of the dark. Hearing that sound, the Spook paused, and we waited outside the door a long time until the crying finally subsided and was replaced by another very faint sound. I could hear the breath whistling out through Meg's teeth as she exhaled.

"She's all right now," I said quietly to my master. "She's asleep. I can hear her snoring."

"Nay, lad!" said the Spook, giving me one of his withering glances. "It's more like singing than snoring!"

Well, it certainly sounded like snoring to me, and all I could think was that the Spook didn't like even the slightest criticism of Meg. Anyway, that said, we went up, locked the gate behind us, and packed our things for the journey.

We went east, climbing deeper into the clough, until it grew so narrow that we were almost walking in the stream and there was just a tiny crack of gray sky above us. Then, to my surprise, we came to some steps cut into the rock.

They were narrow, steep steps, slippery with patches of ice. I was carrying the Spook's heavy bag, which meant that, if I slipped, I only had one hand free to save myself.

Following my master, I managed to get to the top in one piece, and it was certainly worth the climb because I was back in the fresh air again, with wide-open spaces on every side. The wind was gusting fit to blow us right off the moor, and the clouds were dark and menacing, racing so close above our heads that it felt like you could almost reach up and touch them.

As I told you, being a moor, Anglezarke was high but a lot flatter than the fells we'd left behind in Chipenden. There were some hills and valleys though, some of them very strange shapes. One in particular stood out because it was a smallish mound, too rounded and smooth to be natural. As we passed close to it, I suddenly recognized it as the barrow where I'd seen the Hursts' son.

"That's where I saw Morgan," I told the Spook. "He was standing right on top of it."

"No doubt he was, lad. He always was fascinated by

that barrow and just couldn't stay away. They call it the Round Loaf, you know, because of its shape," said the Spook, leaning on his staff. "It was built in ancient times, by the first men who came to the County from the west. They landed at Heysham, as you well know."

"What's it for?" I asked.

"Few know for sure, but many are daft enough to make a guess. Most think it's just a barrow where an ancient king was laid to rest with all his armor and gold. Greedy folks have dug deep pits, but for all their hard work, they found nothing. Do you know what the word Anglezarke means, lad?"

I shook my head and shivered with cold.

"Well, it means 'pagan temple.' The whole moor was a vast church, open to the skies, where that ancient people worshipped the old gods. And, as your mam told you, the most powerful of those gods was called Golgoth, which means Lord of Winter. This mound, some say, was his special altar. To begin with, he was a powerful elemental force, a spirit of nature who loved the cold. But because he was worshipped so long and so fervently, he became aware and willful, sometimes lingering long after his allotted season and threatening a year-long grip of ice and snow. Some even think that it was Golgoth's power that brought about the last Ice Age. Who knows the truth? In any event, in the depths of winter, at the solstice, fearing that the cold would never end and that spring would never return, people made sacrifices to appease him. Blood sacrifices, they were, because men never learn."

"Animals?" I asked.

"Humans, lad—they did it so that, gorged on the blood of those victims, Golgoth would fall satisfied into a deep sleep, allowing spring to return. The bones of those sacrificed still remain. Dig anywhere within a mile of this spot and it won't be long before you find bones aplenty.

"This mound is something else that's always bothered me about Morgan. He couldn't keep away from the place and was always interested in Golgoth—far too much for my liking—and he probably still is. You see, some folks think Golgoth could be the key to achieving magical supremacy, and if a mage like Morgan were to tap into the power of Golgoth, then the power of the dark could overwhelm the County."

"And you think Golgoth is still here, somewhere on the moor. . . ."

"Aye. It's said that he sleeps far beneath it. And that's why Morgan's interest in Golgoth is dangerous. The thing is, lad, the old gods wax strong when they're worshipped by foolish men. Golgoth's power waned when that worship ceased and he fell into a deep slumber. A slumber we *don't* want him waking from."

"But why did the people stop worshipping him? I thought they were afraid that the winter would never end?"

"Aye, lad, that's true, but other circumstances are sometimes more important. Perhaps a stronger tribe moves onto the moor with a different god. Or maybe crops fail and a people have to move on to a more fertile area. The reason is lost in time, but now Golgoth sleeps. And that's the way I want it to stay. So keep away from this spot, lad, that's my advice. And let's try to keep Morgan away from it, too. Now come on, there can't be much daylight left, so we'd better press on."

With those words, the Spook led us away, and an hour later we came down off the moor and moved northward, arriving at Stone Farm before dark. William, the farmer's son, was waiting for us at the end of the lane, and we made our way up the hill toward the farm just as the light was beginning to fail. But before visiting the farmhouse, the Spook insisted on being taken up to the place where the body had been found.

A track from the back farmyard gate led straight up onto the moor, which was dark and threatening against the gray sky. Now that the wind had dropped, the clouds were moving sluggishly and looked heavy with snow.

About two hundred paces brought us to a clough far smaller than the one where the Spook's house was built but no less gloomy and forbidding. It was just a narrow ravine full of mud and stones, split in two by a fast-moving shallow stream.

There seemed nothing much to see, but I didn't feel at ease and neither did William. His eyes were rolling in his head and he kept spinning around suddenly, as if he thought something might be sneaking up on him from behind. It was funny to watch, but I was too scared to manage even a smile.

"So this is the place?" asked the Spook as William came to a halt.

William nodded and indicated a patch of ground where the tussocks of grass had been flattened.

"And that's the boulder we lifted from his head," he said, pointing at a large lump of gray rock. "It took two of us to lift it!"

The rock was big and I stared at it gloomily, scared to think that something like that could drop from the sky. It made me realize how dangerous a stone-chucker could be.

Then, very suddenly, stones did start to fall. The first was a small one, the noise of it hitting the grass so faint that I only just heard it above the gurgling of the stream.

I looked up into the clouds just in time to see a far larger stone fall, narrowly missing my head. Soon stones of all sizes were dropping around us, some large enough to do us serious damage.

The Spook pointed toward the farm with his staff and, to my surprise, began to lead the way back down the clough. We moved fast, and I struggled to keep up, the bag getting heavier with every step, the mud slippery beneath my feet. We only came to a breathless halt when we reached the farmyard.

The stones had stopped falling, but one of them had already done some damage. There was a cut on the Spook's forehead and blood was trickling down. It wasn't serious and no threat to his health, but seeing him injured like that made me worried.

The stone-chucker had killed a man, and yet somehow my master—who wasn't in his prime—was going to have to deal with it. I knew he really was going to need his apprentice tomorrow. I knew it would be a terrifying day.

○ ○ ○

Henry Luddock made us very welcome when we got back to the farm. Soon we were seated in his kitchen in front of a blazing log fire. He was a big, jovial, red-faced man who hadn't let the threat from the boggart get him down. He was sad at the death of the shepherd he'd hired but was kind and considerate toward us and wanted to play the host by offering us a big supper.

"Thanks for the offer, Henry," the Spook told him, declining politely. "It's very kind of you, but we never work on a full stomach. That's just asking for trouble. But you just go ahead and eat what you want anyway."

To my dismay, that's exactly what the Luddock family did. They sat down and tucked into big helpings of veal pie, while a measly mouthful of pale yellow cheese and a glass of water each was all the Spook allowed us.

So I sat there nibbling my cheese, thinking about Alice in that house where she was so unhappy. If it hadn't been for this boggart, the Spook might have dealt with Morgan and made things better. But with a stone-chucker to face, who knew when he would get around to it now?

There were no spare bedrooms at the Luddocks', and the Spook and I spent an uncomfortable night, each wrapped in a blanket on the kitchen floor, close to the embers of the fire. Cold and stiff, we were up the following morning well before dawn and set off for the nearest village, which was called Belmont. It was downhill all the way, which made progress easy, but I knew that soon we'd have to retrace every step, making the hard climb back up to the farm.

Belmont wasn't very large—just a crossroads with half a dozen houses and the smithy we'd come to visit. The blacksmith didn't seem very pleased to see us, but that was probably because our knocking got him out of bed. He was big and muscular like most smiths, certainly not a man to trifle with, but he looked at the Spook warily and seemed ill at ease. He knew my master's trade, all right.

"I need a new ax," said the Spook.

The smith pointed to the wall behind the forge, where a number of ax heads were displayed, roughly shaped, ready for their final finish.

The Spook chose quickly, pointing to the biggest. It was a huge double blade, and the blacksmith looked my master up and down quickly, as if judging whether he was big and strong enough to wield it.

Then, without further ado, he nodded, grunted, and set to work. I stayed by the forge, watching while the blacksmith heated, beat, and shaped that ax head on his anvil, every so often quenching it in a tub of water with a great sizzle and cloud of steam.

He hammered it onto a long wooden shaft before sharpening it at the grindstone, the sparks flying. In all, it was almost an hour before the blacksmith was finally satisfied and passed the ax to my master.

"Next I need a large shield," said the Spook. "It has to be big enough to protect the two of us, yet light enough for the lad to hold at arm's length above his head."

The blacksmith looked surprised but went into his store at the back and returned with a large circular shield. It was made of wood with a metal rim. It also had an iron center boss with a spike, so the blacksmith began by removing this and replacing it with more wood to make the shield lighter. Then he covered the outside of the shield with tin.

By gripping its outer edge, I was now able to hold the shield above my head with both arms outstretched. The Spook said that wouldn't do because my fingers could get hurt and I might drop the shield. So the usual leather strap was replaced by two wooden handles just inside the rim.

"Right, let's see what you can do," said the Spook.

He made me hold the shield in different positions at different angles, and then, satisfied at last, he paid the blacksmith and we set off back toward Stone Farm.

We went up onto the fell right away. The Spook had to leave his staff behind because he had his hands full carrying the ax and his own bag. I was struggling with the heavy shield, glad that he didn't expect me to carry his bag as well. We climbed until we reached the place where the man had died. Then the Spook paused and looked hard into my eyes.

"You need to be brave now, lad. Very brave. And we have to work quickly," he told me. "The boggart's living under the roots of an old thorn tree up yonder. We have to cut down and burn the tree to drive it out."

"How do you know that?" I asked. "Do stone-chuckers usually live under tree roots?"

"They live anywhere that takes their fancy. But generally boggarts do like living in cloughs, and particularly under the roots of thorn trees. The shepherd was killed at the foot of this clough right here. And I know there's a thorn tree farther up, because that's exactly where I dealt with the last one, almost nineteen years ago, when young William was just a babe in arms and Morgan was my apprentice. But that's given us a problem, because whereas that boggart listened to a bit of friendly persuasion and moved on when I asked, this is a rogue stone-chucker that's already killed, so words won't be enough."

So then, heading due north, we entered the western edge of the clough, the Spook setting a fast pace ahead of me: soon we were both breathing hard. The mud gradually gave way to loose stones, making it difficult underfoot.

At first we kept close to the top of the clough, but then the Spook led the way down the scree until we reached the edge of the stream. It was shallow and narrow, but still it boiled across the stones, rushing downward with such force that it would have been difficult to cross. We continued upward against its flow, the banks on either side rising up steeply until only a narrow crack of sky was visible overhead. Then, despite the noise of the stream, I heard the first pebble drop into the water just ahead.

It was something I'd been expecting, and soon there were others, forcing me to take the shield from my back and try to hold it over our heads. The Spook was taller than me, so I had to hold it up high, and it wasn't long before my shoulders and arms began to ache. Even though I held it at arm's length, the Spook was forced to stoop, and progress wasn't comfortable for either of us.

Soon we came in sight of the thorn tree. It wasn't particularly big, but it was an ancient tree, black and twisted, with gnarled roots that resembled claws. It stood defiant, having survived the worst of the weather for a hundred years or more. It was a good place for a boggart to make its home, especially a stone-chucker like this, a type that avoided human company and liked to be alone.

The falling stones were getting larger by the minute, and just as we reached the tree, one bigger than my fist clanged onto the shield, nearly deafening me.

"Hold it steady, lad!" the Spook shouted.

Then the stones stopped falling.

"Over there . . ." My master pointed, and in the darkness below the tree's branches I could see the boggart starting to take shape. The Spook had told me that this type of boggart was really a spirit and had no flesh, blood, and bone of its own; but sometimes, when it tried to scare people, it covered itself with things that made it visible to human eyes. This time it was using the stones and mud from beneath the tree. They rose up in a big whirling wet cloud and stuck to it so that its shape could be seen.

It wasn't a pretty sight. It had six huge arms, which, I suppose, were pretty useful for throwing stones. No wonder it could hurl so many so fast. Its head was enormous, too, and its face was covered with mud, slime, and pebbles that moved when it scowled at us, just as if an earthquake were taking place underneath. There was a black slit for a mouth and two large black holes where its eyes should have been.

Ignoring the boggart and wasting no time, as stones started to shower down again, the Spook went straight for the tree, the ax already swinging down as he reached it. The gnarled old wood was tough, and it took quite a few blows to lop off its branches. I'd lost sight of the boggart, being too busy trying to hold up the shield and ward off the worst of the stones that came our way. The shield seemed to be getting heavier by the minute, and my arms were trembling with the effort of holding it aloft.

The Spook attacked the trunk, striking at it in a fury. I

knew then why he'd chosen an ax with a double-blade: he swung it both forehand and backhand in huge scything arcs, so that I felt in danger of my life. Looking at him, you'd never have guessed he was so strong. He was a long way from being young, but I knew then, by the way the ax-blade bit deep into the wood, that despite his age and recent ill health he was still at least as strong as the blacksmith and would have made two of my dad.

The Spook didn't chop the tree right down; he split the trunk, then put down the ax and reached into his black leather bag. I couldn't see what he was doing properly because the stones began to rain down harder than ever. I glanced sideways and saw the boggart begin to ripple and expand: huge bulging muscles were erupting all over its body like angry boils. And, as more mud and pebbles flew up, it almost doubled in size. Then two things happened in quick succession.

The first was that a huge boulder fell out of the sky to our right and buried itself half in the ground. If that had landed on top of us, the shield would have been useless.

We'd both have been flattened. The second was that the tree suddenly burst into flames. As I said, I didn't get a chance to see how the Spook managed it, but the result was certainly spectacular. The tree went up with a great *whoosh* and flames lit up the sky, sparks crackling away in every direction.

When I looked left, the boggart had vanished, so with trembling arms I lowered the shield and rested its lower edge on the ground. No sooner had I done so than the Spook picked up his bag, leaned the ax against his shoulder, and, without a word or a look behind him, set off down the fell.

"Come on, lad!" he called after me. "Don't dawdle!"

So I picked up the shield and followed, not risking even a glance backward.

After a while the Spook slowed down, and I caught up with him. "Is that it?" I asked. "Is it over?"

"Don't be daft!" he said, shaking his head. "It's only just begun. That was just the first step. Henry Luddock's farm is safe now, but that boggart will strike again somewhere else very soon. There's a lot worse to come yet!"

I was disappointed, because I'd thought the danger was over and our task completed. I'd been really looking forward to a hot, tasty meal, but now the Spook had dashed my hopes, because we'd have to carry on fasting.

As soon as we got back, he told Henry Luddock that he'd got rid of the boggart. The farmer thanked him and promised to pay him the following autumn, directly after the harvest; five minutes later, we were on our way back to the Spook's winter house.

"Are you sure that boggart will come back? I really thought the job was done," I told the Spook as we crossed the moor, the wind blustering at our backs.

"In truth, the job's half done, lad, but the worst is yet to come. Just as a squirrel buries acorns to eat later, a boggart stores reserves of power where it lives. Mercifully, that's now gone, burned away with the tree. We've won the first big battle, but after a couple of days spent gathering strength, it'll start plaguing somebody else."

"So are we going to bind it in a pit?"

"Nay, lad. When a stone-chucker kills so casually, it needs to be finished off for good!"

"Where will it get new strength from?" I asked.

"Fear, lad. That's how it'll do it. A stone-chucker feeds upon the fear of those it torments. Some poor family nearby is in for a night of terror. I don't know where it'll go and who it'll choose, so there's nothing I can do about it and no warnings to be given. It's just one of the things we have to accept. Like killing that poor old tree. I didn't want to do it, but I had little choice. That boggart'll keep moving, gathering strength, but within a day or two it'll find itself a new, more permanent home. And that's when somebody will come and ask us for help."

"Why did the boggart become rogue in the first place?" I asked. "Why did it kill?"

"Why do *people* kill?" asked the Spook. "Some do and

some don't. And some who start out good end up bad. I reckon this stone-chucker got fed up with being just a hall-knocker and lurking around buildings scaring people with raps and bumps in the night. It wanted more; it wanted the whole hillside to itself and planned to drive poor old Henry Luddock and his family out of their farm. But now, because we've destroyed its home, it'll need a new one. So it'll move farther down the ley."

I nodded.

"Well, maybe this'll cheer you up," he said, pulling a piece of yellow cheese out of his pocket. He broke off a small piece and handed it to me. "Chew on this," he told me, "but don't swallow it all at once."

Once back at the Spook's house, we brought Meg up from the cellar and I settled back into my routine of chores and lessons. But there was one big difference. As we were expecting boggart trouble, the fast continued. It was torture for me to watch Meg cook her own meals while we went hungry. We had three full days of starving ourselves, until my stomach thought my throat had been cut, but at last, about noon on the fourth day, there came a loud knocking on the back door.

"Well, go and see to it, lad!" commanded the Spook. "No doubt it's the news we've been waiting for."

I did as I was told, but when I opened the door, to my astonishment, I found Alice waiting there.

"Old Mr. Hurst sent me," Alice said. "There's boggart trouble down at Moor View Farm. Well? Aren't you going to ask me in?"

CHAPTER VIII
THE STONE-CHUCKER'S RETURN

THE Spook had been right in his prediction, but he was as surprised as I'd been when I showed our visitor into the kitchen. "The boggart's turned up at the Hursts' farm," I told him. "Mr. Hurst's asked for help."

"Come through to the parlor, girl. We'll talk there," he said, turning to lead the way.

Alice smiled at me, but not before she'd glanced toward Meg, who had her back to us and was warming her hands over the fire.

"Sit yourself down," my master said to Alice, closing the parlor door. "Now tell me all about it. Start at the beginning and take your time."

"Ain't much to tell," Alice began. "Tom's told me enough about boggarts for me to be sure that it's a stone-chucker. It's been throwing rocks at the farm for days— it ain't safe to go out. Risked my life just getting out to fetch you. The yard's full of boulders. There's hardly a pane of glass left, and it's knocked three pots off the chimney stack. It's a wonder nobody's been hurt."

"Hasn't Morgan tried to do anything about it?" asked the Spook. "I taught him enough of the basics about boggarts."

"Ain't seen him for days. Good riddance to bad rubbish!"

"Sounds like it's what we've been waiting for," I said.

"Aye, reckon so. You'd best prepare the herb tea. Make it as strong as last time."

I stood up and opened the cupboard next to the fireplace, taking out the big brown glass bottle. As I turned around, I could see the disapproval on Alice's face. The Spook saw it, too.

"No doubt, as usual, the lad's told you all about my private business. Therefore you'll know what he's going to do and why it's necessary. So take that look off your face!"

Alice didn't reply but followed me into the kitchen and watched me make the herb tea while the Spook went into his study to bring his diary up to date. By the time I'd finished, Meg was dozing in her chair, so I had to wake her gently by shaking her shoulder.

"Here, Meg," I told her as she opened her eyes. "Here's your herb tea. Sip it carefully so that you don't burn your mouth."

She accepted the cup, but then stared at it thoughtfully. "Haven't I already had my tea today, Billy?"

"You need an extra cup, Meg, because the weather's getting colder by the day."

"Oh! Who's your friend, Billy? She's such a pretty girl! What lovely brown eyes!"

Alice smiled when she called me "Billy" and introduced herself. "I'm Alice, and I used to live at Chipenden. Now I'm staying at a farm nearby."

"Well, come and visit us whenever you want," Meg invited her. "I don't get much female company these days. I'd be glad to see you."

"Drink your tea, Meg," I interrupted. "Sip it while it's hot. It's best for you that way."

So Meg began to sip the potion, and it didn't take that long for her to finish the lot and nod off to sleep.

"Better get her down the steps into the cold and damp!" Alice said, an edge of bitterness in her voice.

I didn't get a chance to reply, because the Spook came out of the study and lifted Meg from her chair. I took the candle and unlocked the gate while he carried her down to her room in the cellar. Alice stayed in the kitchen. Five minutes after our return, the three of us were on the road.

❍ ❍ ❍

Moor View Farm had taken a battering. Just as Alice had described, the yard was full of stones and almost every pane of glass had been smashed. The kitchen window was the only one still intact. The front door was locked, but the Spook used his key and had it open in seconds. We searched for the Hursts and found them cowering in the cellar; of the boggart there was no sign at all.

The Spook wasted no time.

"You'll have to leave here right away," he told the old farmer and his wife. "I'm afraid there's nothing else for it. Just pack essentials and get yourselves gone. Leave me to do what's necessary."

"But where will we go?" Mrs. Hurst asked, close to tears.

"If you stay, I can't guarantee your lives," the Spook told them bluntly. "You've relatives down in Adlington. They'll have to take you in."

"How long before we can come back?" asked Mr. Hurst. He was worried about his livelihood.

"Three days at the most," answered the Spook. "But don't worry about the farm. My lad'll do what's necessary."

While they packed, my master ordered me to do as many of the farm chores as possible. Everything was quiet: no stones were falling, and it seemed that the boggart was resting. So, making the best of that situation, I started by milking the cows; it was nearly dark by the time I'd finished. When I walked into the kitchen, the Spook was sitting at the table alone.

"Where's Alice?" I asked.

"Gone with the Hursts, where else? We can't have a girl getting under our feet when there's a boggart to be dealt with."

I was really tired, so I didn't bother to argue with him. I'd just half hoped that Alice would have been allowed to stay.

"Sit yourself down and take that glum look off your face, lad. It's enough to turn the milk sour. We need to be ready."

"Where's the boggart now?" I asked.

The Spook shrugged. "Resting under a tree or a big boulder, I suppose. Now that it's dark, it won't be long before it arrives. Boggarts can be active in daylight and, as we found to our cost up on the fell, will certainly defend themselves if provoked. But night is their favorite time and when they're at their strongest.

"If it is the same boggart we met up at Stone Farm, then things are likely to get rough. For one thing, it'll remember us as soon as it gets close, and it'll want revenge for what we did. Breaking windows and knocking a few chimney pots down won't be enough. It'll try to smash this farmhouse to the ground, with us inside it. So it'll be a fight to the finish. Anyway, lad, cheer up," he said, catching a glimpse of my worried face. "It's an old house, but it's built of good County stone on very strong foundations. Most boggarts are even more stupid than they look, so we're not dead yet. What we need to do is weaken it further. I'll offer myself as a target. When I've sapped its strength, you finish it off with salt and iron, so get your pockets filled, lad, and be ready!"

I'd used that old salt-and-iron trick myself when I'd faced the old witch Mother Malkin. The two combined substances were very effective against the dark. Salt would burn the boggart; iron would bleed away its power.

So I did as my master instructed, filling my pockets from the pouches of salt and iron that he kept in his bag.

Just before midnight, the boggart attacked. A big storm had been brewing for hours, and the first distant rumbles had given way to crashes of thunder overhead and flashes of sheet lightning. We were both in the kitchen, sitting at the table, when it happened.

"Here it comes," muttered the Spook, his voice so low that he seemed to be talking more to himself than to me.

He was right: a couple of seconds later the boggart came ranting and raving down the fell and rushed at the farmhouse. It sounded as if a river had burst its banks and a flood was racing toward us.

The kitchen window blew in, scattering shards of glass everywhere, and the back door bulged inward as if some great weight were leaning against it. Then the whole house shook like a tree in a storm, leaning first one way, then the other. I know that sounds impossible, but I swear it happened.

Next there was a ripping and popping noise overhead and the tiles began to fly off the roof and crash down into the farmyard. Then, for a few seconds, everything became quiet and still, as if the boggart were resting or thinking what to do next.

"Time to get this over with, lad," said the Spook. "You stay here and watch through the window. Things'll turn nasty out there for sure."

I thought things were pretty nasty already, but I didn't say so.

"At all costs, whatever happens," continued my master, "don't go outside. Only use the salt and iron when the boggart comes into the kitchen. If you use it outside in this weather, he won't get the full impact. I'll lure the boggart inside. So be ready."

The Spook unlocked the door and, carrying his staff, went out into the farmyard. He was the bravest man I'd ever met. I certainly wouldn't have liked to face that boggart in the dark.

It was pitch black out there, and in the kitchen all the candles had blown out. Being plunged into total darkness was the last thing I wanted, but fortunately we still had a lantern. I brought it near to the window, but it didn't cast much light out into the yard. The Spook was some distance away, so I still couldn't see all of what was happening and had to rely on flashes of lightning.

I heard the Spook rap three times with his staff on the flags; then, with a howl, the boggart flew at him, rushing across the farmyard from left to right. Next there was a cry of pain and a sound just like a branch snapping. When the lightning flashed again, I saw the Spook on his knees, his hands held up in front of him, trying to protect his head. His staff lay on the flags some distance from him, broken into three pieces.

In the darkness I heard stones hitting the flags close to the Spook and more tiles falling off the roof above him. He cried out in pain maybe two or three times, and despite having been told to watch from the window and wait for the boggart to come inside, I wondered if I should go out and try to help. My master was having a hard time of it and seemed certain to come off worst.

I stared out into the darkness, trying to see what was happening, hoping for lightning to light up the yard again. I just couldn't see the Spook at all. But then the back door began to creak open very slowly. Terrified, I moved away from it, retreating until my back was against the wall. Was the boggart coming for me now? I placed the lantern on the table and got ready to reach into my breeches pockets for the salt and iron. A dark shape slowly crossed the threshold into the kitchen, and I froze, petrified, but then sucked in a breath as I saw the Spook on his hands and knees. He'd been crawling toward the door in the shadow of the wall. That's why I hadn't been able to see him.

I rushed forward, slammed the door shut, then helped him to the table. It was a struggle, because his whole body seemed to be trembling and there wasn't much strength in his legs. He was a mess. The boggart had hurt him badly: there was blood all over his face and a lump the size of an egg on his forehead. He rested both hands against the table's edge, struggling to keep on his feet. When he opened his mouth to speak, I could see that one of his front teeth was missing. He wasn't a pretty sight.

"Don't worry, lad," he croaked. "We've got him on the run. He hasn't much strength left, and now it's time to finish him off. Get ready to use the salt and iron, but whatever happens, don't miss!"

By "on the run," the Spook meant he'd offered himself as a target and the boggart had used up a lot of its energy in trying to destroy him and was now a lot weaker. But how much weaker? It would still be very dangerous.

At that very moment the door burst open again, and this time the boggart did come in. The lightning flashed, and I saw the round head and the six arms caked in mud. But there was a difference: it looked much smaller now. It had lost some of its power, and the Spook hadn't suffered in vain.

My heart hammering and my knees trembling, I moved forward to face the boggart. Then I reached into my pockets and pulled out two handfuls and hurled them straight at the boggart. Salt from my right hand; iron from my left.

Despite what it had cost him, the Spook had done everything by the book. Firstly he'd burned the boggart's tree, taking away its store of energy. Secondly he'd offered himself as a target outside, bleeding away even more of the boggart's strength. But I had to finish the job inside. And I couldn't afford to miss.

There was only the draft from the window and open door, and my aim was good. The cloud of salt and iron struck the boggart full on. There was a scream, so loud and shrill that it set my teeth on edge and almost burst my eardrums. The salt was burning the creature, the iron sapping the last of its power. The next moment the boggart disappeared.

It was gone. Gone forever. I'd finished it off!

But my relief was short-lived. I saw the Spook stagger

and knew that he was about to fall. I tried to reach him—I really tried. But I was too late. His knees buckled; he lost his grip on the table and collapsed backward, banging his head on the kitchen flags very hard. I struggled to lift him, but he was a dead weight, and I noticed, to my dismay, that his nose was bleeding badly.

I began to panic. At first I couldn't hear him breathing. Then, at last, I made out the breath fluttering very faintly in his throat. The Spook was seriously hurt and needed a doctor urgently.

CHAPTER IX
INTIMATIONS OF DEATH

I ran all the way down the hill to the village in the torrential rain, the thunder crashing overhead and vivid streaks of lightning forking the sky.

I hadn't a clue where the doctor lived and, in desperation, knocked on the first door I came to. There was no answer, so I hammered on the next one with my fists. When that brought no answer either, I remembered that the Spook's brother, Andrew, had a shop somewhere in the village. So I ran farther down toward the center, stumbling across the cobbles and through the rivulets of rainwater that were cascading down the hill.

It took me a long time to find Andrew's place. It was smaller than the Priestown one he'd rented, but it was in a good location, in Babylon Lane, just around the corner from what seemed to be the village's main row of shops. A flash of lightning illuminated the sign above the window.

ANDREW GREGORY

MASTER LOCKSMITH

I rapped hard on the shop door with my knuckles and, when that brought no response, seized the handle and rattled it violently, still to no avail. I wondered if Andrew was away doing a job somewhere. Maybe staying overnight in another village. Then I heard the sash window of a bedroom above the next shop being raised, and a man's angry voice called out into the night.

"Be off with you! Be off at once! What do you mean making all that commotion at this time o' night when decent folk need their sleep?"

"I need a doctor!" I shouted up toward the dark oblong of the window. "It's urgent. A man could be dying!"

"Well, you're wasting your time here! That's a locksmith's shop!"

"I work for Andrew Gregory's brother. He lives in the house up the clough, on the edge of the moor. I'm his apprentice!"

The lightning flashed again, and I glimpsed the face above and saw fear etched into it. The whole village probably knew that Andrew's brother was a spook.

"There's a doctor lives on the Bolton Road, about a hundred yards or so to the south!"

"Where's the Bolton Road?" I demanded.

"Go down the hill to the crossroads and turn left.

That's Bolton Road. Then keep going. It's the last house on the row!"

With that, the window was slammed shut, but it didn't matter: I had the information I needed. So I sprinted down the hill, turned left, ran on, breathing hard, and was soon knocking on the door of the last house in the row.

Doctors are used to being woken up in the middle of the night for emergencies, so it didn't take him long to answer the door. He was a small man with a thin black mustache and hair that was turning gray at his temples. He was holding a candle and nodded as I spoke, seeming very calm and businesslike. I told him that the injured man was at Moor View Farm, but when I explained who needed help and why, his manner changed and the candle began to shake in his hand.

"You get back, and I'll follow you as soon as I can," he said, closing the door in my face.

I went back up toward the moor, but I was worried. The doctor was clearly scared at having to treat a spook. Would he do as he'd promised? Would he really follow me to the farm? If he didn't, the Spook could die. For all I knew he might be dead already, and with a heavy heart I trudged up the hill as fast as I could. By then the worst of the storm had moved away and all that could be heard were distant rumbles of thunder over the moor and the occasional flash of sheet lightning.

I needn't have worried about the doctor. He was true to his word and reached the farm only fifteen or so minutes after me.

But he didn't stay long. When he examined the Spook, his hands shook so badly I didn't need the wide-eyed expression on his face to tell me that he was terrified. Nobody likes to be near a spook. I'd also told him what had happened in the yard and kitchen, which made it even worse. He kept looking around as though he expected to see the boggart creeping up on him. I would have found it funny if I hadn't felt so sad and worried.

He did help me carry the Spook up the stairs and get him to bed. Then he put his ear against the Spook's chest and listened carefully. When he stood up, he was shaking his head.

"Pneumonia is creeping into his lungs," he said at last. "There's nothing I can do."

"He's strong!" I protested. "He'll get better."

He turned to me with an expression on his face that I'd seen doctors use before. It was a professional face, a mixture of compassion and calm, a mask adopted when they have to break bad news to relatives of the seriously ill.

"I'm afraid the prognosis is very bad, boy," he said, patting me gently on the shoulder. "Your master is dying — it's unlikely that he'll survive the night. But death comes to us all in the end, so I'm afraid we have to accept it. Are you here alone?"

I nodded.

"Will you be all right?"

I nodded again.

"Well, I'll send someone up here in the morning," he said, picking up his bag and preparing to go. "He'll want washing," he added ominously.

I knew what he meant by that. It was a County tradition to wash the dead before burial. It had always seemed a daft idea to me. What was the point of washing someone when they were just going to end up in a coffin in the ground? I was angry and almost told him as much, but I managed to control myself and went and sat beside the bed, listening to the Spook gasping for breath.

He couldn't be dying! I refused to believe it. How could he die after all he'd been through? I just wasn't prepared to accept it. The doctor was wrong, surely? But no matter how hard I tried to convince myself that the doctor was mistaken, I began to despair. You see, I remembered what Mam had said about intimations of death. I remembered the smell in Dad's room, that stench of flowers, and how Mam had said it was a sign of the approach of death. I had her gift and I could smell it now, because it was coming from the Spook, and it was getting stronger and stronger by the minute.

◎ ◎ ◎

But when daylight came, my master was still alive and the woman sent by the doctor to wash his body couldn't keep the disappointment from her face.

"I can't stay longer than noon. I've another one to do this afternoon!" she snapped, but then she told me to get a clean bedsheet and rip it into seven pieces, and to bring her a bowl of cold water.

After I'd done what she asked, she took a strip of the sheet, folded it until it was no bigger than the palm of her hand, and dipped it into the water. Then she used it to bathe the Spook's forehead and chin. It was hard to tell whether she'd done that to make him feel better or to save herself a bit of time washing the body later.

That done, she sat down beside the bed and started knitting what looked like baby clothes. She talked a lot, too, telling me the story of her life and boasting about her two jobs. Besides washing the dead and preparing them for burial, she was also the local midwife. She had a bad cold and kept coughing all over the Spook and blowing her red nose into a large, mottled handkerchief.

Just before noon, she started to pack her things ready to go. "I'll be back in the morning to lay him out," she said. "He won't survive a second night."

"Is there no hope at all?" I asked her, aware that the Spook hadn't opened his eyes since banging his head.

"Listen to him breathing," she told me.

I listened carefully. His breathing sounded harsh, with a faint rattle to it. It was as if his windpipe were constricted.

"That's a death rattle," she said. "His time in this world is coming to an end."

At that moment there was a knock on the front door and I went down to see who it was. When I opened the door, Alice was standing close to the step, her woolen coat buttoned up to the neck and her hood pulled forward.

"Alice!" I said, really glad to see her. "The Spook got hurt dealing with the boggart. He bashed the back of his head and the doctor thinks he's going to die!"

"Let me look at him," Alice said, pushing past me.

"Maybe it ain't as bad as he thinks. Doctors can be wrong. Is he upstairs?"

I nodded and followed Alice up to the front bedroom. She went straight across to the Spook and put her hand on his forehead. Then she lifted his left eyelid with her thumb and peered at his eye very closely.

"Ain't hopeless," Alice said. "I might just be able to help. . . ."

The woman picked up her bag and prepared to leave, indignation furrowing her brow. "Well, I've seen it all now!" she exclaimed, staring down at Alice's pointy shoes. "A little witch offering help to a spook!"

Alice looked up, her eyes blazing with anger, opened her mouth wide, and showed her teeth. Then she hissed at the woman, who took two rapid steps away from the bed.

"Don't expect him to thank you for it!" she warned Alice, backing out of the bedroom door before running down the stairs.

"Ain't got much with me," Alice said when the woman had gone. She unbuttoned her coat and pulled a small leather pouch from her inside pocket. It was fastened with string, and she untied it and shook a few dried leaves onto her palm. "I'll make him up a quick potion for now," she said.

When she'd gone down to the kitchen, I sat at the Spook's bedside, doing what I could to help him. His whole body was burning up, and I kept mopping his brow with the wet cloth to try and bring the fever down. There was a constant trickle of blood and mucus from his nose, and it kept running down into his mustache, so it was a full-time job just keeping him clean. All the time his chest was rattling and the smell of flowers was as strong as ever, so I began to feel that, whatever Alice said, the nurse was right and he hadn't long to go.

After a while Alice came back upstairs carrying a cup half full of a pale yellow liquid, and I lifted the Spook's head while she poured a little of it into his mouth. I wished Mam were here, but I knew that Alice was the next best thing: as Mam had once told me, she knew her stuff regarding potions.

The Spook choked and spluttered a bit, but we managed to get most of it down him. "It's a really bad time of year, but I might be able to find something better," Alice said. "It's worth going out to look. Not that he deserves it, the way he's treated me!"

I thanked Alice and saw her to the front door. It wasn't raining anymore, but there was a chill in the damp air. The trees were bare and everything looked bleak. "It's winter, Alice. What can you find when hardly anything is growing?"

"Even in winter there are roots and bark you can use," Alice replied, buttoning up her coat against the cold. "That's if you know where to look. I'll be back as soon as I can."

I went back up to the bedroom to sit with the Spook, sad and lost. I know it sounds selfish, but I couldn't help starting to worry about myself. I couldn't possibly manage to complete my apprenticeship without the Spook. I'd have to go north of Caster to where Arkwright practiced his trade and ask him to take me on. As he'd once been the Spook's apprentice and had lived at Chipenden like me, perhaps he'd do it, but there was no guarantee. He might already have an apprentice. After thinking that, I felt worse. Really guilty. Because I'd just been thinking about myself, not my master.

Then, after about an hour, the Spook suddenly opened his eyes. They were wild and bright with fever, and to begin with I don't think he knew who I was. He still remembered how to give orders, though, and began shouting them out at the top of his voice as if he thought I was deaf or something.

"Help me up! Get me up! Up! Up! Do it now!" he shouted as I struggled to help him up into a sitting position and to pack the pillows behind his back. He began to groan very loudly, and his eyes rolled in his head and went right up into his skull until only the whites were visible.

"Get me a drink!" he shouted. "I need a drink!"

There was a jug of cold water on the bedside table, and I filled a cup half full and held it gently to his lips.

"Sip it slowly," I advised, but the Spook took a big gulp and spat it out onto the bedclothes.

"What's this rubbish? Is this all I deserve?" he roared, his pupils coming back into view to fix me with a wild, angry stare. "Bring me wine. And make it red. That's what I need!"

I didn't think it was a good idea at all, what with him being so ill, but he insisted again. He wanted wine and it had to be red.

"I'm sorry, but there is no wine," I explained, keeping my voice calm so as not to get him even more agitated.

"Of course there's no wine here! This is a bedroom!" he shouted. "Down in the kitchen, that's where you'll find it. If not, try the cellar. Go and look. And be quick about it. Don't keep me waiting."

There were about half a dozen bottles of wine in the kitchen, and all of them were red. The trouble was, there was no sign of a corkscrew—not that I looked too hard. So I took the bottle back up to the bedroom, thinking that would be the end of it.

I was wrong: as soon as I came near the bed, my master snatched the bottle from me, put it to his mouth, and pulled the cork out with his remaining teeth. For a moment I thought he'd swallowed it, but suddenly he spat it out with such force that the cork bounced off the bedroom wall opposite.

Then he began to drink and, as he drank, he talked. I'd never seen the Spook drink alcohol before, but now he couldn't get the stuff down his throat fast enough. He became more and more excited, the talk giving way to ranting. It didn't make much sense because he was raving with the fever and the drink. A lot of it was in Latin, too, the language I was still struggling to learn. At one point he kept making the sign of the cross with his right hand, the way priests do.

Back at our farm, wine was something we drank rarely. Mam makes her own elderberry wine, and it's really good. It only comes out on special occasions, though: when I lived at home, I was lucky to be given half a small glass twice a year. The Spook finished off a whole bottle in less than fifteen minutes, and later he was sick—so sick that he nearly choked to death there and then. Of course, I had to clean up the mess using the other strips of sheet.

Alice came back soon after that and made up another potion with the roots she'd found. We worked together and managed to get it down the Spook's throat, and within moments he was asleep again.

That done, Alice sniffed the air and wrinkled up her nose. Even after I'd changed the bedclothes the room still stank to high heaven, so that I couldn't smell the flowers anymore. At least, that's what I thought at the time. I didn't realize that the Spook was on the mend.

So the doctor and nurse were both proved wrong: within hours the fever had gone and my master was coughing up thick phlegm from his lungs, filling handkerchiefs as quickly as I could find them, so I ended up tearing another sheet into strips. He was on the slow road to recovery. And once again we owed it all to Alice.

CHAPTER X
BAD NEWS

THE Hursts returned the following day but looked lost and bewildered, as if they didn't know how to start clearing up the mess. The Spook spent most of his time sleeping, but we couldn't let him stay in a room with the wind howling in through the broken window, so I took some money from his bag and gave

· 195 ·

it to Mr. Hurst to pay for some of the repairs.

Workmen were employed from the village: a glazier fitted new glass to the bedroom and kitchen windows, while Shanks boarded up the rest temporarily to keep the elements out. I had a busy day myself, making up the fires in the bedrooms and one downstairs in the kitchen, helping with the farm chores, too, especially the milking. Mr. Hurst did some work, but his heart wasn't in it. It seemed as if he didn't enjoy life anymore and had lost the will to live.

"Oh dear! Oh dear!" he kept muttering wearily to himself. And once I heard him say quite distinctly, as he looked up at the barn roof, his face filled with anguish, "What did I do? What did I do to deserve this?"

That night, just after we'd finished our supper, there were three loud raps on the front door, and they brought poor Mr. Hurst to his feet so suddenly that he almost fell backward over his chair.

"I'll go," Mrs. Hurst said, laying her hand gently on her husband's arm. "You stay here, love, and try to keep calm. Don't go upsetting yourself again."

By their reaction I guessed it was Morgan at the door. And there was something about the manner of the three loud raps that chilled me to the bone. My suspicions were confirmed when Alice looked at me, turned down the corners of her mouth, and mouthed silently the word "Morgan."

Morgan swaggered into the room ahead of his mother. He was carrying a staff and bag. Wearing his cloak and hood, he looked every inch a spook.

"Well, this *is* cozy. And if it isn't the young apprentice himself," he said, turning to me. "Master Ward, we meet again."

I nodded in reply.

"So what's been happening here, old man?" Morgan taunted Mr. Hurst. "That farmyard's a disgrace. Have you no pride in yourself? You're letting this place go to rack and ruin."

"Ain't his fault. Stupid or something, are you?" Alice snapped, hostility heavy in her voice. "Any fool can see it's the work of a boggart!"

Morgan frowned angrily and glared at her, raising his stick a little, but Alice returned his gaze with a mocking smile.

"So the Spook sent his apprentice to deal with it, did he?" Morgan said, turning toward his mother. "Well, that's gratitude for you, isn't it, old woman? You take in a little witch for him, and he can't even be bothered to come and help bind your boggart. He always was a cold-hearted wretch."

I was on my feet in an instant. "Mr. Gregory came right away. He's upstairs because he was badly hurt dealing with the boggart —"

Immediately I knew that I'd said too much. Suddenly I felt afraid for my master. Morgan had threatened him in the past, and now the Spook was weak and defenseless.

"Oh, so you *can* speak," he said, mocking me. "If you ask me, your master's clearly past it. Hurt binding a boggart? Good Lord, that's the easiest trick in the book! But that's what age does. Clearly the old fool's past his best. I'd better go upstairs and have a word with him."

With that, Morgan crossed the kitchen and began to climb the wooden stairs to the bedrooms. I leaned across and whispered that Alice should stay where she was. Then I left the kitchen and made for the stairs. At first I thought that Mrs. Hurst was going to ask me to stay, but she simply sat down and buried her face in her hands.

I began to creep up the stairs, but they were creaky, so I only climbed three before pausing to listen to Morgan's raucous laughter from above, followed by the sound of the Spook coughing. Then the stair creaked behind me, and I turned and looked down to see Alice with her finger against her lips to signal silence.

Next the Spook's voice came from the bedroom above. "Still digging into that old mound?" I heard him ask. "It'll be the death of you one day. Have more sense. Keep well clear while you've still got breath left in your body."

"You could make it easy for me," Morgan replied. "Just give me back what's mine. That's all I ask."

"If I gave you that, you'd do untold damage. That's if you survived. Why does it have to be this way? Stop meddling with the dark and sort yourself out, lad! Remember the promises you made to your mother. It's still not too late to make something of your life."

"Don't pretend to care about me," answered Morgan. "And don't you dare talk about my mother. You never cared one jot about any of us, and that's the truth. Nobody except that witch. Once Meg Skelton came into the picture, my poor mother didn't have a chance. And where did that get you? And where did it get her but condemned to a life of misery?"

"Nay, lad. I cared about you and I cared about your mother. I loved her once, as you well know, and all my life I've done my level best to help her. And for her sake I've tried to help you, despite all that you've done!"

The Spook started to cough again, and I heard Morgan curse and start to walk toward the door. "Things are different now, old man, and I will have what's owed to me," he said. "And if you won't give it to me, then I'll use other means."

Alice and I turned together and went back down the

stairs. We just made it into the kitchen before his boot scuffed against the top stair.

As it was, Morgan didn't even look at us. With a face like thunder, ignoring his mam and dad, he strode straight through the kitchen and into the hallway. We all listened quietly as he drew back a bolt, unlocked a door in the hall, and started stamping about in the room behind. After a few moments we heard him come out again, then lock and bar the door. A moment later he'd left the house; the front door slammed shut behind him.

At the table nobody spoke, but I couldn't help glancing at Mrs. Hurst. So the Spook had loved her once, too. That would make three women he'd been involved with! And that was one reason why Morgan seemed to bear a grudge against him.

"Let's get you up to bed, love," Mrs. Hurst said to her husband, her voice soft and affectionate. "A good night's sleep is what you need. You'll feel much better in the morning."

With that, the two of them left the table, poor Mr. Hurst shuffling toward the door with his head bowed. I felt really sorry for them both. Nobody deserved a son like Morgan. His wife paused in the doorway and looked back at us. "Don't be too late coming up, you two," she said, and we both nodded politely and then listened to them climbing the stairs together.

"Well," said Alice, "That just leaves the two of us. So why don't we go and look at Morgan's room? Who knows what we might find?"

"The room he just went in?"

Alice nodded. "Strange noises sometimes come from it. I'd like to see what's inside."

So she picked up the candle from its holder on the table and led the way out of the kitchen, through the living room, and into the hallway.

There were two rooms that led from that hallway. With your back to the front door, you could go right into the living room; on the left was another door painted black. It had a bolt on the outside.

"This is it," Alice whispered, touching the door with the tip of her left pointy shoe and drawing back the bolt. "If it hadn't been locked, I would've had a nosy round in there already. But now it ain't no problem. Your key'll soon get that open, Tom." She pointed at the lock.

My key did unlock the door, and I eased it open. It was quite a big room, longer than it was wide, with one boarded-up window at the far end, hung with heavy black curtains. The floor was flagged like the rest of the downstairs, but there were no rugs or carpets. And there were only three items of furniture in the room: a long wooden table with a straight-backed chair at each end.

Alice led the way into the room.

"Not much to see, is there?" I said. "What did you expect to find?"

"Ain't sure, but I thought there'd be something more," Alice began. "Sometimes I hear bells ringing in here. Mostly little bells, they are, ones that you could hold in your hand. But I once heard a funeral bell that sounded big enough to be clanging from a church tower. Then there's often the sound of water dripping and a girl crying. I suppose that's his dead sister."

"You hear the sounds when he's inside the room?"

"Mostly, but even when he ain't home I sometimes hear a dog barking and growling or even snuffling right up close to the door like it's trying to get free. That's why the Hursts always keep it bolted. I think they're scared that something nasty might get out."

"I don't feel anything here now, though," I told Alice. There was no sense of the cold that warns me when something from the dark is close. "The Spook says Morgan's a necromancer who uses the dead. He talks to them and makes them do his bidding."

"Where does he get his power from? Don't use bone or blood magic like a witch," Alice said, wrinkling her nose, "and he don't have a familiar either. I'd be able to sniff it out for sure if it was one of them. So what is it, Tom?"

I shrugged. "Maybe it's Golgoth, one of the old gods. You heard what the Spook just said about Morgan digging into that mound and that it would be the death of him? Well, it's a barrow called the Round Loaf and it's high up on the moor. Maybe he's trying to summon Golgoth like the ancients did. Maybe Golgoth wants to be summoned and is helping him in some way. But Morgan can't do it yet, because the Spook has something that he needs. Something that would make it easier."

Alice nodded thoughtfully. "That could be it, Tom, but some of the things they said were puzzling, too. Don't see Old Gregory and Mrs. Hurst together. Find it hard to believe that they were a couple."

I found it hard to believe, too. Very hard. Anyway, there was nothing much to see, so we left the room and locked and bolted it behind us. There were mysteries to be solved—secrets in the Spook's past—and I was growing more and more curious.

Morgan didn't show his face at Moor View Farm again, but it was another week before we could travel back to the Spook's house. Shanks was sent for, and we made the journey back with the Spook riding on the little pony and Alice and me walking behind.

Shanks refused to set foot in the house and went straight back to Adlington, leaving the Spook with us. I'd already told my master how Alice's potions had probably saved his life. He hadn't said anything, but he didn't object now when we both helped him up to his bedroom. He still wasn't himself, and it was going to take some time for him to recover fully. The journey back had taken it out of him, too. He wasn't steady on his legs, and he stayed up in his room for a couple of days.

One thing that surprised me was that at first he never even mentioned Meg. I didn't remind him about her, though: I didn't fancy having to go down the steps to the cellar by myself. As she'd spent the whole summer sleeping down there, a few more days wouldn't matter much. So I had to do most of the chores. Alice helped a bit, but not as much as I'd have liked.

"Just because I'm a girl don't mean that I have to do

all the cooking!" she snapped when I suggested that she'd be better at it than me.

"But I can't cook, Alice," I told her. "Mam did it at home, the Spook's boggart did it at Chipenden, and Meg did it here."

"Well, now's your chance to learn," said Alice with a smile. "And as for Meg, I bet she wouldn't be so keen on doing all the cooking without all that herb tea!"

Then, on the morning of the third day, the Spook finally came wearily downstairs and sat himself down at the table while I did my best to cook the breakfast. Cooking was a lot harder than it looked, but not quite as hard as the bacon ended up.

We ate in silence until, after a few minutes, the Spook pushed his plate away from him. "It's a good job I've not much appetite, lad," he said, shaking his head. "Because hunger would force me to eat all that, and I'm not sure I'd survive the experience."

Alice roared with laughter and I smiled and shrugged, pleased to see my master so clearly on the mend. As bacon went, I'd tasted better, but I was hungry enough to eat anything, and so was Alice. I began to cheer up, because it looked like the Spook was going to let her stay.

The following morning the Spook finally decided that it was time to wake Meg. He was still unsteady on his feet, so I went down the steps with him and helped bring Meg back up to the kitchen while Alice heated some water. The effort proved too much for him, and his hands started to shake so much that he had to take himself back off to bed.

I helped Alice get Meg's bath ready. "Thank you, Billy," Meg said as we began to fill it with hot water. "You're such a considerate boy. And your pretty friend is so helpful, too. What's your name, dear?"

"They call me Alice," she replied with a smile.

"Well, Alice, do you have any family living nearby? It's nice to keep close to family. I wish I had. But now they live so far away."

"I don't see my family now. They were bad company, and I'm better off without them," Alice said.

"Surely not!" Meg exclaimed. "Why, what on earth was wrong, dear?"

"They were witches," Alice replied with a wicked little sideways grin toward me.

I was really annoyed. That kind of talk might jog Meg's memory. Alice was doing it on purpose.

"I knew a witch once," said Meg, a dreamy look in her eyes. "But it was such a long time ago. . . ."

"I think your bath's ready now, Meg," I told her, grabbing Alice's arm and leading her away. "We'll go to the study so that you can have some privacy."

Once in the Spook's study, I rounded on Alice angrily. "What did you have to say that for? She might start to remember that she's a witch herself."

"Would that be so bad?" Alice asked. "Ain't fair, treating her the way he does. She'd be better off dead. Already introduced to her, I was, but she'd forgotten me already."

"Better off dead? More than likely she'd end up in a pit," I retorted angrily.

"Well, why don't you just give her a *little* bit less of the herb tea—so that she has a better life and don't keep forgetting everything? Get the dose just right and she wouldn't remember everything, but things could be a lot better for her. Let me do it, Tom. Ain't too difficult. I'll just give her a little less each day until we get it right—"

"No, Alice! Don't you dare!" I warned. "If the Spook found out he'd send you back to the Hursts in the blink of an eye. Anyway, it's just not worth the risk. Something might go badly wrong."

Alice shook her head. "But it ain't right, Tom. Something's got to be done sooner or later."

"Well, later rather than sooner. You won't do anything about the herb tea, will you? Promise me."

Alice smiled. "I promise, but I think you should talk to Old Gregory about it. Will you do that?"

"It's not the right time to do it now, when he's still ill. But I will when I think the time is right. He won't listen, though. This has been going on for years. Why would he change it now?"

"Just speak to him, that's all I ask."

So I agreed, even though I knew I'd be wasting my time and would just make the Spook angry for nothing. But Alice was starting to worry me. I wanted to trust her, but she certainly had a bee in her bonnet about Meg.

The Spook came down late in the afternoon and managed to eat some broth, then spent the evening wrapped in a blanket in front of the fire. When I went up to bed, he was still there, and Alice was helping Meg to wash the pots ready for breakfast.

The following morning, which was a Tuesday, the Spook gave me a short Latin lesson. He didn't look too well: he tired very quickly and went back to bed, so I was left to study by myself for the rest of the day.

Then, late in the afternoon, there was a knock on the back door. I went to answer it and found Shanks, the Spook's delivery man, waiting there. He had a very nervous expression on his face and kept glancing over my left shoulder, as if he expected somebody to appear behind me at any moment.

"I've brought Mr. Gregory's order," he said, nodding back toward his pony with its load of brown sacks. "And I've got a letter for you. It was delivered to the wrong house, and they were away on business. They've just got back so it must be over a week old."

I looked at him in amazement. Who could be sending me a letter here? He reached into his jacket pocket, pulled out a crumpled envelope and handed it to me. I was worried, because I recognized my brother Jack's handwriting on the envelope and knew it would have cost a small fortune to send the letter by the post wagon: it had to be something serious. It was bad news for certain.

I tore open the envelope and unfolded the letter, which was short and to the point.

Dear Tom,
Our dad's taken bad ways again. He's sinking fast.
All his sons are here but you, so you'd best come
home right away.
Jack

Jack always was blunt, and those words made my heart drop right down into my boots. I couldn't believe that Dad was going to die. I couldn't even imagine it. The world wouldn't be the same without him. And if Jack's letter had been down in the village for a week, waiting to be read, I might already be too late. While Shanks unloaded our provisions, I ran inside, went up to the Spook's bedroom, and, with shaking hands, showed him the letter. He read it, then gave a long sigh.

"I'm sorry to hear your bad news," he said. "You'd best get off home right away. At a time like this your mam will need you by her side."

"What about you?" I asked. "Will you be all right?"

"Don't worry about me, I'll be right as rain. No, you get off while there's some daylight left. You'll want to be down off the moor long before nightfall."

When I went down to the kitchen, Alice and Meg were whispering together. Meg smiled when she saw me. "I'm going to make you both a special supper tonight," she said.

"I won't be here for supper, Meg," I told her. "My dad's ill, and I've got to go home for a few days."

"Sorry to hear that, Billy. Snow's on its way for sure, so wrap up warm against the cold. Frostbite can make your fingers fall off."

"How bad is it, Tom?" Alice asked, looking concerned, so I handed her the letter and she read it quickly.

"Oh, Tom! I'm so sorry," she said, coming across to give me a hug. "Maybe it won't be quite as it seems. . . ."

But when our eyes met, I could tell that she was just saying that to make me feel better. We both feared the worst.

I got ready to set off for home. I didn't bother with my bag—I left that in the study—but I took my staff; in my pocket, in addition to a big piece of crumbly yellow cheese for the journey, I had my tinderbox and a candle stub. You never knew when they might come in useful.

After saying good-bye to the Spook, I walked to the back door with Alice. To my surprise, rather than saying farewell then, she tugged her coat from the hook and pulled it on.

"I'll come down to the end of the clough with you," she said, giving me a sad smile.

So we walked down together. We didn't speak. I was numb and fearful, while Alice seemed really subdued. When we reached the bottom of the clough and I turned toward Alice to say good-bye, to my surprise, I saw that there were tears in her eyes.

"What's wrong, Alice?"

"Ain't going to be here when you get back. Old Gregory's sending me away. I'm off to stay at Moor View Farm again."

"Oh, I'm sorry, Alice. He didn't say anything to me about that. I thought everything was all right."

"He told me last night. Says I'm getting too close to Meg."

"Too close?"

"I think it might be because he saw us chatting together, that's all. Who knows what's going on inside

Old Gregory's head? Just thought I'd tell you. So that you'll know where to find me when you get back."

"I'll call in to see you first thing," I told her. "Even before I go back to the Spook's house."

"Thanks, Tom," Alice said, taking my left hand briefly to give it an affectionate squeeze.

With that, I left her and continued down, pausing once to look back. She was still there watching me, so I gave her a wave. Alice hadn't offered any final words of comfort. She hadn't mentioned my dad. We both knew there was nothing to say, and I dreaded what I would find at home.

Dusk came quickly, helped by a bank of thick, heavy cloud from the north. It was getting dark as I left the heights of the moor; somehow I managed to lose my bearings and missed the track I'd intended to take.

Down below was a copse of trees and a low drystone wall with a small building some way beyond it—probably a farmhand's cottage, which meant that there would most likely be a small road or track leading from it down the hill. I clambered up onto the wall but hesitated before dropping down on the other side. For one thing, it was well over six feet high, and I discovered I was now looking down at a large graveyard. It wasn't a cottage in the distance, either. It was a small chapel.

I shrugged and dropped down among the gravestones. After all, it might be a bit creepy, but I was the Spook's apprentice and I had to get used to places like this, even if it was almost dark. I began to weave my way through the graves, moving downhill, and it wasn't long before my feet were crunching along a gravel path on the approach to the chapel.

It should have been straightforward. The path led down the side of the chapel; beyond that, it meandered through the gravestones toward two huge yew trees that formed an archway over a gate. I should have kept walking, but there was a glimmer of light showing in the small stained-glass chapel window, evidence of the flickering of a candle. And as I passed the door, I noticed that it was slightly ajar, and I distinctly heard a voice from within.

A voice that called out a single word: "Tom!"

It was a deep voice, a man's voice, a voice that was used to being obeyed. I didn't recognize it.

Even though it seemed unlikely, I felt that I was being called. And who could be inside the chapel who knew my name, or that I was passing by in the dark at that moment? There shouldn't have been anyone in the chapel at that time of night. It would only be used occasionally, for short services before burials.

Almost before I realized what I was doing, I went up to the chapel door, opened it, and walked in. To my surprise there was nobody there, but immediately I noticed something really strange about the layout inside. Instead of rows of benches facing toward the altar, with an aisle between them, the benches were in four long rows against the wall, and they were directly opposite a single large confessional box against the wall to my right, which had two large candles positioned like sentries at either side of it.

The confessional box had the usual two entrances, one for the priest and one for the penitent. A confessional box is really two rooms with a dividing screen so that, although the priest can hear confessions through a grille, he can't see the face of the person making the confession. But there was something strange here. Someone had removed the doors so that I was facing two oblongs of utter blackness.

As I stared at the doorways, feeling very uneasy, someone stepped out of the darkness of the priest's entrance on the left and walked toward me. He wore a cloak and a hood just like the Spook.

It was Morgan, although the voice that called me hadn't been his. Was there somebody else in the chapel? As he approached, I had a sudden feeling of intense cold. Not the routine cold that told me something from the dark was close. It was different somehow. It reminded me of the cold I'd experienced when facing the evil spirit called the Bane in Priestown.

"We meet again, Tom," Morgan said with a faint,

mocking smile. "I'm sorry to hear the news about your father. But he had a good life. Death comes to us all in the end."

My heart lurched inside my chest and I stopped breathing. How did he know about Dad's illness?

"But death isn't the end, Tom," he said, taking another step toward me. "And for a while we can still talk to the ones we love. Would you like to speak to your father? I could summon him for you now, if that's what you want. . . ."

I didn't reply. What he was saying was only just starting to sink in. I felt numb.

"Oh, I'm sorry, Tom. Of course, you don't know, do you?" Morgan continued. "Your father died last week."

CHAPTER XI
MAM'S ROOM

MORGAN smiled again, but my heart lurched up into my mouth and I was filled with panic; the world spun about me. Without thinking, I turned and ran for the door. Once through it, I continued on down the path, my feet crunching on the gravel. When I reached the gate, I turned and looked back. He was standing in the open doorway of the chapel. His face was in darkness so I couldn't see his expression, but he lifted his left hand and waved to me. The sort of wave you might give to a friend.

I didn't wave back. I just opened the gate and carried on down the hillside, a mixture of thoughts and emotions running through my head. I was distraught to think that my dad might already be dead. Could Morgan be right about that? He was a necromancer, so had he summoned some ghost who'd told him that? I refused to believe it and tried to push it to the back of my mind.

And why had I run away? I should have stayed and told him what I thought of him. But a lump had surged into my throat and my legs had carried me through the door before I'd had time to think. It wasn't that I'd been afraid of him, even though it had been really creepy to hear him say things like that in the chapel, with candles flickering behind him. It was being confronted with news like that.

○ ○ ○

I don't remember much about the rest of the journey, apart from the fact that it seemed to be getting colder and windier. By the evening of the second day, the wind had veered to the northeast and the sky seemed heavy with snow.

Snow didn't actually start to fall until I was within half an hour of home. The light was beginning to fail, but I knew the way like the back of my hand and it didn't hinder my progress. By the time I opened the gate to the yard, there was a white blanket covering everything and I was chilled to the bone. Snow always makes everything seem quiet, but a special evening stillness seemed to have fallen over the farmhouse. I entered the yard, and the stillness broke as the dogs began to bark.

There was nobody about, though a light was flickering in one of the back bedroom windows. Was I too late? My heart was down in my boots, and I feared the very worst.

Then I saw Jack. He came stomping across the yard toward me. He was scowling, his bushy eyebrows meeting above his nose.

"What kept you?" he demanded angrily. "It doesn't

take over a week, does it? Our brothers have been and gone. And James lives halfway across the County! You were the only one not to arrive —"

"Your letter went to the wrong address. I got it a week late," I explained. "But how is he? Am I too late?" I asked, holding my breath but already reading the truth in Jack's face.

Jack sighed and bowed his head as if unable to meet my eyes. When he raised his head again, his eyes were glinting with tears. "He's gone, Tom," he said softly, all the harshness and anger gone. "He died peacefully in his sleep a week yesterday."

Before I knew it, he was hugging me and we were both crying. I was never going to see my dad again; never hear his voice, his old stories and wise sayings; never shake his hand or ask his advice; and the thought was unbearable. But as I stood there, I remembered someone who'd feel that loss even more than I did.

"Poor Mam," I said, when I could finally speak again. "How's she been?"

"Bad, Tom. Very bad," Jack said, shaking his head sadly. "I've never seen Mam cry before, and it was a terrible sight to see. She was beside herself, didn't eat or sleep for days. And the day after the funeral she packed a bag and left, saying she had to get away for a while."

"Where's she gone?"

Jack shook his head, his face filled with misery. "I only wish I knew," he said.

I didn't say anything to Jack, but I remembered what Dad had once told me: that Mam had her own life to lead and that after he was dead and buried she'd probably return to her own country. And he'd said that when the time came I should be brave and let her go with a smile. I just hoped that she'd not gone already. Would she go without saying good-bye to me? I hoped not. I just had to see her again, even if it was for the last time.

It was the worst supper I could ever remember having at home.

It was so sad not having Mam and Dad at the table,

and I kept glancing at Dad's empty chair. The baby was already upstairs in her cradle, so there were just the three of us, Jack, Ellie, and me, sitting at the table and picking slowly at our food.

When I caught her eye, Ellie smiled sadly but was really quiet. I had a feeling that she wanted to say something to me but was biding her time.

"It's a really good hot pot, Ellie," I told her. "I'm sorry to waste it, but I can't eat much. I just don't feel hungry."

"Don't worry, Tom," she said kindly. "I understand. None of us have any appetite. Just eat what you can manage. It's important to keep your strength up at a time like this."

"It's probably not the right time, but I wanted to say congratulations, you two. Last time I was here, Mam told me you're expecting another baby and that it's a boy."

Jack smiled sorrowfully, his voice subdued. "Thanks, Tom. If only Dad could have lived to see his grandson born. . ." Then he cleared his throat as if he were about to say something important. "Look," he began. "Why don't you stay with us for a few days until the weather improves? You don't have to get back tomorrow, do you? The truth is, I could do with a bit of help on the farm. James stayed for a couple of days, but he had to get back to work."

James was the second oldest of my brothers; a blacksmith. I doubted that he'd stayed on after the funeral because Jack *really* needed help with the farmwork. It wasn't like spring planting, or the autumn harvest, when you used all the help you could get. No, Jack wanted me to stay for the same reason he'd needed James. Despite the fact that he hated spooks' business and wasn't usually happy to have me around, he needed me now to fill the emptiness, the loneliness of being here without Dad and Mam.

"I'd be glad to stay for a few days," I told him with a smile.

"That's really good of you, Tom. I appreciate it," he said, pushing his plate away even though he'd hardly cleared a third of it. "I'll get off to bed now."

"I'll be up later, love," Ellie said to Jack. "You don't mind if I stay down a bit and keep Tom company, do you?"

"Not at all," he said.

When he'd gone up, Ellie gave me a warm smile. She was as pretty as ever, but she looked sad and tired, the strain of the past week having taken its toll. "Thanks for agreeing to stay awhile, Tom," she said. "He needs to talk about the old times with one of his brothers. That's how you grieve, by talking it through over and over again. But I also think he needs you because he believes that if you're here, Mam's more likely to come back. . . ."

I hadn't thought of that. Mam could sense things. She would know that I was staying at the farm. She really might come back to see me.

"I hope she does."

"So do I, Tom. But listen, I want you to be very patient with Jack. You see, there's something he's not told you yet. There was a surprise in your dad's will. Something he didn't expect. . . ."

I frowned. A surprise? What could that be? The whole

family knew that once Dad died, Jack, as the eldest son, would inherit the farm. There was no point in dividing it up among the seven of us and making it smaller and smaller. It was the County tradition. It always went to the eldest son, with the farmer's widow being guaranteed a home for life.

"A *pleasant* surprise?" I asked uncertainly, not knowing what to expect.

"No, not the way Jack sees it. But I don't want you to take this the wrong way, Tom. He's only thinking of me and little Mary and, of course, his unborn son," she said, smoothing her hand across her belly. "You see, Jack hasn't inherited the whole house. One room has been left to you."

"Mam's room?" I asked, already guessing the answer. It was the room where Mam kept her private things; where she'd kept the silver chain that she'd given to me in the autumn.

"Yes, Tom," Ellie said. "That locked room directly below the attic. That room and everything contained within it. Even though Jack owns the house and land, you're always to be allowed access to that room and to stay there whenever you want. Jack went pale when the will was read. It means you could even live here, had you such a mind."

I knew that Jack wouldn't want me near the house much in case I brought something with me; something from the dark. I couldn't argue against that, because it had happened once before. The old witch Mother Malkin had actually found her way down into our cellar last spring. Jack and Ellie's baby daughter, Mary, had been in real danger.

"Did Mam say anything about that?" I asked.

"Not a word. Jack was too upset to talk about it, and then she left the following day."

I couldn't help thinking that giving the room to me now meant that she'd be leaving soon; going off to her own country and leaving us forever. That was, if she hadn't gone already.

⌾ ⌾ ⌾

The following morning I got up very early, but Ellie was down in the kitchen before me. It was the smell of frying sausages that brought me down the stairs. Despite all that had happened, my appetite was beginning to return.

"Have a good night's sleep, Tom?" she asked, giving me a big smile.

I nodded, but it was a white lie. It had taken me a long time to drop off, and then I'd kept waking up. And each time I'd opened my eyes, the pain had come to me again, as if I was realizing for the first time that Dad was dead.

"Where's the baby?" I asked.

"Mary's upstairs with Jack. He likes to spend a bit of time with her each morning. Gives him a good excuse to start work a bit later, too. You won't get much done today anyway," she said, gesturing toward the window. Snowflakes were whirling down, and the room was brighter than on a summer's day as the light reflected off the snow piled deep in the yard.

Soon I was tucking into a plate of sausage and eggs. While I was eating, Jack came down and joined me at the table. He nodded and started on his own breakfast; Ellie went off into the front room, leaving us alone. He picked at his food, chewing it slowly, and I started to feel guilty because I was able to enjoy my own breakfast.

"Ellie told me that you know about the will," Jack said at last.

I nodded but didn't say anything.

"Look, Tom, as the eldest son, I'm the executor of the will and it's my duty to make sure that Dad's wishes are carried out, but I wonder if we could come to some arrangement," he said. "What if I buy the room from you? If I could raise the money, would you sell it to me? And as for Mam's things inside it, I'm sure Mr. Gregory would let you store them at Chipenden. . . ."

"I need time to think, Jack," I told him. "It's all come as a shock. Too much has happened too quickly. Don't worry, I've no plans to keep coming back here. I'll be too busy."

Jack reached into his breeches pocket and pulled out a bunch of keys. He placed them on the table in front of me. There was a large key and three smaller ones. The first was for the door of the room; the other three for the boxes and chests inside.

"Well, there are the keys. No doubt you'll be wanting to go up and see your inheritance."

I reached across and pushed the keys back toward him. "No, Jack," I said. "You keep them for now. I'll not go into that room until I've spoken to Mam."

He looked at me in astonishment. "Are you sure?"

I nodded and he thrust the keys back into his pocket, and nothing more was said about it.

What Jack had said was sensible enough. But I didn't want his money. To buy me out, he'd need to raise a loan and, financially, things would be difficult enough now that he had to run the farm by himself. As far as I was concerned, he could have the room. And I was sure the Spook would let me keep Mam's boxes and chests at Chipenden. But I suspected that it was Mam's wish that the room should be mine, and this was the only thing that stopped me from agreeing immediately. It was in Dad's will but had probably been her decision. Mam always had a very good reason foreverything she did, so I couldn't make up my mind properly until I'd talked to her face-to-face.

That afternoon I went to visit Dad's grave. Jack was going to come with me, but I managed to talk him out of it. I wanted time on my own. An hour or so to think and grieve alone. And there was something else I needed to know. Something that I couldn't do if Jack came with me. He wouldn't have understood, or at best, he would have been really upset.

I timed my walk so that I would arrive at sunset, with just enough light to find the grave. It was a bleak snow-covered graveyard about half a mile from the church. The churchyard itself was full, so they'd consecrated this as additional holy ground. It was really just a small field bounded by a hawthorn hedge with a couple of sycamores on its western boundary. It was easy to find Dad's grave in the front line of burial plots advancing month by month across the field. His grave didn't have a stone yet, but they'd marked it temporarily with a simple cross, his name carved deeply into the wood.

JOHN WARD
RIP

For a while I stood near that wooden cross, thinking of all the happy times we'd had as a family; remembering being small, with Mam and Dad happy and busy and all my brothers living at home. I recalled the last time I'd spoken to Dad and how he'd told me that he was proud to have such a brave son and that, although he hadn't any favorites, he still thought that I'd turn out the best of all.

Tears came into my eyes, and I wept aloud at the side of the grave. But as it grew dark, I took a deep breath and steadied myself, focusing on what had to be done. This was spooks' business.

"Dad! Dad!" I called into the darkness. "Are you there? Can you hear me?"

Three times I called exactly the same, but on each

occasion the only sounds I could hear were the wind whistling through the hawthorn hedge and a lone dog barking far in the distance. So I sighed with relief. Dad wasn't here. His spirit wasn't bound here. He wasn't a graveside lingerer. I just hoped he'd gone to a better place.

I hadn't really made up my mind about God. Maybe God existed and maybe He didn't. If He did, would He bother to listen to me? I didn't usually pray, but this was Dad, so I made an exception.

"Please, God, give him peace," I said softly. "It's what he deserves. He was a good, hardworking man, and I loved him."

Then I turned and, very sadly, made my way back home.

I stayed at the farm for almost a week. When the time came for me to leave, it was raining, the snow turning to slush in the yard.

Mam hadn't come back, and I wondered if she ever would. But my first duty was to get back to Anglezarke and see how the Spook was. I just hoped he was continuing to recover. I told Jack and Ellie that I'd visit them in the spring and that we'd talk about the room then.

I began the long walk south, thinking of Dad and how much things had altered. It didn't seem that long since I was living at home happily with my parents and six brothers, and Dad was strong and fit. Now it was all changing. All falling apart.

In one sense I could never visit home again, because it wouldn't be there anymore. It was all too different now. The buildings would still be the same, and so would the view of Hangman's Hill from my old bedroom window. But without Dad and Mam it simply wouldn't be home.

I knew I'd lost something forever.

CHAPTER XII
NECROMANCY

THE farther south I traveled, the colder it got, the rain gradually turning back to snow. I was tired and wanted to go directly to the Spook's house, but I'd promised Alice I'd visit her first, and I intended to keep my word.

By the time Moor View Farm was in sight, it was already dark. The wind had dropped and the sky was clear. The moon was up and the snow made everything much brighter than usual; beyond the farmhouse, the lake was a dark mirror reflecting the stars.

The farm itself was in darkness. Most County farmers go to bed early in winter, so it was what I'd been expecting. I was hoping that Alice would have sensed my approach, though, and sneaked out to meet me. I climbed over the boundary fence and crossed a field toward the cluster of dilapidated buildings. A cattle shed loomed up before me, and hearing an unusual sound, I halted just outside the open doorway. Someone was crying.

I stepped into the doorway and the animals within edged away nervously. Immediately the stink hit me. It wasn't the usual warm animal smell, plus a few dozen healthy cowpats. It was scour, a digestive illness that cattle and pigs are prone to. It is treatable, but these cattle were ill and neglected. Things had got even worse since I'd last been here.

It was then that I realized someone was watching me.

To my left, lit by a shaft of moonlight, Mr. Hurst was sitting hunched on a milking stool. There were tears running down the old man's cheeks, and he was staring up toward me, misery etched into his face. I took a step backward as he came to his feet.

"Get you gone! Leave me be!" he cried, shaking his fist at me while trembling from head to foot.

I was shocked and upset. He'd always been so meek and mild, never giving me or Alice so much as a cross word. Now he looked desperate and at the end of his tether. I walked away, my head bowed low. I felt very sorry for him. Morgan must have been treating him really badly: no doubt that was why he was upset and embarrassed. I didn't know what to do but thought I'd better speak to Alice about it.

I moved on until I came to the yard. The house was still in darkness, and I wasn't sure what to do. Alice must have been in a very deep sleep not to be aware that I was close by. I waited for a moment, my breath steaming in the cold air.

I walked up to the back door and rapped on it twice. I didn't need to knock again. After a few moments the door opened slowly, creaking on its hinges, and Mrs. Hurst peered out at me, blinking into the moonlight.

"I need to speak to Alice," I told her.

"Come in, come in," she invited, her voice weak and hoarse.

There was a mat just inside the door, so I stepped into the small hallway and, after smiling and thanking her politely, stamped the snow off my boots as best I could. Ahead were the two internal doors. The one on the right was closed; but the door to Morgan's room was partially open, and I saw candlelight flickering beyond.

"Go through," she said, pointing toward it.

For a moment I hesitated, wondering what Alice was doing in Morgan's room, but I went in anyway. The air was heavy with the reek of tallow, and for some reason the first thing I noticed was a thick candle made of black wax, which was set into a big brass candlestick. It was positioned in the center of the long wooden table with its two facing chairs, one at each end.

I'd expected to see Alice there, but I was mistaken. Seated at the near end of the table, and facing away, toward that candle, was a hooded figure. He turned in my direction and I saw a beard and a mocking smile. It was Morgan.

Once again my instinct was to run for it, but I heard two sounds behind me. The first was the door being closed firmly. The second was the heavy bolt being slotted home. Ahead of me was the window covered with a heavy black curtain and no other door. I was locked in the room with Morgan.

I looked about me, glancing down at the bare stone flags, then across to the waiting empty chair. The room was cold, and I shivered. There was a fireplace, but it was filled with gray ashes.

"Take a seat, Tom," Morgan said. "We've a lot to talk about."

I didn't move, so he gestured at the chair opposite him.

"I came here to speak to Alice," I told him.

"Alice has gone," Morgan said. "She left three days ago."

"Gone? Gone where?" I asked.

"She didn't say. She wasn't a very talkative girl, that Alice. Didn't even bother to say she was leaving. Now, Tom, the last time you entered this room you came uninvited like a thief in the night with that girl at your side. But we'll forget that, because now you're very welcome. So I'll say it again. Sit yourself down."

Filled with dismay, I sat down but kept my staff upright by my left side, gripping it firmly. How did he know that we'd been in his room? And I was really worried about Alice. Where could she have gone? Surely not back to Pendle? I looked across and met Morgan's gaze. Suddenly, with a smile, he pulled the hood back from his face to reveal his unruly thatch of hair. There seemed a lot more gray in it than last time. In the candlelight his face was craggy and the lines were far deeper.

"I'd offer you wine," he said, "but I don't drink when I'm working."

"I don't usually drink wine," I told him.

"But no doubt you eat cheese," he said, a mocking grin on his face.

I didn't reply, and his expression became serious. Suddenly he leaned forward, pursed his lips, and blew hard. The candle flickered and went out, plunging the room into absolute darkness while the smell of tallow intensified.

"There's just you, me, and the dark," Morgan said. "Can you stand it? Are you fit to be my apprentice?"

They were the exact words the Spook had said to me in the cellar of the haunted house in Horshaw, the place where he'd taken me on the very first day of my apprenticeship. He'd done it to judge whether or not I was made of the right stuff to become a spook. They were the words he'd spoken the moment the candle went out.

"I'll bet that when you first walked down the steps into the cellar, he was sitting in the corner and stood up the moment you came near," Morgan continued. "Nothing changes. You, me, and two dozen others or more.

Predictable stuff. The old fool! No wonder nobody sticks with him for long."

"You stayed three years," I said softly into the darkness.

"Found your voice again, Tom? That's good," Morgan said. "I see that he's been talking about me. Did he have anything good to say?"

"Not really."

"That doesn't surprise me. And did he tell you why I gave up my apprenticeship as a spook?"

By now my eyes had adjusted to the dark, and I could just make out the shape of his head facing me across the table. I could have told him that the Spook said he'd lacked discipline and wasn't up to the job, but instead I decided to ask a few questions of my own.

"What do you want from me? And why has the door been barred?" I asked.

"So that you can't run away again," Morgan said. "So that you've no choice but to stay and face what I have to show you. You're quite the apprentice, I hear. You and I both know that your master doesn't appreciate that. So this is the first lesson of your new apprenticeship. You'll have had some dealings with the dead, but now I'm going to add to your knowledge. And add to it significantly."

"Why would you want to do that?" I challenged him. "Mr. Gregory's teaching me all I need to know."

"First things first, Tom," Morgan replied. "Let's talk about ghosts first. What do you know about them?"

I decided to humor him. Maybe if I let him get what he wanted to say off his chest, I could be on my way to the Spook's house.

"Most ghosts are bound close to their bones; others to the place where they either suffered or committed some terrible crime while still on earth. They aren't free to wander at will."

"Well done, Tom," Morgan said, an edge of mockery back in his voice. "And I bet you've written it all down in your notebook, too, like a good little apprentice. Well, here's something that the old fool won't have taught you. He won't have mentioned it because he doesn't like to think about it. So here's the big question. Where do the dead go after death? And I don't mean bound ghasts and ghosts. I mean the other dead. The vast majority. People like your father."

At the mention of my dad I sat up straight and stared hard at Morgan. "What do you know of my dad?" I asked angrily. "How did you know he was dead?"

"All in good time, Tom. All in good time. I have powers your master can only dream of. But you haven't answered my question. Where do the dead go after death?"

"The Church says heaven, hell, purgatory, or limbo," I replied. "I'm not sure about all that, and Mr. Gregory never talks about it. But I believe that the soul survives death."

Purgatory was a place where souls went to be cleansed, suffering until they were fit to enter heaven. Limbo was more mysterious. Priests thought that those who weren't baptized went there. It was supposed to be for souls that weren't really evil but, through no real fault of their own, weren't fit to enter Heaven.

"What does the Church know?" Morgan said, a sneering tone entering his voice. "That's about the only thing Old Gregory and I do agree on. But you see, Tom, of the four places you've just mentioned, limbo is by far the most useful for somebody like me. It takes its name from the Latin word *'limbus,'* which means edge or fringe. You see, wherever they're heading, the majority of the dead first have to pass through limbo, which is on the edge of this world, and some find it very hard to do. Some of the weak, the fearful, and the guilty retreat, falling back into this world to become ghosts, joining the lingerers who are already trapped on earth. They are the easiest to control. But even the strong and the good must struggle and fight to pass through limbo. It takes time, and while they're delayed, I have the power to reach any soul there that I choose. I can stop it from passing on. I can make it do what I want. If need be, make it suffer.

"The dead have had their lives. It's over for them. But we're still living and can use them. We can profit from them. I want what Gregory owes me. I want his house in

Chipenden with that big library of books that contains so much knowledge. And then there's something else. Something even more important. Something that he's stolen from me. He has a grimoire, a book of spells and rituals, and you're going to help me get it back. In return, you can continue your apprenticeship, with me training you. And I'll teach you those things he's never even dreamed of. I'll put *real* power at your fingertips!"

"I don't want you training me," I snapped angrily. "I'm happy with things just the way they are!"

"What makes you think that you've any choice in the matter?" Morgan said, his voice suddenly cold and threatening. "I think it's time to show you just what I can do. Now, for your own safety, I want you to sit perfectly still and listen carefully. Whatever happens, don't attempt to leave that chair!"

The room became very quiet, and I did as I was told. What else could I do? The door was locked and he was bigger and stronger than I was. I could use my staff against him, but with no real guarantee of success. It was best to play along with him for now, until I could get away and back to the Spook.

A faint sound came out of the darkness. Something between a rustling and a pattering. It was a bit like mice scampering around under the floorboards. But there weren't any floorboards, just heavy stone flags, and I could feel the room start to grow colder. Usually this would be a sign that something was approaching— something that didn't belong in this world. But once again, this cold was different, just as it had been when we'd talked in the chapel.

Suddenly a bell tolled somewhere in the air far above our heads. It was deep and mournful, as if calling the bereaved to a funeral, and so loud that the table vibrated. I could feel it resonating through the flags beneath my feet. The bell tolled nine times in all, each peal fainter than its predecessor. This was followed immediately by three loud raps on the table. I could make out the shape of Morgan, and he didn't seem to be moving. The raps were repeated, louder than ever, and the heavy brass candlestick fell over, rolled across the tabletop, and crashed to the floor.

In the darkened room, the silence that followed was almost painful and I felt as if my ears were about to pop. I was holding my breath, and all I could hear was the thumping inside my head, the rapid beating of my heart. The strange cold intensified, and then Morgan spoke into the darkness.

"Sister of mine, be still and listen well!" he commanded.

Then I heard the patter of dripping water. It sounded as if there was a hole in the ceiling and it was dripping onto the center of the tabletop, where the candle had been.

Next a voice answered. It seemed to come from Morgan's mouth. I could just about make out the outline of his head and I could swear that his jaw was moving, but it was a girl's voice and there was no way a grown man could have imitated its pitch and intensity.

"Leave me be! Let me rest!" cried the voice.

The noise of dripping water grew louder, and there

was a faint splashing, as if a puddle had formed on the tabletop.

"Obey me and then I'll let you rest," cried Morgan. "It's another I wish to speak to. Bring him to this place and then you may return from whence you came. There's a boy with me in this room. Can you see him?"

"*Yes, I see him,*" the girl's voice answered. "*He has just lost someone. I sense his sadness.*"

"The boy's name is Thomas Ward," Morgan said. "He mourns his father. Bring his father's spirit to us now!"

The cold began to lessen, and the water ceased its dripping. I couldn't believe what I'd just heard. Was Morgan really going to summon Dad's spirit? I felt a sense of outrage.

"Aren't you looking forward to speaking to your father one more time?" Morgan demanded. "I've already spoken to him, and he told me that all your brothers visited his deathbed to say good-bye but you, and that you even missed his funeral. He was sad about that. Very sad. Now you'll both have a chance to put things right."

I was stunned by that. How could Morgan possibly know what had happened? Unless he really had been in contact with Dad's spirit . . .

"It wasn't my fault!" I said, angry and upset. "I didn't get the message in time."

"Well, now you're about to get the chance to tell him that yourself."

It started to grow colder again. Then a voice spoke to me across the table. Morgan's jaw was moving again but, to my dismay, it was Dad's voice that came out of his mouth. There was no mistaking it. Nobody could possibly have mimicked somebody else's voice so perfectly. It was as if Dad were sitting facing me in the chair opposite.

"*It's dark,*" Dad cried, "*and I can't even see my hand before my face. Someone light a candle for me, please. Light a candle so that I can be saved.*"

I felt terrible thinking of Dad alone and afraid in the dark. I tried to call out and reassure him, but Morgan spoke first.

"How can you be saved?" he said, his voice deep and

powerful and filled with authority. "How can a sinner such as you go to the light? A sinner who always worked on the Lord's day?"

"*Oh, forgive me! Forgive me, Lord!*" Dad cried. "*I was a farmer and there were jobs to be done. I worked my fingers to the bone, but there were never enough hours in a day. I'd a family to provide for. But I always paid my tithes, holding nothing back that belonged to the Church. I always believed, truly I did. And I taught my sons right from wrong. I did all that a father should.*"

"One of your sons is here now," Morgan said. "Would you like to speak to him one last time?"

"*Please. Please. Yes. Let me speak to him. Is it Jack? There were things I should have said to him while I lived. Things unsaid that I would say now!*"

"No," Morgan said. "Jack isn't here. It's your youngest son, Tom."

"*Tom! Tom! Are you there? Is it really you?*"

"It's me, Dad. It's me!" I cried, a lump coming up into my throat. I couldn't bear the thought of Dad suffering in the darkness like that. What had he done to deserve this?

"I'm sorry I didn't get home in time. Sorry I didn't go to your funeral. The message reached me too late. If you've anything to say to Jack, tell me. I'll give him your message," I said, the tears starting to prick behind my eyes.

"Just tell Jack I'm sorry about the farm, son. Sorry that I didn't leave it all to him. He's my eldest lad, and it was his birthright. But I listened to your mam. Tell him I'm sorry that I left that room to you."

There were tears running down my face now. It was a shock to hear that Mam and Dad hadn't been in agreement about the room. I wanted to promise Dad that I'd make it right by giving the room to Jack, but I couldn't because I had to take into account Mam's wishes. I had to talk to her first. But I tried to make Dad feel better. It was the best I could do.

"Don't worry, Dad! It'll be all right. I'll talk to Jack about it. It won't cause any trouble in the family. None at all. Don't you worry. It'll be fine."

"You're a good lad, Tom," Dad said, his voice full of gratitude.

"A good lad!" Morgan interrupted. "He's anything but that. This is the son that you gave to a spook! Seven sons you had and not one did you offer to the Church!"

"Oh! I'm sorry! I'm so sorry!" Dad's voice cried out in anguish. *"But none of my lads had a vocation. None wanted to be priests. I struggled to find a good trade for each, and when it came to the last of my sons, his mam wanted him apprenticed to a spook. I was strong against it, and we argued over that more than we'd ever argued before. But I gave in finally, because I loved her and couldn't deny her what she'd set her heart on. Forgive me! I was weak and put earthly love before my duty to God!"*

"That you did!" Morgan cried out in a loud voice. "There is no forgiveness for one such as you, and now you must suffer the pains of hell. Can you feel the flames starting to lick at your flesh? Can you feel the heat starting to build?"

"Nay, Lord! Please! Please! The pain is too much to bear! Please spare me. I'll do anything! Anything!"

I came to my feet, filled with anger. Morgan was doing this to Dad. Making Dad believe he was in hell. Making him experience terrible pain. I couldn't allow it to continue.

"Don't listen to him, Dad!" I shouted. "There are no flames. There is no pain. Go in peace! Go in peace! Go to the light! Go to the light!"

I took four rapid steps down the left side of the table and, with all my strength, swung my staff toward the hooded figure and struck him a terrible blow. Without uttering a sound, he fell away to the right and I heard the chair tumble onto the flags.

Quickly I pulled my tinderbox and the candle stub from my pocket. Within moments I managed to light the candle. I held it up and looked about me. The chair had fallen sideways and a black cloak was draped across it and down onto the flags. But of Morgan there was no sign! I prodded it with my staff, but it was as empty as it looked. He'd vanished into thin air!

I noticed something on the tabletop. The wood was dry as a bone and there was no trace at all of the water that had seemed to drip and puddle there, but where the brass candlestick had stood was a black envelope.

Setting the candle down on the edge of the table, I reached across and picked up the envelope. It was sealed, but on it were the words:

To My New Apprentice, Tom Ward

I tore open the envelope and unfolded the piece of paper within.

Well, now you've seen what I am capable of. And what I have just done, I can do again. I have trapped your father in limbo. Thus I can reach him anytime I choose and make him believe anything I want. There is no limit to the pain that I can inflict upon him.

If you would save him from this, obey my will. Firstly, I need something from Gregory's house. Up in the attic, locked inside his writing desk, there is a wooden box and within it a grimoire, which is a book of powerful spells and rituals. It's bound in green leather and has a silver pentacle embossed on the front cover—three concentric circles with a five-pointed star within. It is mine. Bring it to me.

Secondly, say nothing to anyone of what you have seen.
Thirdly, you must accept that you are now my apprentice,
bound to my service for a period of five years from this day
forth—or your father will suffer. To signal your acceptance,
rap three times upon the tabletop. The door is unlocked and,
whatever your decision, you are free to go. The choice is
yours.

Morgan G.

I couldn't bear the thought of Dad's spirit in torment.
But neither did I want to be Morgan's apprentice. I was
reluctant to rap on the table, but it would gain me some
time. Morgan would think I'd agreed to what he'd
demanded, and it would save Dad from suffering now
while I consulted the Spook. He would know what to do
for the best.

I took a deep breath and rapped three times upon the
table. I held my breath and listened, but there was no
acknowledgement. The room was utterly still and silent.

I tried the door and it opened. I hadn't heard it happen, but the bolt had been pulled back. I went back to the table, picked up my tinderbox, blew out the candle, and put both into my pockets. Then, clutching my staff, I left the room and opened the front door.

I almost fell over in amazement. It was broad daylight! Sunlight was dazzling back from the snow, and it was at least two hours after dawn! It had only seemed like fifteen minutes or so that I'd been in the room with Morgan, and yet the same number of hours had gone by.

There was no way I could begin to explain it. The Spook had told me that Morgan was a dangerous man who'd dabbled with the dark. But the Spook hadn't said he was capable of the things I'd seen. Morgan was a powerful and dangerous mage with real magical powers, and I shivered at the thought of having to face him again. Within moments I was trudging through the deep snow as fast as I could, heading uphill toward the Spook's house.

CHAPTER XIII
TRICKERY AND BETRAYAL

SOON the house was directly ahead, with brown smoke rising from the chimney pots telling me that warm welcoming fires were waiting within.

I knocked at the back door. My key would open most locks, but I didn't use it. As I'd been away for a while, it seemed more polite to wait to be invited in. I knocked three times before the door was finally opened by Meg, who smiled at me before stepping back to welcome me inside.

"Come in quickly out of the snow, Tom!" she exclaimed. "It's good to see you back."

Once inside, I removed my cloak and sheepskin jacket, leaned my staff in the corner, and stamped the snow from my boots.

"Sit yourself down," Meg said, guiding me across the flags to the fireplace. "You're shivering with cold. I'll make you a cup of hot soup to warm your bones. That'll have to do for now — I'll cook you a nice big meal later."

I was trembling more than shivering, upset by what had happened in Morgan's room, but gradually I began to calm down. I did as I was told and warmed my hands at the fire, watching my boots begin to steam. "It's good to see you've still got all your fingers!" Meg said.

I smiled. "Where's Mr. Gregory?" I asked, wondering if he'd been called away on spook's business. I hoped he had, because that would mean he was fit and well again.

"He's still in bed. He needs all the rest he can get."

"So he's not that much better yet?"

"He's improving slowly," Meg answered. "But it'll take time. These things can't be rushed. Try not to disturb or burden him too much. He needs to rest and sleep as much as he can."

She brought across a steaming cup of hot chicken soup, so I thanked her and sipped it slowly, feeling it begin to warm my insides.

"How's your poorly dad?" she asked suddenly as she settled herself down in her rocking chair. "Is he getting better now?"

I was surprised that she'd remembered that, and her question brought tears to my eyes again. "He died, Meg," I told her. "But he'd been very ill."

"That's sad, Tom. I'm so sorry. I know what it's like to lose family. . . ."

I felt the pain of losing Dad wrench my stomach and thought of what Morgan had done to his spirit. Dad didn't deserve that. I couldn't let it happen again. I had to do something.

Meg fell silent and stared into the flames. After a while she closed her eyes and started humming a tune very quietly under her breath. When I'd finished the soup, I went across and put the cup on the table.

"Thanks, Meg. That was really good," I told her.

She didn't reply and seemed to be asleep. It was something she often did, fall asleep in her rocking chair near the hearth.

I didn't know what to do now. I'd hoped to speak to my master about Morgan, but he was clearly not well enough to be bothered with it. I didn't want to trouble him and make him worse. Perhaps while he was sleeping I could just take a look at this grimoire; check it was where Morgan had said. Maybe something in there would help me to decide what to do. One thing was clear: with my master so ill and Alice gone, I was on my own, and it was down to me to do the right thing by my dad. He was all that mattered, and I had to do something to stop him from suffering at the hands of Morgan. I would start by looking for the grimoire.

The Spook was upstairs sleeping, and I might not get a better chance to look for it. One part of me felt bad about even thinking of taking it without telling the Spook. But there would be a time for explanations later. Dad was all that mattered now. I couldn't bear the thought of him being tortured by Morgan again.

But when I started to leave the kitchen, Meg suddenly opened her eyes and leaned forward to poke the fire. "I'm just going up to see Mr. Gregory," I told her.

"No, Tom, we don't want to disturb him yet," she said. "You just sit by the fire and warm yourself after that long walk you've had in the cold."

"Well, I'll just go and get my notebook from the study first," I said.

But I went into the parlor rather than the study. If the Spook was still in bed, Meg hadn't had her herb tea yet. I needed her to sleep for a while so that I could hunt for the grimoire, and herb tea was the easiest way to do it. So I took down the big brown glass jar from the cupboard and poured three-quarters of an inch of the mixture into a cup. Then I went into the kitchen and began to heat the water.

"What's this?" Meg asked with a smile as I held the cup toward her.

"It's herb tea, Meg. Drink it down. It'll stop the cold from getting into your bones."

The only warning I got was when the smile slipped from her face. Meg dashed the cup from my hand, and it smashed to pieces on the kitchen flags. Then she got to her feet, gripped my wrist, and dragged me close. I tried to pull away, but she was too strong. I felt that she could snap my arm without trying too hard.

"Liar! Liar!" she shouted, her face only inches from my own. "I'd hoped for better from you, but you're no better than John Gregory! Don't say I didn't give you a chance. You've proved yourself to be just the same. You'd take away my memory, too, wouldn't you, boy? But now I remember everything. I know what I was and I know what I am!"

With our faces almost touching, Meg sniffed at me very loudly. "I know what you are, too," she said, her voice hardly more than a whisper now. "I know what you're thinking. I know your darkest secret thoughts, the ones you couldn't even tell your own mother."

Her eyes were staring hard into mine. They weren't points of fire like Mother Malkin's had been when we'd come face-to-face in the spring, but they seemed to be growing larger. She was a lamia witch and her body was stronger than mine, and now her mind was beginning to control me, too.

"I know what you could be one day, Tom Ward," she whispered, "but that day's still a long way off. You're just a boy, while I've walked this earth more years than I care to remember. So don't try any of John Gregory's tricks on me, because I know them all. Every last one!"

She spun me around so that I was facing away from her and let go of my arm, quickly transferring her grip to my neck.

"Please, Meg! I didn't mean any harm," I pleaded. "I wanted to help you. I'd talked to Alice about it. She wanted to help you, too—"

"It's easy to say that now. Was giving me that filthy mixture to drink the way to help me? No, I don't think so. No more of your lies, or it'll be the worse for you!"

"But they're not lies, Meg. Remember, Alice comes from a family of witches. She understood you and really felt sorry for what was happening. I was going to speak to Mr. Gregory about you and—"

"Right, boy! I've heard enough excuses!" snapped Meg. "It's down to the cellar with you. Let's see how *you* like it down there in the dark. It's just what you deserve. I want you to know what I went through. I didn't sleep the whole time, you see. I kept waking up to spend long hours thinking, alone in the dark. Too weak to move, too weak to climb to my feet—trying desperately to remember all that you and John Gregory would like me to forget—I could still think and feel, knowing that it would be long, tedious, lonely months before anybody came to the door to let me out. . . ."

At first I struggled, trying my best to resist, but it was useless: she was just too strong. Still gripping me by the neck, she marched me down the cellar steps, my feet hardly touching the floor, until we reached the iron gate. She had the key, and we were soon beyond it and descending deeper underground.

She hadn't bothered with a candle, and although I can find my way in the dark a lot better than most people, at each corner it grew darker and more difficult to see. The thought of the cellar below terrified me. I remembered her sister, the feral lamia witch, still imprisoned in the pit; I didn't want to be anywhere near her. But to my relief, when we turned the third corner, she brought me to a halt by the three doors.

With another key she opened the left-hand door, thrust me inside, and locked it behind me. Then I heard her unlock the cell next to mine and go inside. She didn't stay very long. Soon that door slammed shut, and she began to climb the steps. After a few moments there was the sound of the iron gate clanging shut; more steps, growing fainter and fainter; and then silence.

I waited a few moments in case she came back for some

reason, then fumbled in my pockets for the stub of candle and my tinderbox. Seconds later the candle was alight, and I looked around at my cell. It was small, no more than eight paces by four, with a heap of straw in the corner to serve for a bed. The walls were built from blocks of stone, and the door was constructed of sturdy oak, with a square inspection hole near the top sealed with four vertical iron bars.

I sat down on the stone floor in the corner to think things through. What had happened while I'd been away? I felt certain that the Spook was now in the cell next to mine, the one where Meg spent her summers. Why else would Meg have gone in there? But how had the Spook ended up in Meg's power? He still hadn't been well when I'd left for home. Maybe he'd forgotten to give Meg her herb tea and she'd recovered her memory? Perhaps she'd put something in *his* food or drink—the same thing he'd been using all those years to keep her docile, most likely.

Not only that—there'd been Alice's influence. She'd

kept chatting to Meg, talking to her about coming from a family of witches. Sometimes they'd whispered together. What had they been discussing? If Alice had had her way, Meg's dose of herb tea would have been reduced. Well, I didn't blame Alice for what had happened, but her presence in the Spook's house certainly wouldn't have helped the situation.

When I'd returned, Meg had only been pretending to be confused and had been playing a game with me. Had she really been giving me what she'd called a chance? If I hadn't tried to give her the herb tea, would she have treated me any differently? And then it hit me. When I got back to Anglezarke, I'd been so wrapped up in my thoughts of Morgan and Dad, I'd been completely blind to the evidence—signs I could see only too clearly now. Meg had called me Tom, not Billy, for the first time ever. And she'd remembered about my dad. Why hadn't I picked up on that at the time? I should have been on my guard. I'd let my heart rule my head, and now the whole County was in danger. A lamia witch free to roam once more, and neither a spook nor an apprentice to stop her. What was done was done, but somehow I had to put it right.

There was good news and bad news, but most of it was bad. Meg had sniffed me out using her powers as a witch. She knew a lot about me, but she hadn't bothered to search me or she'd have found the tinderbox and candle. She'd have found the key, too—the key that could open most doors as long as they weren't too complex. So that was the good news. I could get out of my cell. I could open the door to the Spook's cell, too.

The bad news was that the key wouldn't be good enough to get me through the gate. Otherwise the Spook wouldn't have kept a special one on top of the bookcase in the library. And Meg had that key now. Even if I could get us both out of our cells, we were still trapped in the cellar. So what I needed to do now was clear enough. I had to talk to the Spook. My master would know what to do for the best.

So I used the key to open the door of my cell. It didn't

make much noise, but the cell door seemed to stick and, despite my best efforts, jerked open, making a noise that echoed up and down the steps. I hoped Meg would be upstairs by the kitchen fire and wouldn't have heard. Taking the candle, I tiptoed out into the corridor and held it up to the bars of the Spook's cell. I peered inside but couldn't see much. There was a bed in the corner and a dark bundle on top of it. Was it the Spook?

"Mr. Gregory! Mr. Gregory!" I called through the bars, putting urgency into my voice while still trying to keep its volume as low as possible.

A deep groan came from the bundle, and it moved slowly. It sounded like the Spook, all right. I was just going to call again when I heard a sudden sound from the steps below. I turned and listened. For a moment there was silence. Then I heard it again. Something was moving up the steps toward me.

A rat? No, it sounded too large for that. Suddenly it stopped. Was I mistaken? Had I just imagined the sound? Fear can play tricks on the mind. As the Spook always says, it's important to recognize the difference between waking and dreaming.

Without realizing it, I'd been holding my breath. Now, when I breathed out, the movement up the steps began again. I couldn't see around the corner, so I could only judge what it was by the sounds it was making. It wasn't like something dragging itself up, so it couldn't be a dead witch that had somehow managed to get free. It wasn't the sound of boots, so it couldn't be a ghast or a ghost coming up the steps, or even a human being who'd been hiding down there for some reason. It was a sound I'd never heard in my life before.

Something was moving, then stopping; moving again, then halting just as quickly. Something that was scuttling upward on more than just two legs! What else could it be? It had to be the feral lamia witch! After years in that pit, she'd have a frantic need for human blood. And she was coming for me!

In a panic, without thinking, I ran back into my cell, pulled the door closed, and locked it quickly. Next I blew out the candle—otherwise she would see the light and be attracted to it. But was I even safe inside a locked cell? If the witch had managed to escape from the pit, she must have been able to bend the bars. Then I realized that Meg might simply have released her sister from the pit, and for a moment I felt a bit better. But I didn't even get time to sigh with relief. You see, I remembered something that the Spook had said about the gate:

"The iron would stop most of 'em getting past this point. . . ."

The lamia witch was the most dangerous thing in the cellar. So, if she'd a mind to escape, maybe even the iron trellis gate wouldn't be enough to stop her for long! As for the bars of my cell, they didn't bear thinking about. My only hope was that the witch was still relatively weak after being in the pit for so long.

I kept perfectly still and listened, doing my best to breathe quietly. I could hear her approaching, scuttling and halting, scuttling nearer and nearer. I pressed myself back into the corner and stopped breathing altogether.

Something touched the door lightly. The next contact with the wood was stronger, and there was a scratching sound, as if sharp claws were biting in, trying to get a purchase. It was as if something was clawing its way up the door. I'd run into my own cell without thinking, and now I wished I'd locked myself in the other cell with the Spook. I might have been able to wake him up and ask him what to do.

It was dark. Very dark. So dark that, inside my cell, I couldn't tell where the door ended and the walls on either side began. But the oblong, dissected by the four vertical bars, was slightly paler than its surroundings, so there had to be some light on the stairs, shedding a faint illumination of the wall beyond my cell.

A shape moved across the oblong. It was in silhouette, but I could see enough to tell that it was something like a hand. I heard it grip the bars. But it wasn't as if flesh and muscle came into contact with them. There was a rasp, almost as if a file had scraped against iron, followed by an explosive hiss of anger and pain. The lamia witch had touched iron, and the hurt she was suffering would be severe. Only her will was holding her there. Next, something big moved up in front of the bars, like the disk of a dark moon eclipsing the pale light beyond. It had to be the witch's head. She was peering at me through the bars, but it was too dark to see her eyes!

There was another rasp, and the door groaned and creaked. I trembled with fear. I knew what was happening. She was trying to bend the bars or pull them right out of the wooden door.

If I'd had my staff of rowan wood I could have jabbed at the witch through the bars and perhaps driven her off. But I had nothing. My silver chain was in my bag, but it was no use to me there. I'd nothing here that I could use to defend myself.

The door groaned and creaked as the pressure on it grew, and I heard it start to buckle. The witch hissed again and made a snuffling, croaking sound. She was eager to get inside, desperate to drink my blood.

But to my relief, there was a sudden clang of metal

from up the steps, and the lamia let go of the bars and dropped out of sight. I heard the echo of approaching footsteps, and candlelight flickered on the wall beyond the bars.

"Back! Back!" I heard Meg shout from beyond the door, followed by the sound of the feral lamia scuttling away down the steps.

Next there was the flicker of candlelight and the click of pointy shoes following the creature down. I stayed where I was, crouched in the corner. After a while the footsteps approached again, and I heard a bucket being placed on the floor and a key turning in the lock of my cell door.

Just in time, before Meg opened the door, I pushed my candle stub and tinderbox back into my pockets. Now I was glad that I hadn't locked myself in the Spook's cell, or she'd have known about my key.

Meg stood framed in the doorway, holding up her candle. With her other hand, she beckoned me to her. I didn't move. I was too scared.

"Come here, boy," she said, chuckling to herself. "Don't worry. I won't bite!"

I came to my knees, but my legs felt too wobbly to allow me to stand.

"Will you come to me, boy? Or do I have to come to you?" Meg asked. "The first is far easier and less painful."

This time terror brought me to my feet. She might be "domestic," but Meg was still a lamia witch whose favorite food was probably blood. The herb tea had made her forget that. But she knew exactly what she was now. And she knew what she wanted. There was compulsion in her voice, a power that sapped my will and made me cross the cell to the open door.

"It's lucky for you that I decided to feed Marcia when I did," she said, pointing down to the bucket.

I looked down. It was empty. I don't know what had been inside it, but there was a film of blood in the bottom.

"Almost left it until later, but then I remembered how desperate she'd be to get at you, what with you being so young. John Gregory doesn't have half the attraction," she said with a thin, cruel smile, nodding toward the next cell and confirming for me that the Spook really was in there.

"He really cares about you," I told Meg desperately. "He always has. So please don't treat him like this! In fact, he loves you. He really *loves* you!" I said, repeating the words again. "He actually wrote it down in one of his notebooks. I wasn't meant to find it, but I did and read it anyway. It's the truth."

I could remember what he'd written word for word. . . .

"How could I put her into the pit, when I realized that I loved her better than my own soul."

"Love!" sneered Meg. "What does a man like that know about love?"

"It was when you first met and he was about to put you into a pit because it was his duty. He couldn't do it, Meg! He couldn't do it because he loved you too much. It went against everything he'd been taught and believed, but he still saved you from the pit! He only gave you the tea because there was no other choice. The pit or tea—he chose what he thought was best, because he cares about you so much."

Meg gave a hiss of anger and peered down into the bucket as if she wanted to lick it clean or something. "Well, that was a long time ago, and he certainly has a funny way of showing it," she said. "Perhaps now he'll understand just what it's like to be locked down here half the year. Because there's no hurry now. I'm going to take a long time thinking over just what to do with him. As for you, you're just a boy, and I don't blame you that much. You don't know any better because that's how he's trained you. And it's a hard life. A difficult trade.

"I'd let you go," she went on. "But you wouldn't be able to leave it there, would you? It's the way you've been made. The way you've been brought up. You'd go for help. You'd want to rescue him. Folks round here don't think much of me. Perhaps I've given them good reason in the past, but most deserved what they got. They'd come after me in a mob. Too many for me to do anything about. No, if I let you go, it could be the end of me. But

I will promise you one thing. I won't give you to my sister. You don't deserve that."

So saying, she gestured that I should move back; then she closed the door and locked it again.

"I'll bring something for you to eat later," she said through the bars. "Maybe by then I'll have thought what's the best thing to do about you."

It was hours and hours before she returned, and in that time I'd had a chance to think and plan.

I was listening very carefully, and I heard Meg start to descend the steps. Outside it would just be getting dark. I imagine she was bringing me an early supper. I hoped it wouldn't be my last. I heard her unlock the gate and the clang of it opening. I concentrated very hard then, noting the time that elapsed between the second clang of the gate being closed and the *click, click* of her pointy shoes resuming.

I had two plans. The second one was filled with risk, so I hoped the first one worked.

I had a glimpse of candlelight through the bars and Meg put something down outside my cell, unlocked the door, and opened it. It was a tray with two bowls of steaming soup and two spoons.

"I've thought of something, Meg," I said, trying my first plan, which was to win her round with words. "Something that could make things a lot better for both of us. Why don't you give me the run of the house? I could make the fires and bring in the water. I could help a lot. What will you do when Shanks delivers the groceries? If you answer the door, he'll know you're free. But if I answer, he'll never guess. And if anyone comes on spooks' business I could just say that he's still ill. If you had me to answer the door, it would be a long time before anybody knew you were free. You'd have plenty of time to decide what to do about Mr. Gregory."

Meg smiled. "Take your soup, boy."

I bent down, lifted the bowl from the tray, and helped myself to one of the spoons. When I stood upright, Meg waved me back and started to pull the cell door shut.

"A good try, boy," she said, "but how long would it be before you took advantage and tried to free your master? Not long, I'll bet!"

Meg locked the door. My first plan had failed already. I'd no choice now but to try the second. I put my bowl of soup on the floor and pulled my key from my pocket. I could hear Meg already turning her own key in the lock of the Spook's cell. I waited, taking a chance, hoping against hope.

I was right! She went straight into the Spook's cell. I'd guessed that he might be too weak or groggy to be able to stand and come to the door. She might even be going to feed him herself. So, wasting no time, I unlocked my own door, pushed it carefully open, and stepped outside. Mercifully it didn't stick and make a noise this time.

I'd thought everything through carefully, weighing all the risks in my mind. One option would have been to go straight into the Spook's cell and try to deal with Meg. Under normal circumstances, together, my master and I might have been a match for her, but I suspected that the

Spook would be too weak to help. And we had nothing to fight her with: no rowan staff and no chain.

So I'd decided to go and get the silver chain from my bag in the study and try to bind Meg. To achieve that, I was counting on two things. One was that the feral lamia wouldn't scamper up the steps and catch me before I got through the iron gate. The second was that Meg hadn't locked the gate after her. That's why I'd been concentrating hard. The gate had clanged and the heels had started clicking downward almost immediately afterward. She hadn't had time to lock it. Or at least, I didn't think so!

I tiptoed at first, just one step up at a time, and kept glancing back over my shoulder: at the cell, to see if Meg was coming out; then at the corner of the steps, to see if feral Marcia was after me. I was hoping that she was still too full after her morning meal. Or that she wouldn't come up from the cellar while Meg was there. Perhaps she was afraid of her sister. She'd certainly gone back down the steps at Meg's command.

At last I reached the gate and gripped the cold iron.

Was it locked? To my relief, it yielded, and I pulled it open, trying to keep the movement as smooth as possible. But the Spook had known what he was doing when he'd had it built on the steps. There was a clang, and the whole house above seemed to reverberate like a bell.

Immediately Meg rushed out of the Spook's cell and ran up the steps toward me, her arms raised, fingers splayed and arched like talons. For a moment I froze. I couldn't believe how fast she was moving. Another couple of seconds and it would have been too late, but I ran, too. Ran and ran without looking back. Right to the top of the steps, then through the house to the kitchen, aware that Meg was close at my heels, hearing her foot-steps behind and expecting to feel her nails cut into my skin at any moment. There was no time to go into the study for my bag. I wouldn't have a hope of unfastening it and getting my silver chain out in time. At the back door I snatched up my cloak, jacket, and staff, unlocked the door, and raced out into the freezing cold.

I'd been right. It was dusk, but there was still plenty of

light to see by. I kept glancing backward, but there was no sign of pursuit. I struggled down the clough as fast as I could manage, but it was hard work. The snow was starting to freeze hard underfoot, and there was a lot of it.

When I reached the bottom of the slope, I halted and looked back again. Meg hadn't followed me. It was bitterly cold and the wind was gusting from the north, so I put on my sheepskin jacket, pulling my cloak over the top. Then I paused for thought, my breath steaming into the cold air.

I felt like a coward for leaving the Spook behind at the mercy of Meg, and I had to make up for what I'd done. Somehow I had to rescue the Spook and get him out of her clutches. But I needed help to do that. And help was close by: living and working in Adlington was the Spook's brother, Andrew, who'd helped me before in Priestown. He was the locksmith who'd made the Spook a key to the Silver Gate that imprisoned the Bane. Making a key for the iron gate to the Spook's cellar should be far easier. And that was exactly what I needed.

I was going to have to sneak back into the winter house, get through the gate, and let the Spook out of his cell, something that was easier said than done. There was a feral lamia on the loose — not to mention Meg.

Trying not to think too much about the difficulties ahead, I trudged on through the snow toward Adlington. It was downhill all the way. But soon I'd have to return.

CHAPTER XIV
SNOWBOUND

THE cobbled streets of Adlington Village were buried under six inches or more of snow. In the fading light, delighted children were out in force, laughing, screeching and shouting, making slides or hurling snowballs at one another. Other people were less happy. A couple of shawled women passed me, stepping nervously

· 295 ·

on the snow-laden pavement with bowed heads, eyes watching their feet. They were clutching empty baskets and heading down toward Babylon Lane for some last-minute shopping. I followed in the same direction until I reached Andrew's shop.

As I lifted the latch and pushed open the door, a bell tinkled. The shop was empty, but I heard someone approaching from the back. There was the *click, click, click* of pointy shoes, and to my astonishment, Alice walked in and came up to the counter, a big smile on her face.

"Good to see you, Tom! I wondered how long it would take you to find me."

"What are you doing here?" I asked in astonishment.

"Working for Andrew, of course! Gave me a job *and* a home," she answered with a smile. "I mind the shop so he can have more time in his workshop. Do most of the cooking and cleaning, too. He's a good man, Andrew."

I fell silent for a moment and Alice must have read the expression on my face, because her smile quickly faded and she looked concerned. "Your dad . . ." she said.

"When I got there, Dad had already passed away. I was too late, Alice."

I couldn't say anymore because my voice failed and a lump came up into my throat. But in an instant, Alice reached across and put her hand on my shoulder. "Oh, Tom! I'm so sorry," she told me. "Come through to the back and warm yourself by the fire."

The living room was comfortable, with a settee, two comfy armchairs, and a generous coal fire blazing in the grate. "I like a good fire," Alice said happily. "Andrew's more careful with the coal than I am, but he's away on a job and won't be back until well after dark. While the cat's away . . ."

I leaned my staff in the corner before sinking into the settee, which faced the fire directly. Instead of sitting down beside me, Alice knelt by the fire, her knees on the hearthrug, so that her left side was toward me.

"Why did you leave the Hursts?" I asked.

"Had to get away," Alice said with a scowl. "Morgan kept pestering me to help him in some way, but wouldn't say exactly how. Got a grudge, he has. Had some sort of a plan to get back at Old Gregory."

I thought I probably knew what she was talking about, but I decided not to say anything to her. I'd promised Morgan I'd tell no one about his plans. He was a necromancer who used spirits to find things out. I couldn't take the chance. I couldn't tell Alice in case he found out and made Dad suffer again.

"He wouldn't leave me alone," continued Alice. "That's why I left. Couldn't stand the sight of him one minute longer. So I thought of Andrew. But that's enough about me, Tom. I'm sorry about your dad. Do you want to talk about it?"

"It was hard, Alice. I even missed Dad's funeral. And Mam's gone off somewhere, and nobody knows where she is. She could have gone back to her own land, and I might never see her again. I feel so lonely. . . ."

"Been lonely most of my life, I have, Tom. So I know what that feels like. We've got each other, though, ain't we?" she asked, reaching across to hold my hand. "We'll always be together. Even Old Gregory won't be able to stop that!"

"The Spook's in no position to do anything at the moment," I said. "When I got back, Meg had turned the tables. He's the one locked up now. I need Andrew to make me a key so that I can get the Spook out of there. I need your help. You and Andrew are the only people I can turn to."

"Seems to me he finally got what was coming to him," Alice said, pulling her hand away from mine, a faint smile turning up the corners of her mouth. "Got a good dose of his own medicine!"

"I can't just leave him there," I told Alice. "And what about the other lamia? The feral one? Meg's sister? She's out of her pit and free to roam the steps behind the gate. What if she were to get out of the house? She could come down here, to the village. Nobody would be safe, and there are a lot of children living here."

"But what about Meg?" Alice asked. "Ain't that simple, is it? Don't deserve to go in a pit. Don't deserve to spend the rest of her life sipping herb tea, either! One way or another that's got to stop."

"So you're not going to help?"

"Didn't say that, Tom. It just needs thinking about, that's all."

Soon after dark, Andrew returned. I was waiting for him in the shop when he came in.

"What's this then, Tom?" he asked, stamping the snow from his boots and rubbing his hands together to get the blood circulating properly again. "What does that brother of mine want now?"

Andrew always looked like a well-dressed scarecrow, his limbs gangly and awkward, but he was kind and easy-going and really good at his job.

"He's in trouble again," I told Andrew. "I need you to make a key so we can get him out of it. And it's really urgent."

"A key? A key for what?"

"The gate on the cellar steps in his house. Meg's got him imprisoned down there."

SNOWBOUND

Andrew shook his head and clicked his tongue. "Can't say I'm surprised. It was bound to happen one day. Just astonished that it's taken so long! I always thought Meg would get the better of him in the end. He cares about her too much and always has. He must have let his guard down."

"But you will help?"

"Of course I will. He's my brother, isn't he? But I've been out in the cold most of the day, and I can't do much till I've warmed my bones and got some hot food in my belly. You can tell me all about it when we've eaten."

I'd not sampled much of Alice's cooking, apart from rabbits cooked in the embers of a fire outdoors, but judging by the appetizing smell of stew wafting in from the kitchen, I was in for a real treat.

I wasn't disappointed. "It's really good, Alice," I said, tucking in right away.

Alice smiled. "Aye, better than that muck you fed me in Anglezarke."

We laughed, then ate in silence until there wasn't a

301

scrap of food left. It was Andrew who spoke first.

"I haven't got a key to that gate," he told me. "The lock and key were crafted by a locksmith from Blackrod a good forty years ago or more. He's dead now, but he'd a reputation second to none, so we're facing a very complex mechanism. I'll need to go to the house and take a look myself. The easiest way would be for me to try and pick the lock and let you through the gate."

"Could we go tonight?" I asked.

"The sooner the better," he said. "But I'd like to know exactly what we're up against. Where's Meg likely to be?"

"She usually sleeps in a rocking chair by the fire in the kitchen. But even if we get past Meg safely and through the gate, there's another problem. . . ."

So I told him about the feral lamia loose in the cellar. He kept shaking his head as if he couldn't believe just how bad things were.

"How will you deal with her? Use that silver chain of yours?"

"I haven't got it," I told him. "It's in my bag. And the

bag's probably still in its usual place in the Spook's study. But I've got my staff. It's made of rowan wood, and if I'm lucky it'll keep a lamia at bay."

Andrew shook his head and didn't look too happy. "That's hardly a plan, Tom. It's far too dangerous. I can't pick a lock while you fight off two witches. But there is another way," he said. "We could get a dozen or so of the men from the village to go with us and sort out Meg once and for all."

"No," Alice said firmly. "That ain't the way. It's too cruel."

I knew she was remembering when the mob from Chipenden had attacked the house where she'd been living with her aunt, Bony Lizzie. Alice and her aunt had sniffed them out and just had time to escape, but everything had gone up in flames and they'd lost all their possessions.

"Mr. Gregory wouldn't want that, I'm sure of it," I said.

"That's true enough," Andrew said. "It's the safest way, but John would probably never forgive me. All right, looks like we're back to the first plan."

"Here's something you ain't thought of," Alice said. "A witch like that can't sniff *you* out at a distance, Tom. Don't work on a seventh son of a seventh son, do it? Most likely I'd be all right, too — that's if I do decide to go with you. But Andrew's different. Once he approaches the house, she'll sniff him out and be ready."

"If she's asleep, we might just get away with it," I said, but I didn't feel that confident.

"Even asleep, it's too much of a risk," Alice said. "Just you and me should go, Tom. We might be able to find the key and wouldn't have to pick the lock at all. Where does the Spook keep it?"

"On top of the bookcase usually, but Meg might be keeping it on her now."

"Well, if it's not there we'll get your bag from the study and bind her with a silver chain so we can get it off her. Either way, we wouldn't need you, Andrew. Me and Tom can do that."

Andrew smiled. "That would suit me," he said. "I like

to keep my distance from that house and its cellar. But I can't let you do it all by yourselves without some support. Best thing is if I give you a head start and follow on later. If you don't come to the door within half an hour, I *will* go back to Adlington and get a dozen big lads from the village. John will just have to live with the consequences of that."

"All right," I said. "But the more I think about it, the more I'm afraid that going in through the back door's too risky," I told Alice. "As I said, at night Meg sleeps in the kitchen, in a chair by the fire. She'd be bound to hear us, and we'd have to walk past her to get to the study. The front door would be slightly better, but there's still a big risk of waking her. No—there's a much better way. We could go in through one of the back bedroom windows. The best one's on the floor directly under the attic, where the cliff's very close to the window ledge. The window catches in the bedrooms are mostly rusty or broken. I think I could reach across and force the window open and climb in."

"It's madness," Andrew said. "I've been in that bed-room, and I've seen the gap between the cliff and the ledge. It's too wide. Besides, if you're worried about turning a key in the lock of the back door, just imagine how much noise you'd make forcing open a window!"

Alice grinned as if I'd said something really daft, but I soon wiped the smile off her face.

"Meg wouldn't hear us if someone were to knock hard on the back door at the very moment that I forced the window. . . ." I said.

I watched Andrew's mouth open as what I was suggesting slowly dawned on him.

"Nay," he said, "you don't mean . . ."

"Why not, Andrew?" I asked him. "After all, you are Mr. Gregory's brother. You've reason enough to visit the house."

"Aye, and I could end up down in the cellar, a prisoner with John!"

"I don't think so. My guess is that Meg won't even answer the door. She doesn't want anyone from the village to know that she's free, or she could attract a mob. You could knock at the door four or five times before you go away, giving me all the time I need to get in through the window."

"Could just work, that," said Alice.

Andrew pushed his plate away and didn't speak for a long time. "One thing still bothers me," he said at last. "That gap between the cliff and the window ledge. I can't see you managing it. It'll be slippery, too."

"It's worth a try," I said, "but if I can't do it, we could return later and risk the back door."

"We might be able to make things easier by using a plank," Andrew said. "I've got one out back that should do the job. Alice would need to anchor it to the ledge with her foot while you crawled across. It wouldn't be easy, but I've also got a small crowbar that's made for the job," he added.

"So it's worth a try," I said, trying to appear braver than I felt.

It was agreed, and Alice seemed to have made up her

mind to help. Andrew fetched the plank from the yard. But when we opened the front door to set off, a blizzard was raging outside. Andrew shook his head.

"It'd be madness for you to go now," he said. "That blizzard's worthy of Golgoth himself. Drifts will form and it'll be dangerous up on the moor. You could get lost and freeze to death. No, best wait till tomorrow morning. Don't worry," he said, clapping me on the shoulder. "That brother of mine's a survivor, as we well know. Otherwise he wouldn't have lasted as long as he has."

There were only two bedrooms above the shop one for Andrew and one for Alice, so I slept on the settee in the living room, wrapped in a blanket. The fire died in the grate and the room first became chilly, then bitterly cold. I lost count of the number of times I woke up in the night. On the last occasion, dawn light was glimmering behind the curtains, so I decided to get up.

I yawned and stretched and walked up and down a bit to get the stiffness out of my joints. It was then that I heard a noise from the front. It sounded as if someone had rapped three times on the shop window.

When I walked into the shop, it was bright with light reflecting off the snow. There'd been drifts in the night, all right, and the snow was heaped right up to the base of the window. And there, leaning against the glass, was a black envelope. It had been positioned in such a way that I could see what was written upon it. It was addressed to me! It had to be from Morgan.

One part of me wanted to just leave it there. But then I realized that the streets would start to get busy soon and anyone could walk by and see it. They might pick it up and read it, and I didn't want a stranger knowing my business.

There was so much snow piled against the front door that I couldn't open it and had to go out through the back door, open the yard gate, and walk around. It was only as I prepared to plunge into the drift that I realized something very odd. There were no footprints. Facing me was a large mound of snow without a mark upon its surface. How had the letter got there?

I retrieved the letter and, in doing so, gouged out a deep channel in the snow. I went around to the back again and into the kitchen, tore open the letter and read it.

I'll be in St George's churchyard, just west of the village. If you want what's best both for your dad and your old master, don't keep me waiting. Don't make me come to you. You won't like it.
Morgan G.

I hadn't noticed the signature on his last letter, but now it caught my eye. Had he changed his name? The initial of his second name should have been H for Hurst.

Puzzled, I folded up the letter and pushed it into my pocket. I wondered about waking Alice and showing her the letter. Perhaps I should take her with me. But the last person she'd want to see now was Morgan. She'd already said how she'd left Moor View Farm because she couldn't stand him another minute. And I knew I couldn't really tell Alice even if I wanted to: I was afraid of Morgan and what he might do to Dad. To be honest, I was also scared about what he might do to me. With so much power, he was really dangerous—not someone to disobey. So I pulled on my cloak, picked up my staff, and went out, heading directly for the churchyard.

It was an old church, almost hidden by the ancient yew trees clustered about it. Some of the stones marked the graves of locals who'd died centuries earlier. I saw Morgan in the distance, silhouetted against the gray sky, leaning on his staff, his hood up against the cold. He was in the newest part of the churchyard, where those who'd died relatively recently were buried.

At first he didn't acknowledge me. His head was bent down toward a grave, his eyes closed as if he were praying. I stared down, too, in astonishment. The churchyard was either inches or feet deep in snow, the result of last night's wind, but this grave was completely free of it, just an oblong of wet soil. It was almost as if it had been freshly dug. I looked around but could see no sign of a spade or any other implement that could have been used to clear away the snow.

"Read the inscription on the stone!" Morgan commanded, looking at me for the first time.

I did as I was told. Four bodies had been buried in the same grave, stacked one above the other as was the County custom, in order to save space in the churchyard and ensure that kin were together in death. Three were children, but the last one was their mother. The children had died fifty or so years earlier, aged two, one, and three years old, respectively. The mother had died recently, and her name was Emily Burns, the woman the Spook had once been involved with. The woman he'd taken from one of his own brothers, Father Gregory.

"She had a hard life," Morgan said. "Lived most of it in Blackrod, but when she knew she was dying, she came here to spend her last months with her sister. Losing three children like that broke her heart, and even after all those intervening years she never fully recovered. Four others lived, though. Two are working in Horwich and have families of their own. The eldest left the County ten years ago, and I've heard nothing of him since. I was the seventh and the last. . . ."

It took a few moments before it all started dropping into place. I remembered what the Spook had said to him in the bedroom at the Hursts':

"I cared about you and I cared about your mother. I loved her once, as you well know. . . ."

I also remembered how he'd signed his letter to me with the initial G.

"Yes," he said. "Soon after I was born, my father left the family home for the last time. He never married my mother. Never gave us his name. But I took it anyway."

I looked up at him in astonishment.

"Yes," he said with a grim smile. "Emily Burns was my real mother. I'm John Gregory's son."

Morgan stared into the distance as he spoke. "He left us. Left his children. That's not what a father should do, is it?"

I wanted to defend the Spook, but I didn't know what to say. So I said nothing.

"He did provide for us financially, though," Morgan said. "I'll give him that. We managed for a while, but then my mother had a breakdown and couldn't cope. Each of us was fostered out to a family. I drew the short straw and ended up with the Hursts. But when I was seventeen, my father came back for me and took me on as his apprentice.

"For a while, I'd never been happier. I'd wanted a father for so long and now I had one, so I was desperate to please him. I tried really hard at first, but I suppose I couldn't forget what he'd done to my mother, and gradually I began to see through him. After three years he was starting to repeat himself. I already knew everything he did and more besides. I knew I could be better and stronger than him. I'm the seventh son of a seventh son of a seventh son. A three times seven."

I heard the note of arrogance in his voice, and it annoyed me. "Is that why you didn't write your name on the bedroom wall at Chipenden like all the other apprentices?" I blurted out. "Is it because you think you're better than the rest of us? Better than the Spook?"

Morgan smirked. "I won't deny it. That's why I left to follow my own path. I'm mainly self-taught, but I'm still learning. And I can do things that old fool never even dreams of. Things that he's afraid to try. Think about it! Knowledge and power like mine—and the assurance that your father rests in peace. That's what I'm offering you in return for a little bit of help."

I was astonished by all that Morgan was telling me. If what he said was true, it showed the Spook in a really bad light. I already knew that he'd left Emily Burns for Meg. But now I'd just discovered that he was a father, who'd had seven sons by her but had left them all. I felt hurt inside and let down. I kept thinking about my own dad, who'd stayed with his family and worked hard all his life. And now he could suffer at the whim of Morgan. I was upset and angry. The graveyard seemed to lurch up into the sky, and I almost fell.

315

"Well, my young apprentice, have you brought it for me?"

My face must have looked blank.

"The grimoire, of course. I asked you to bring it to me. I hope you've obeyed me, or your poor father will really suffer."

"I haven't been able to get it. Mr. Gregory has eyes in the back of his head," I said, hanging my head.

I certainly wasn't going to tell Morgan that my master was at the mercy of Meg. If he thought the Spook was out of the way, he might just go and help himself to the grimoire. Yes, my master might have some terrible dark secrets, but I was still *his* apprentice and I respected him. I needed more time. Time to rescue my master and tell him all about Morgan. Together we'd defeated the stone-chucker; surely together we could stop Morgan.

"I need more time," I said. "I can do it, but I need to wait for an opportunity."

"Well, don't take too long about it. Bring the book to me next Tuesday night, soon after sunset. Remember the chapel in the graveyard?"

I nodded.

"Well, that's where I'll be waiting."

"I don't think I can do it that quickly—"

"Find a way!" he snarled. "And do it without Gregory realizing that it's gone."

"What will you do with it?" I asked.

"Well, Tom, when you bring it to me you'll find out, won't you? Don't let me down! If you start to waver, think of your poor father and what he could be made to suffer. . . ."

I knew how cruel Morgan could be. I'd seen the way he'd reduced poor Mr. Hurst to tears; heard Alice's account of how he'd dragged the old man to his room and locked him inside. If Morgan could hurt my dad, he would do it, I was in no doubt about that.

And then, as I stood there trembling, right inside my head I heard once again my father's anguished voice as, all around me, the air shivered and moved.

"Please, son, I'm begging you, do as he asks or I'll be tortured for all eternity. Please, son, just get it for him."

As the voice faded away, Morgan smiled grimly. "Well, you heard what your father said. So you'd better be a dutiful son."

With that he smiled grimly, turned on his heel, and left the graveyard.

I knew that it was certainly wrong to steal the grimoire for Morgan, but as I watched him go, I knew that I'd no choice. Somehow I'd have to get it as we rescued the Spook.

CHAPTER XV
DOWN TO THE CELLAR

WHEN I got back to Andrew's premises, Alice was in the kitchen cooking breakfast. It was ham and eggs, and it smelled wonderful.

"You were out early this morning, Tom," she said.

"I was aching after sleeping on the settee," I lied. "I needed to stretch my legs a bit."

"Well, you'll feel a lot better after your breakfast."

"I can't, Alice. It's best to fast when you're about to face the dark."

"Can't believe a few mouthfuls would do you that much harm!" she protested.

I didn't bother to argue. There were things she'd told me about witchcraft that I took with a pinch of salt, while there were things the Spook considered to be the gospel truth that brought a smile of derision to her face. So I just kept my silence and watched her and Andrew eat while my mouth watered.

After breakfast we set off straightaway for the Spook's house. It was still mid-morning, but the light was deteriorating fast, the sky heavy with dark clouds. It looked like more snow was on the way.

We left Andrew at the foot of the clough. He was going to wait ten minutes to allow us time to get up onto the moor above the house. Later, after he'd knocked at the door, he'd move away and watch from a distance, hoping to see us emerge and signal our success.

"Good luck, but don't keep me waiting too long," Andrew said, "or I'll freeze to death!"

I waved good-bye and, carrying the plank and my staff, and with the small crowbar tucked away in the inside pocket of my jacket, set off up the side of the moor. As we trudged upward, me in the lead and Alice on my heels, the snow crunched under our feet, and it was starting to freeze harder. I began to worry about the climb down to the house. It would be slippery and dangerous.

Soon we started to descend a path into the clough. This path then became a ledge, with the cliff on our left and a sheer drop to our right.

"Watch your step, Alice!" I warned. It was a long way down. One slip, and we'd need scraping up with a spade.

A few moments later, and we came in sight of the house; there we halted. As agreed, we were waiting for the sound of Andrew approaching from the front.

It was about five minutes before we heard boots crunching through the freezing snow far below. Somewhere down there, a very nervous Andrew would be walking around the side of the house and up to the back door. Quickly I stood up and began to carry the plank toward the house. When we arrived at the rear, facing the back window, I knelt down and tried to position the plank. I managed to rest the far end on the window ledge first time. What bothered me was that the ledge wasn't that wide. I was scared that the plank might slip off as I crossed and I'd fall down into the yard below. So it was important that Alice steady it on the cliff edge.

"Put your foot on that!" I whispered, indicating the near edge of the plank.

Alice did as I asked. I hoped it would prevent it from moving. Handing Alice my staff, I knelt on the plank and prepared to crawl across. It wasn't far, but I was nervous, and at first my limbs refused to obey me. It was a long way down to the snow-covered flags below. At last I began to crawl along, trying not to look down at the sheer drop. Soon I was kneeling close to the window ledge; once there, I tugged the small crowbar from my jacket pocket and positioned it at the bottom of the window frame. At that very moment Andrew knocked loudly on the back door almost directly below me.

Three loud raps echoed down the clough. At each rap I worked the bar, trying to lever the sash window upward. In the pause that followed I became perfectly still.

Rap! Rap! Rap!

Again I worked at the window, but without a hint of success. I began to wonder how many times Andrew would knock before his nerve failed him. Maybe the catch was stronger than I'd anticipated. How many chances would we get? Maybe the witch would answer the door after all. If so, I wouldn't want to be in Andrew's shoes.

Rap! Rap! Rap!

This time, at last, I was successful. I levered the window up and, once there was a sufficient gap, lifted it with both hands.

Rap! Rap! Rap! came the sound from below. Had I looked down I could have seen Andrew, but I fixed my gaze upon the window ledge and pulled myself through the window and into the room before returning the crowbar to my pocket. Alice leaned across and handed my staff to me, then came across the plank faster than I had. Once inside we heaved it across, just in case Meg came out into the yard and saw it from below. Then we closed the window.

That done, we sat together on the floor in the gloom, listening carefully. There were no more raps on the front door. I hadn't heard it opening, so I hoped Andrew had got away safely. The sound I dreaded now was that of Meg climbing the stairs. Had she heard the window being forced?

I'd already agreed with Alice that, if we got inside the house safely, we'd wait for fifteen minutes or so before making our move. The first step would be to get my bag from the Spook's study. Once the silver chain was in my hands, our chances of success were much higher.

But I hadn't told Alice what Morgan wanted me to do. I hadn't told her about the grimoire, because I knew she'd say I was a fool to give it to him. But it was all very well for her to talk like that. It wasn't *her* dad who might suffer. His voice pleading in the dark kept coming back to haunt me. It was all too much to bear.

If I could rescue the Spook and somehow bind Meg, I was going to come back up to the attic. I had to do it. It was betraying the Spook, but I couldn't let Dad suffer anymore. So we waited and waited, listening nervously to every creak of the old house.

When about a quarter of an hour had passed, I tapped Alice lightly on the shoulder, stood up carefully, picked up my staff, and moved cautiously toward the bedroom door.

It wasn't locked and I eased it open and stepped out onto the landing. It was even gloomier on the stairs, with a pool of darkness waiting for us below. I moved downward, one slow step, pausing to listen before taking a second one. That became the pattern: step, pause, and listen; step, pause, and listen. At one point the stair creaked beneath my feet. We froze and waited for five minutes at least, thinking that we might have awakened the witch. And when Alice's feet caused a second creak from that same stair, we had to repeat the process! It took a long time, but at last we reached the ground floor.

Moments later we were inside the Spook's study. It was brighter in there, and I could see my own bag still in the corner where I'd left it, but of the Spook's bag there was no sign. I took the silver chain and coiled it around my left hand and wrist, ready for throwing. That was my throwing arm: when practicing in the Spook's garden, I could cast the chain over a post eight feet away, nine times out of ten. So now, face-to-face with either the feral lamia or Meg, I had a good chance of success. An attack by both at the same time would be a different story, and I didn't like to think about that.

Next I leaned forward and put my lips close to Alice's ear.

"See if the key is on top of the bookcase," I whispered, pointing up to the spot.

There was a chance that Meg would keep the key to the gate close by her side, but I was remembering what the Spook had once told me about her: that she was methodical and always kept things in their proper place. He'd been talking about pots and pans, knives and forks. Would she do the same thing with the key? It was well worth checking to see.

So while Alice carried a chair across and positioned it next to the bookcase, I stood guard by the open door, my chain at the ready. She climbed up onto the chair and felt carefully across the upper surface of the top shelf before smiling broadly and holding up the key.

I'd been right! We had the key to the gate!

Still gripping the chain, I picked up my staff and cautiously led the way out of the study to the steps down to the cellar. I'd expected Meg to be awake, but I could hear the sound of her breathing in the kitchen, the air whistling out of her mouth as she exhaled. She was sound asleep, and so far our luck had more than held.

One option would have been to go straight into the kitchen and bind Meg while she was still sleeping, but I needed the chain to face the threat from the feral lamia in the cellar. We moved slowly down the steps, Alice now in the lead, until we reached the gate. This was a dangerous moment, and I'd already explained how a clang from the gate could resonate right through the house. But Alice inserted the key into the lock very carefully and twisted it without a sound. She managed to do the same when moving the gate, which we left open in case we needed to get out of the cellar fast.

It was very dark below, and I tapped Alice lightly on the shoulder, the signal to halt. I pushed the chain back into my pocket, leaned my staff carefully against the wall, and using my tinderbox, lit a candle stub and handed it to Alice. Once again I followed one step behind her, chain and staff at the ready. The candle was a calculated risk because, although the steps spiraled down, a glimmer of light might reach the cellar to alert the feral lamia. But we really needed some light to attend to the Spook properly and get him out of his cell. As it happened, it proved to be the right decision.

Suddenly Alice gasped, came to a sudden halt and pointed downward. A cold draft was coming up the steps from the cellar, making the candle flame dance and flicker, and by its light I glimpsed a dark shape moving rapidly up the steps toward us. For a moment, my heart racing, I thought it was the feral lamia: I stepped down alongside Alice, raised my left hand, and prepared to cast the silver chain.

But as the draft from below ceased, the light steadied and I saw that the rapid movement of the dark shape was an illusion caused by the flicker of the flame. Something *was* moving up the steps, but it was crawling; dragging itself so incredibly slowly that it would take a long time to reach the gate.

It was Bessy Hill, the other live witch—the one who'd been in the pit next to the feral lamia. Her gray hair was long and greasy and heaving with small black insects, while her tattered gown was stained with mildew and patches of slime. She was slowly dragging her body up the stairs, but although she'd managed to get free of her grave, years of surviving on a diet of slugs, worms, and other creepy crawlies meant that she hadn't much power at her disposal. Of course, it might have been a very different story if we'd blundered into her in the dark.

We came to a halt. If she managed to get a grip on one of our ankles, it would be hard to pry her off. She wanted blood desperately and would fasten her teeth into any warm flesh that came near. A mouthful of blood would immediately make her much stronger and more danger-ous. It was scary, but we had to get past her.

I moved downward nervously, gesturing to Alice that she should follow behind me. The steps were broad, and we were able to give the witch a wide berth. I wondered how she'd managed to escape from her pit. One possibil-ity was that the feral lamia had bent the bars for her. Or maybe Meg had released her. As we passed, I glanced down at her quickly. Her head was facing us, but her eyes were tightly closed. Her mouth was open, though, and her long purple tongue was protruding down onto the step, as if licking something from the damp stone. She sniffed, snuffled, twisted her head up, and tried to lift her hand. When she opened her eyes, they were like points of fire burning in the dark.

We moved down quickly, leaving her behind. When we reached the landing with the three doors, I handed my staff to Alice. She accepted it with a grimace. She didn't like to touch rowan wood. But I was already pulling my own key from my pocket, and it was the work of a moment to unlock the door to the Spook's cell.

Until then I'd been worried that he might not be there. I thought that Meg might have moved him somewhere else, even putting him in a pit in the cellar. But there he was, sitting on the bed with his head in his hands. As the candle flickered light into the cell, he looked toward us, but his expression was one of bewilderment. After glancing down the steps and listening carefully to check that the lamia wasn't coming up, I went into the cell with Alice, and we helped the Spook to his feet. He made no resistance as we tugged him to the door. He didn't seem to recognize either of us, and I guessed that Meg had only recently given him a strong dose of the potion.

My chain was back in my pocket now—not the best place for it if the lamia attacked, but I had no choice.

Progress up the steps was slow as the Spook shuffled upward, Alice and I supporting him by each elbow. I kept glancing back, but there were no threatening sounds from below. When we came to the witch on the stairs, she was asleep, eyes tightly closed, snoring loudly through her open mouth. Climbing the steps had exhausted her for now.

Soon we reached the gate. Once through it, Alice locked it carefully and quietly again, and I took the key from her and slipped it into my pocket. We continued up until we arrived at the ground floor. The sound of Meg's breathing from the kitchen reassured me that she, too, was still asleep, so I now had an important decision to make. Either I could help Alice to get the Spook clear of the house, or I could enter the kitchen and bind Meg with the silver chain.

If I succeeded in binding her, it would be over and the house would be back in our hands. But trying it was filled with risk. Meg might wake up suddenly—and nine times out of ten wasn't quite ten out of ten! I might miss, and Meg was incredibly strong. The Spook was in no condition to help, and the three of us would be at Meg's mercy. So I pointed down the passageway to the front door.

Moments later I had the door open and helped Alice to get the Spook outside. Next I took the candle from her, shielding it close to my body to stop it from going out.

"I've got something to do back in the house," I told her. "I won't be long, but get Mr. Gregory away from here. Andrew should be waiting farther down the clough—"

"Don't be daft, Tom!" Alice exclaimed, her face filled with concern. "What could be so important as to make you want to go back in there?"

"Trust me, Alice. It's got to be done. I'll see you back at Andrew's—"

"There's something you ain't told me," Alice complained. "What is it? Don't you trust me?"

"Go on, Alice, please. Just do as I say. I'll explain it all to you later."

Reluctantly Alice moved off down the hill, guiding the Spook by the elbow. She didn't look back, and I could tell that she was really angry with me.

CHAPTER XVI
UP TO THE ATTIC

ONCE inside, I closed the door behind me and started to climb the stairs. In my right hand I held the candle; in my left was my rowan staff. The silver chain was still in the left pocket of my sheepskin jacket. I moved up faster than we'd come down, but I was still careful. I didn't want to wake Meg. I had another worry, too. My key would be too big for the lock of the Spook's desk. I was going to have to force it open with the crowbar, and that was likely to make more than just a bit of noise.

As I climbed upward, I began to feel more and more uneasy. Meg was still sleeping, but she might wake up at any time. If she followed me up the stairs, I could always reposition the plank and make my escape through the back bedroom window. But would I hear her coming in time? Alice was right. On the face of it, this was a daft thing to do. But I kept thinking of Dad and forced my legs to keep climbing the stairs.

It wasn't long before I was standing close to the attic door. I was just about to open it and go in when I heard a faint sound. It sounded like a sort of scratching. . . .

I listened nervously, with my left ear close to the door, and heard the scratching sound again. What could be making a noise like that? I'd no choice but to ignore it and try to get what Morgan wanted. I began to turn the handle. Only then, as I slowly stepped into the room, did I realize that I should have escaped with Alice and the Spook while I still had the chance. I should have told my master everything that had happened with Morgan and followed his advice. The Spook would have known how best to help Dad.

All my instincts now told me to run. It was as if a voice were screaming "Danger! Danger! Danger!" over and over again inside my head. When I stepped inside, I almost closed the door behind me. I felt a strong urge to do it, but somehow I managed to resist. It was gloomy, so I lifted the candle above my head in order to see better; then there was a sudden blast of cold air and it guttered out.

Above, I could see the square pale outline of the skylight. It was wide open, and there was a cold breeze wafting downward into my face. Six small birds were perched on the edge of the skylight. They were silent, as if waiting patiently for something. And below them was the horror of that room.

The floorboards were scattered with feathers, splattered with blood and littered with fragments of dead birds. It was as if a fox had got into a chicken coop. There were wings, legs, heads, and hundreds and hundreds of feathers. Feathers falling through the air, swirling around my head, stirred by the chill breeze that was blowing through the skylight.

When I saw something much larger, I wasn't surprised. But the sight of it chilled me to the bone. Crouching in the corner, close to the writing desk, was the feral lamia, eyes closed, the top lids thick and heavy. Her body seemed smaller somehow, but her face looked far larger than the last time I'd glimpsed it. It was no longer gaunt but pale and bloated, the cheeks almost two pouches. As I watched, the mouth opened slightly and a trickle of blood ran down her chin and began to drip onto the floorboards. She licked her lips, opened her eyes, and looked up at me as if she had all the time in the world.

She'd been feeding. Feeding on the birds. She'd opened the skylight and then summoned the birds to her clawed, clutching hands, compelling them to fly to where she was waiting. Then, she'd begun to drink their blood, one by one, keeping the ones still alive close by with a spell of compulsion. They had wings but had lost the will to fly away.

I'd no wings, though I did have legs. But my legs wouldn't obey me and I stood, rooted to the spot with fear. She came toward me very slowly. Maybe it was because she was heavy, being so bloated with blood. Maybe she felt there was no hurry.

Had she scurried across the floor toward me, it would have been over. I'd never have left that attic. But she moved slowly. Very slowly. And the horror of watching her approach was enough to break the spell. Suddenly I was free. I could move. Move faster than I'd ever moved before.

I had no thought of using either my chain or staff. My legs acted quicker than I could think. As the lamia crawled across the floorboards, I turned and ran. And as I ran, there was a flutter of wings from behind: my escape had released the waiting birds from the spell. Terrified, my heart hammering, I bounded down the stairs, making enough noise to wake the dead. But I didn't care. I just had to get outside and away from the lamia. Nothing else mattered. All my courage had gone.

But someone was waiting for me in the shadows at the foot of the stairs.

Meg.

Why hadn't I turned off the stairway into the back bedroom? I should have concentrated. Thought carefully. Instead I'd panicked and missed my chance to escape. The feral lamia was too bloated with blood to move quickly. I'd have been able to open the window, position the plank, and crawl across it to safety. And now my heavy feet thumping down the stairs had awakened Meg.

She was there, between me and the front door. While somewhere behind me, probably already descending the stairs, was the feral lamia. Meg looked up at me, her pretty face widening into a smile. There was enough light to see that it wasn't a friendly smile. Suddenly she leaned toward me and sniffed loudly three times.

"I once said I wouldn't give you to my sister," she said. "But that's all changed now. I know what you've done. There's a price to pay for that. A blood price!"

I didn't answer, because I was already retreating slowly up the stairs. I was still gripping the stub of candle, so I thrust it into my breeches pocket. That done, I transferred my staff to my right hand and pulled out the silver chain from the left pocket of my sheepskin jacket.

Meg must have seen the chain or sensed it, because suddenly she ran up the stairs directly at me, her hands held before her as if she wanted to rip out my eyes. I panicked, took quick aim, and hurled the chain directly at her. It was a wild shot, and it missed her head completely. But fortunately for me, it fell against her left shoulder and side. At its touch, she screamed out in agony and fell back against the wall.

Seeing my chance, I ran past her and reached the foot of the stairs before turning to face her. At least now I didn't have the threat of her sister at my back. The chain was still on the steps above. All I had now was my staff of rowan wood. It was the most powerful wood of all to use against a witch. But Meg wasn't from the County; she was a lamia witch from a foreign land. Would it be effective against her?

Meg regained her balance and turned to face me. "The

touch of silver is agony to me, boy," she said, her face twisted with fury. "How would you like to feel pain like that?"

She took a step down, and as she did so, quite deliberately trailed the back of her left hand along the wall at her side. As I watched, she scraped her nails hard against the plaster, gouging into it deeply. The plaster was old and very hard. She was showing me what her nails could do to my flesh. As Meg took another step, I readied the staff, pointing it upward, ready to jab at her head and shoulders.

But I was thinking now. Concentrating. And when she attacked, rushing down the steps, I brought the staff quickly down, thrusting it at her feet. Her eyes widened as she saw what I was trying to do, but her momentum was too great: her legs became tangled in the staff and she fell headlong down the stairs. The staff was torn from my hands, but now I had a chance to retrieve the chain, and I leaped over her and ran back up the steps.

I picked up the chain, twisted it around my left wrist, and prepared to throw it again. This time I was determined not to miss.

She smiled at me, her face full of mockery. "You've

missed once already. It's not as easy as throwing at that post in Gregory's garden, is it? Are your hands sweating, boy? Are they starting to shake? You'll only get one more chance. And then you'll be mine. . . ."

I knew that she was just trying to undermine my confidence and make it more likely that I'd miss. So I took a deep breath and remembered my training. Nine times out of ten, I could hit the post. And I'd never missed twice in a row. Only fear could stop me now. Only doubt. So I took a deep breath and concentrated. As Meg came to her feet, I took careful aim.

I cracked the chain in the air like a whip before hurling it straight at the witch. It fell in a perfect widdershins spiral to enclose her head and body. She gave a shriek, but it was cut off suddenly as the silver chain tightened against her mouth and she fell heavily to the floor.

Cautiously I walked down the steps and looked at her closely. To my relief, she was bound fast. I looked into her eyes and saw the pain there. But although the silver chain was hurting her, there was defiance in her eyes, too.

Suddenly her expression changed, and I realized that she was looking beyond me, back up the stairs. At the same time I heard a scuttling and spun around to see Marcia, the feral lamia, moving down the steps toward me.

Once again the fact that she had already drunk her fill of blood saved me. She was still bloated and sluggish. Otherwise she'd have attacked before I'd even had a chance to blink. So I snatched up my rowan staff and moved up the stairs to meet her. Hatred burned from her heavy-lidded eyes, and the four thin limbs beneath her body tensed, ready to spring forward. At first I didn't have time to be afraid and jabbed toward her bloated face with my staff. She couldn't stand the touch of rowan wood and gasped with pain as my third jab struck her just below the left eye. She hissed angrily and began to retreat backward, her long, greasy black hair brushing the stairs on either side of her to leave a slimy, damp trail.

I don't know how long I struggled with her. Time seemed to stand still. Sweat was running from my brow into my eyes and I was breathing hard, my heart hammering from both exertion and fear. I knew that at any moment she might slip beneath my guard or that I might stumble—in which case she'd have been on me in an instant, her sharp teeth sinking into my legs. But at last I backed her up to the attic door, then jabbed again frantically to drive her inside. That done, I slammed the door hard and locked it, using my key. I knew the door wouldn't stop her for long, and as I descended the stairs, I heard her claws already beginning to rip at the wooden door. It was time to escape. I'd follow the others to Andrew's shop. When the Spook had recovered, we'd be able to return and sort things out.

But when I opened the front door, a blizzard was raging outside, snow blasting straight into my face. I might find my way to the edge of the clough, but to go beyond that would be madness. Even if I got down off the moor safely, I could freeze to death trying to find Adlington. Quickly I closed the door. There was just one other option left.

Meg was no bigger than I was and wasn't very heavy. So I decided to take her down into the cellar and put her in the pit. That done, I could lock myself behind the gate with her and be relatively safe from the feral lamia. Or at least for a while. Even the gate wouldn't stop Marcia forever.

However, there was the other witch, Bessy Hill, to worry about. So I left Meg at the top of the cellar steps and had a quick search for the Spook's bag. I found it at last in the kitchen and quickly helped myself to pocketfuls of salt and iron. That done, I carried Meg down to the cellar, holding her across my right shoulder by her legs. In my left hand I carried both my staff and a candle. It took a long time to get her down there, and I was careful to lock the gate behind me. Once again I kept well away from Bessy Hill, who was still snoring on the stairs.

After all that had happened, I felt like dragging Meg by the feet and letting her head bounce on every step. But I didn't. She was probably suffering a lot already because the silver chain was binding her tightly. And in any case, despite everything, the Spook would want her treated as well as possible. So I was careful with Meg.

But when I eased her over the edge of the pit, I couldn't resist saying what I did.

"Dream about your garden!" I told her, making the tone of my voice as sarcastic as possible. Then I left her and, clutching my stub of candle, went back up the steps. Now it was time to deal with the other witch, Bessy Hill. I must have woken her up on my way down, because now she was snuffling and spitting her way slowly up toward the gate again. I reached into my breeches pockets and pulled out a handful of salt and a handful of iron. But I didn't throw them at her; about three steps above her, I scattered a line of salt from wall to wall, then sprinkled the iron on top of it. After that, I moved along the step and carefully mixed them together to form a barrier that the witch would be unable to cross.

Finally I walked up to the gate and sat about three steps below it, just in case the feral lamia came down and tried to reach me through the bars.

I sat there and watched the candle burn lower and lower. Long before it threatened to go out, I was feeling sorry for what I'd said to Meg. My dad wouldn't have liked me being sarcastic like that. He'd brought me up better than that. Meg couldn't be all bad. The Spook loved her and she'd loved him once. And how was he going to feel when he saw that I'd put her in the pit? That *I'd* done something he'd never been able to face doing himself?

After a while the candle finally guttered out, and I was left in the dark. There were faint whispers and scratching sounds from the cellar far below where the dead witches were stirring and, every so often, the sound of the feeble live witch, sniffing and snuffling in frustration, unable to cross the barrier of salt and iron.

I'd almost dozed off when the feral lamia arrived suddenly, having finally clawed her way through the attic door. My night vision is good, but it was really dark on the cellar steps, and all I heard was the rush of her legs scuttling forward and then a bang as a dark shape hurled itself at the gate and started to rasp at the metal. My heart lurched into my mouth. It sounded like she was ravenous again already, so I picked up my rowan staff and desperately jabbed at her through the bars.

At first it made no difference to her frenzy, and I heard the grille groan as the metal bent and yielded. But then I got lucky. I must have jabbed her in a sensitive spot, probably her eye, because she screamed shrilly and fell back from the gate, whimpering her way back up the steps.

When the blizzard stopped and the Spook was strong enough, he'd come back to the house to sort things out — I was sure of that. What I didn't know was when. It would be a long afternoon and a longer night after that. I might even have to spend days there on the stairs. I wasn't sure how many times Marcia would assault the gate.

Twice more she attacked, and after I'd driven her away for the third time she retreated right back up the steps and out of sight. I wondered if she'd gone back up into the house. Maybe she'd go hunting for rats or mice. After a while I had to fight to keep awake. I couldn't afford to sleep, because the gate was already weakened. If I wasn't ready to fend her off, it wouldn't take her long to force her way through.

I was in serious trouble. If only I hadn't gone back for the grimoire, I'd have been safe and sound with the Spook and Alice at Andrew's house.

CHAPTER XVII
HOME TRUTHS

I_T was uncomfortable on the steps and very cold. After a while, according to my calculations, night turned to day again. I was hungry, and my mouth was dry with thirst.

353

How long would I have to spend down there? How long before the Spook came? What if my master hadn't recovered properly and was too ill to come? Then I began to worry about Alice. What if she came back to the house looking for me? She would think the lamia was still trapped in the cellar. She didn't know that it had been in the attic, that it was now loose in the house.

At last I heard noises from somewhere above. Not scuttling legs, but the welcome murmur of human voices and the thump of boots clumping downward and then the sound of something heavy being dragged down the steps. Candlelight flickered around the corner and I came to my feet.

"Well, Andrew! Looks like you won't be needed after all," said a voice that I immediately recognized.

The Spook walked down to the gate. He was dragging the feral lamia behind him, bound tightly in a silver chain. At his side was Andrew, who'd accompanied him down to pick the lock.

"Well, lad, don't stand there gawping," said the Spook. "Open the gate and let us in."

Quickly I did as I was told. I wanted to tell the Spook

what I'd done to Meg, but when I opened my mouth to speak, he shook his head and put a hand on my shoulder.

"First things first, lad," he said, his voice kind and understanding, as if he knew exactly what I'd done. "It's been hard for all of us, and we've a lot to talk through. But the time for that is later. First there's work to be done."

That said, with Andrew in the lead holding the candle aloft, we set off down the steps. As we approached the live witch, Andrew halted and the candle started to quiver in his hand.

"Andrew, give the candle to the lad," said the Spook. "It's best if you go up top and wait at the door for the mason and smith to arrive. Then you can tell them we're down here."

With a sigh of relief, Andrew handed the candle to me, and after nodding in the Spook's direction, walked back up the steps. We continued down until we reached the cellar, with its low ceiling thickly hung with cobwebs. The Spook led the way directly to the feral lamia's pit, where the bars were yawning wide, leaving plenty of space to drop her into the darkness—and the Spook wasted no time in preparing to do just that.

"Staff at the ready, lad!" he commanded.

So I stepped close to his side, the candle in my right hand to illuminate the lamia and the pit, my rowan staff in my left hand positioned to jab downward.

The Spook held the lamia over the gaping bars and, with a sudden jerk, twisted the silver chain to the right, giving it a flick. It unraveled and, with a shrill cry, the lamia fell into the darkness. Immediately the Spook knelt beside the pit and began to fasten the silver chain from bar to bar across the top of the opening to make a temporary barrier that the lamia couldn't cross. From the shadows below, the lamia hissed up at us angrily but made no attempt to scuttle upward; within a few moments the job was done.

"There, that should hold her fast until the mason and the blacksmith arrive," my master said, coming to his feet. "Now let's see how Meg is. . . ."

He walked over toward Meg's pit and I followed, carrying the candle. He looked down and shook his head sadly. Meg was lying on her back looking up at us, her eyes wide and angry, but the chain still bound her tightly and she couldn't speak.

"I'm sorry," I said. "Really sorry. I was —"

The Spook held up his hand to silence me. "Save your words for later, lad. It hurts me to see this. . . ."

I heard the choke in the Spook's voice and caught a glimpse of the grief on his face. I looked away quickly. There was a long silence, but at last he gave a deep sigh.

"What's done is done," he said sadly, "but I never thought it would come to this. Not after all these years. Anyway, let's go and attend to the other one."

We went back up the steps until we reached the live witch, Bessy Hill.

"By the way, that was well thought out, lad!" exclaimed the Spook, indicating the line of salt and iron. "Good to see you using your initiative."

Bessy Hill turned her head slowly to the left and

seemed to be trying to speak herself. The Spook shook his head sadly and pointed downward at her feet.

"There, lad. You take her right foot, I'll take her left. We'll pull her down slowly. Gently, now! We don't want to bang her head. . . ."

We did just that, and it was unpleasant work: Bessy's right foot felt cold, damp, and slimy, and as we dragged her downward she began to snuffle and spit. It didn't take long, though, and soon she was back in her pit. All it needed now was the bent bars to be replaced, and she'd be safe for a long time.

We didn't speak for a while and I guessed that the Spook was thinking about Meg, but soon there was the distant sound of men's voices and heavy boots.

"Right, lad, this'll be the smith and the mason. I'd half a mind to ask you to deal with Meg, but it's not right and I won't shirk what has to be done. So you get yourself back up those steps and light a big fire in every down-stairs room. You've done well—we'll talk later."

On the way up I met the smith and the mason. "Mr.

Gregory's at the bottom of the steps," I told them. They nodded and carried on down. Neither of them looked happy. It was grim work, but it had to be done.

Later, when I went back down into the cellar to tell my master that I'd lit the fires, Meg was still in her pit, but my silver chain was safely back in his possession, and he handed it to me without a word. The stone-and-iron cover had been dragged into place and locked with metal pins driven deep into the ground.

Now she was imprisoned beneath iron bars just as firmly as the other witches. The Spook must have been really sad having to do that, but he'd done it anyway. It had taken him almost a lifetime, but Meg was finally bound.

It was late afternoon before the work was done and the mason and smith had finally gone on their way. The Spook turned to me as he closed the door after them and scratched at his beard.

"There's just one more job before we eat, lad. You

might as well get yourself upstairs and clean up that mess in the attic."

Even after all that had happened, I hadn't forgotten about the grimoire. I hadn't forgotten what Morgan might do to Dad. And here was my chance! So, my hands shaking at the thought of how I was going to betray the Spook and steal the grimoire, I carried a mop and bucket up to the attic. After closing the skylight, I began to clean the floor just as fast as I could. Once the job was done, it would take just a few moments to force the desk and hide the grimoire in my bedroom. I'd never seen the Spook go up to the attic, so I could give it to Morgan without him realizing that it had gone.

Having cleaned the floor of feathers and blood, I turned my attention to the writing desk. Although it was a well-crafted desk, ornate but soundly made, it wasn't going to take me long to get it open. I pulled the small crowbar from my jacket pocket and eased it into the crack between the doors.

At that moment I heard footsteps behind me and

jumped up guiltily to see the Spook standing in the door-way, a look of anger and disbelief on his face.

"Well, lad! What have we here?"

"Nothing," I lied. "I was just cleaning this old desk."

"Don't lie to me, lad. There's nothing worse in this world than a liar. So this is why you went back into the house. The girl couldn't understand it."

"Morgan told me to get the grimoire from your desk in the attic!" I blurted out, and hung my head in shame. "I'm supposed to take it to him on Tuesday night at the graveyard chapel. I'm sorry—really sorry. I never wanted to betray you. I just couldn't bear the thought of what he might do to Dad if I didn't."

"Your dad?" The Spook frowned. "How can Morgan harm your dad?"

"My dad died, Mr. Gregory."

"Yes, the girl told me last night. I was sorry to hear that."

"Well, Morgan summoned Dad's spirit and terrified him—"

361

The Spook held up his hand. "Calm yourself down, lad. Stop gabbling and slow down. Where did all this happen?"

"In his room at the farm. He summoned his sister first, and she brought Dad. It was Dad's voice, and Morgan made him think he was in hell. He did it again in Adlington—I definitely heard Dad's voice inside my head—and Morgan said he'd keep doing it if I didn't obey him. I went back to get the grimoire, but when I got up to the attic, the feral lamia was there feeding on the birds. I ran downstairs in a panic to find Meg there waiting. My first throw of the chain I missed her and thought I was done for."

"Aye, it could have cost you your life," my master said, shaking his head in disapproval.

"I was desperate," I told him.

"I don't care, lad," said the Spook, scratching at his beard. "Didn't I tell you to steer clear of him? You should have told me everything, not sneaked up to steal something on the word of that fool Morgan."

I was hurt by his use of the word "steal." There was no

denying that it would have been theft, but to hear him use that word hurt me badly.

"I couldn't. Meg had you prisoner. Anyway, *you* didn't tell me everything," I said angrily. "Why didn't you tell me Morgan was your son? How can I know who to trust when you keep things like that a secret? You told me he was Mr. and Mrs. Hurst's son—but he isn't, he's yours. The seventh you had with Emily Burns. I did what I did because I love my father. But your son would never do the same for you. He hates you. He wants to destroy you. He says you're an old fool!"

I knew I'd gone too far, but the Spook just smiled grimly and shook his head. "I suppose there *is* no fool like an old fool, and I've certainly sometimes been that, but as for the rest . . ."

He looked at me hard, his green eyes glinting fiercely. "Morgan is no son of mine! He's a liar!" he said, suddenly thumping the top of the desk, his face livid with anger. "He was, he is, and he always will be. He's just trying to confuse and manipulate you. I don't have any children—

I've sometimes regretted that, but if I had a child, do you think I'd deny it? Would your father have disowned one of you?"

I shook my head.

"Would you like to hear the full story, if it means that much to you?"

I nodded.

"Well, I won't deny that I took Emily Burns from my own brother. Or that it hurt my own family badly. My brother particularly. I've never disputed that, and I've little to say in my defense except that I was young. I wanted her, lad, and I had to have her. One day you'll find out what I mean, but only half the fault was mine. Emily was a strong woman, and she wanted me, too. But it wasn't long before she tired of me, just as she'd tired of my brother. She moved on and found herself another man.

"Edwin Furner was his name, and although he was a seventh son of a seventh son, he worked as a tanner. Not everybody qualified to do so follows our trade. It was fine for just over two years, and they were happy together. But very soon after their second child was born, he took himself off for almost a year, leaving her to fend for herself with two young children.

"It would have been better had he stayed away, but he kept turning up again like a bad penny. Each time he went away again, she was expecting another of his children. There were seven in all. Morgan was Furner's seventh. After that he never came back."

The Spook shook his head wearily. "Emily had a hard life, lad, and we still stayed friends. So I helped her out when I could. Sometimes with money, sometimes finding work for her growing lads. As there was no father to fend for them, what else could I do? When Morgan was sixteen, I got him a job at Moor View Farm. The Hursts took to him so much that they eventually adopted him. They had no son of their own, and the farm would have been his. But he couldn't stick to the work and things started to turn sour. It lasted barely a year.

"As I told you, they had a daughter. She was about the

same age and her name was Eveline. Young as they were, Morgan and Eveline fell in love. Her parents would have none of it because they wanted them to be brother and sister, so they beat them both; made their lives not worth living. Finally, unable to stand it any longer, Eveline drowned herself in the lake. After that, Emily begged me to get Morgan away from there and take him on as my apprentice. At the time it seemed a reasonable solution, but I had my doubts and I was proved right. Three years he lasted, until finally he went back to Emily, but he couldn't keep away from Moor View Farm. He still lives there sometimes—at least, that's when he's not making mischief elsewhere.

"The sister must be a lingerer, someone who's not been able to cross over to the other side. And because of that, he's got her in his power. And there's no doubt that he is growing stronger. He certainly seems to have had some power over you. You'd better tell me exactly what's been happening between you."

So I did, and as I talked, the Spook kept prompting me

for details. I began with my meeting with Morgan at the graveyard chapel on the edge of the moor and ended with our conversation at Emily Burns's grave.

"I see," said the Spook when I'd finished. "It's clear enough now. As I told you before, Morgan was always fascinated by that ancient burial mound up on the moor. Dig into it long enough, and you're bound to find something. Well, when he was my apprentice, he finally found a sealed chest with the grimoire inside. And that grimoire contains a ritual that is the only way to raise Golgoth. So that's what he tried to do. Fortunately I got there before the ritual had gone too far and put a stop to it."

"What would have happened if he'd succeeded?" I asked.

"Doesn't bear thinking about, lad. One mistake in the ritual, and he'd have been dead. Better that than completing it successfully. You see, he'd followed the instructions to the letter and drawn a pentacle on the floor of his room in Moor View Farm, a five-pointed star within three concentric circles. So if he got the rest right, he was safe enough inside there. But Golgoth would have materialized on the outside of the pentacle and been loose in the County. Not for nothing was he called the Lord of Winter. It might have been years before summer returned. Freezing death and famine might have been our lot. Morgan offered up the farm dog as a sacrifice. Golgoth never touched it, but the poor animal died of fright.

"So, as I said, I stopped Morgan in time. I terminated his apprenticeship and took the grimoire off him. Then his mother and I made him promise that he would leave Golgoth alone and not try to raise him again. She believed his promise, and for her sake I gave him every chance and always hoped that her faith in him would be justified. But as I'd stopped him part of the way through the ritual, some of the power of Golgoth had already awoken and attached itself to him. Your mother was right—this is going to be a bitter winter. I'm convinced that's to do with Golgoth and Morgan. After Morgan left my care, he turned to the dark, and his powers have steadily increased. And he thinks that the grimoire will give him ultimate power.

"Already he can do things that a man shouldn't. Some are little more than conjuring tricks, like changing the temperature in a room to impress the gullible. But now it seems that he can also bind the dead to his will—not just ghosts, but also spirits that hover in limbo between this life and the other side. It pains me to say this, lad, but it looks very bad. I really do fear that Morgan has the ability to hurt your poor dad's spirit. . . ."

The Spook looked up at the skylight, then down at the writing desk. He shook his head sadly. "Well, lad, get yourself downstairs and we'll talk this through some more."

Fifteen minutes later, my master was sitting there quietly in Meg's rocking chair and pea soup was simmering away in a pan.

"Got much appetite, lad?" he asked.

"I've not eaten since yesterday," I told him.

At that he grinned, revealing the gap where the boggart had knocked out his front tooth, got up, put two bowls on the table and ladled hot soup into them. Soon I was dunking bread into the delicious steaming soup. The Spook didn't bother with the bread, but he did empty his bowl.

"I am very sorry your dad's passed away," he said, pushing the empty bowl away from him. "He should have had nothing to fear after death. Unfortunately, Morgan's using the power of Golgoth to hurt your dad and get at you through him. But don't worry, lad, we're going to put a stop to it just as soon as we can. And as for the other nonsense, Morgan's not my son and never was." He looked straight into my eyes again. "Well, do you believe me?"

I nodded, but I can't have done it convincingly enough, because the Spook sighed and shook his head. "Well, lad, either he's a liar or I am. You'd better decide which one of us it is. If there's no trust between us, there's no point in you carrying on as my apprentice. But one thing's for sure, I wouldn't let you go off with him. Before that I'd take you by the scruff of your neck, give you back to your mother, and let her knock some sense into that thick head."

370

His tone was harsh, and after all that had happened I felt really upset. "You couldn't take me back to my mother," I told him bitterly. "I was too late for the funeral and I didn't even get to see her. Afterward she went off somewhere—maybe back to her own land. I don't think she'll be coming back."

"Well, give her space, lad. She's just lost her husband and needs time to mourn and think. But you'll be seeing her again and not before too long, I'm sure. And that's not prophecy. It's good common sense. If she goes, she goes, but she'll want to say a proper farewell to *all* her sons before she does.

"Anyway, it's a terrible thing that Morgan's been doing, but don't worry—I *will* find him and stop him once and for all."

I was too weary to say anything, so I just nodded my head. I hoped he was right.

CHAPTER XVIII
THE CHAPEL OF THE DEAD

FOR all the Spook's promises, it wasn't possible to deal with Morgan right away. For the next two weeks the weather was so bad, we hardly ever went outdoors. Blizzard after blizzard surged up the clough, whirling snow against the windows and burying the front of the house almost up to the level of the first-floor bedrooms. I was starting to believe that Golgoth had indeed been awakened, and I was grateful that Shanks had had the foresight to deliver extra provisions. When the Tuesday that Morgan had appointed for our meeting arrived, I was nervous and half expected to see him turn up at the house. But the blizzards were so bad that no one would have made it across the moor. Still, every hour trapped in that house felt like torture. I was desperate to get out and find Morgan and put an end to my father's misery.

My master made us carry on with our usual routine of sleeping, eating, and lessons during the blizzard, but something new was added. Every afternoon he descended the steps to the cellar to talk to Meg and take her something to eat. Usually it was just a few biscuits, but sometimes he carried the remainder of our lunch with him. I wondered what the two of them talked about when he was down there, though I knew better than to ask. We'd agreed no more secrets, but I realized the Spook still expected some privacy.

The other two witches had to manage the best they

could, chewing on worms, slugs, and anything else they could grub out of the damp earth, but Meg was still a special case. I half expected that, one day soon, the Spook would give Meg her herb tea again and bring her up from the cellar. She was certainly a far better cook than either of us, but after all that had happened, I couldn't help feeling safer with her down in the pit. I did worry about the Spook, though. Had he gone soft? After all his warnings about not trusting women, here he was breaking all his own rules again. I felt like telling him as much, but how could I when I could see that he was upset about Meg?

He still wasn't eating properly, and one morning his eyes were red and swollen, as if he'd been rubbing them. I even wondered if he'd been crying, and that made me think about how I would behave in a similar situation. What if I were the Spook, with Alice down there in the pit? Wouldn't I be doing the same? I was also wondering how Alice was getting on. If the weather ever improved, I'd decided to ask my master if I could pay a visit to Andrew's shop to visit her again.

Then, unexpectedly, one morning the weather did change. I'd kept thinking about the threat to Dad, hoping that, first chance, we'd be off after Morgan. But it wasn't to be. With the sunshine came spooks' business. My master and I were called away east, to Platt Farm. It was boggart trouble, or so it seemed.

It was an hour or so before we could get started, because first the Spook cut himself a new staff of rowan wood, and when we finally arrived, after a two-hour slog through the deep snow, there was no sign at all that a boggart had been in the vicinity and the farmer apologized profusely for being mistaken, blaming it on his wife, who was prone to sleepwalking. He said she'd moved things in the kitchen and clattered pots and pans to disturb the household, waking up the following morning without any memory of having done so. He seemed embarrassed at having called us out for nothing and almost too eager to pay the Spook for his trouble.

I was furious that we'd wasted precious time and told the Spook as much on the way back. He agreed. "I smell a rat," he said. "Unless I'm mistaken, lad, we've been sent on a wild goose chase. Ever seen anyone so keen to put his hand in his pocket and pay?"

I shook my head and we doubled our pace, the Spook out in the lead, eager to get home. We arrived to find the back door was already open. The lock had been forced. After checking that the cellar door and the gate were still secure, the Spook told me to wait in the kitchen and went upstairs. Five minutes later he came down, shaking his head angrily.

"The grimoire's been taken!" he said. "Well, lad, we certainly know who we're looking for! Who else would it be but Morgan? He's got Golgoth in his power enough to stop the snow, and then he plots and schemes to rob us."

It seemed odd to me that Morgan hadn't tried to steal the grimoire before. It would have been easy enough during the summers, when Meg was locked in the room on the cellar steps and the upper part of the house was empty. But then I remembered what the Spook had told me—the promise Morgan had made to his mother not to try and raise Golgoth again. Perhaps he'd kept his word until his mother died; now after he'd mourned her, he felt free to do whatever he wanted.

"Well, there's little we can do today but get ourselves down to Adlington and ask that brother of mine to come up and fix the door," said the Spook. "But don't mention the grimoire. I'll tell him that in my own time. And on our way, we'll pay a little visit to Moor View Farm. I doubt I'll find Morgan there, but I've a few things I need to ask the Hursts."

I wondered why he didn't want to tell Andrew about the grimoire, but I could tell that he wasn't in the mood for questions.

We set off right away for Moor View Farm. When we arrived, the Spook went in alone to talk to the Hursts and told me to wait in the yard. There was no sign at all of Morgan. My master spent some time in the farmhouse and came out frowning. Tight-lipped, he led the way to Andrew's shop.

The Spook behaved as if it were just a brotherly visit,

making me wonder again why he made no mention at all of what had happened. It was good to see Alice, though. She made us a late supper, and we warmed ourselves in front of the big fire in the living room before seating ourselves at the table. After we'd finished eating, the Spook turned to Alice.

"That was a good supper, girl," he said, giving her a faint smile, "but now I've got private business to attend to with my brother and Tom. So it's best if you take yourself off to bed!"

"Why should I go up to bed?" she asked, bristling with anger. "I live here, not you."

"Please, Alice, do as John says," Andrew said mildly. "I'm sure there's a very good reason for his not wanting you to hear what's about to be said."

Alice gave Andrew a withering look, but it was his house and she obeyed, almost slamming the door and stamping heavily up the stairs.

"The least she knows, the better," said the Spook. "I've just been to see the Hursts and had a bit of a talk with the wife about why young Alice left. It seemed she quarreled with Morgan and went off in a temper, but in the couple of days before that, they'd been quite close and spent a lot of time together in his downstairs room. It may be nothing. It may well be that he just tried to win her over in the way he tried it with the lad," he said, nodding toward me. "Tried and failed. But just in case, it's better that she doesn't hear this. This morning Morgan broke into my house and stole the grimoire."

Andrew looked really concerned and opened his mouth to speak, but I beat him to it. "That's not fair!" I told the Spook. "Alice hates Morgan. She told me so herself. Why else would she have left? There's no way she would have helped him."

The Spook shook his head angrily. "Some lessons are going to take longer to hammer into your daft head than others!" he snapped. "After all this time, you still haven't learned that the girl can never be fully trusted. She'll always need watching. That's why I've made sure she's close by. Other than that, I wouldn't allow her within ten miles of you."

"Look, hang on a minute," Andrew interrupted. "You say Morgan's got the grimoire? How could you be so foolish, John? You should have burned that infernal book while you had the chance! If he tries that ritual again, anything might happen. I was hoping to see a few more summers before my time is up. It should have been destroyed. I just can't understand why you've kept it all these years!"

"Look, Andrew, that's my business, and you'll just have to trust me on that one. Let's just say that I had my reasons."

"Emily, eh?"

The Spook ignored him.

"What's done is done and I wish Morgan had never taken the grimoire and it was still safe under lock and key."

"So do I!" Andrew said, raising his voice and becoming angrier by the second. "Your duty is the County. You've said that often enough. What you've done in keeping that book rather than burning it amounts to a dereliction of that duty!"

"Well, brother, I thank you for your hospitality, but not for those harsh words," the Spook said, an edge of anger in his own voice. "I don't interfere in your business, and you should trust me to do what's best for everyone. I just called here to let you know the situation we're in, but it's been a long hard day and it's time we were off to our beds before we say things we'll really regret!"

With that, we left Andrew's in a hurry. As we walked down the street, I remembered why we'd visited in the first place.

"We didn't ask Andrew to fix the lock," I said. "Shall I run back and tell him?"

"No you won't, lad," said the Spook angrily. "Not even if he were the last locksmith in the County! I'd rather fix it myself."

"Well, now the weather's improved," I asked, "could we start searching for Morgan tomorrow? I'm worried about Dad —"

"Leave that to me, lad," the Spook said, his voice softer. "I've thought of a few places Morgan might have gone to ground. Best thing is if I set off well before dawn tomorrow."

"Can I come with you?" I asked.

"Nay, lad. I've more chance of catching him napping by myself. Trust me. It's for the best."

I did trust the Spook. Although I could see some sense in what he was saying, I still wanted to go with him. I tried one more time to persuade him but realized I was just wasting my breath. If the Spook makes up his mind, you just have to accept it and let him get on with it.

The following morning, when I came down into the kitchen, there was no sign of the Spook. His cloak and staff had been taken, and as promised, he'd left the house long before dawn in search of Morgan. After I'd finished my breakfast, my master still hadn't returned and I realized that his absence provided a chance just too good to miss. I was curious about Meg and decided to pay a quick visit to the cellar to see how she was doing. So I helped myself to the key on top of the bookcase, lit a candle, and went down the steps. I went through the gate and locked it behind me, continuing downward toward the cellar, but when I reached the landing with the three doors a voice suddenly called out from the middle cell.

"John! John! Is that you? Have you booked our passage?"

I came to a sudden halt. It was Meg's voice. He'd released her from the pit and put her in a cell where she'd be more comfortable. So he had softened. No doubt she'd be back in the kitchen within days. But what did she mean by "booked our passage"? Was she going on a voyage? Was the Spook going with her?

Suddenly I heard Meg sniff loudly three times. "Well, boy, what are you doing down here? Come to the door so that I can see you better."

She'd sniffed me out, so it was no use creeping back up the steps. No doubt she'd tell the Spook where I'd been. So I walked up to the cell door and peered inside, taking care not to get too close.

Meg's pretty face smiled at me through the bars. It

wasn't the grim smile she'd given when we'd struggled. To my surprise, it was almost friendly.

"How are you, Meg?" I asked politely.

"I've been better and I've been worse," Meg replied. "No thanks to you. But what's done is done, and I don't blame you for it. You are what you are. You and John have a lot in common. But I will give you one piece of advice—that's if you're willing to listen."

"Of course I'll listen," I told her.

"In that case, heed what I have to say. Treat the girl well. Alice cares about you. Treat her better than John treated me and you won't be sorry. It doesn't need to end up this way."

"I like Alice a lot and I'll do my best."

"See that you do."

"I heard you ask about booking a passage," I said, turning to leave. "What did you mean?"

"That's none of your business, boy," Meg replied. "You could ask John, but I don't think you'll bother because you'd only get the same answer from him. And I don't think he'd want you prowling about down here without his permission, would he?"

With that I muttered good-bye and set off back up the stairs, taking care to lock the gate behind me. So it seemed the Spook still had his secrets, and I suspected he always would. No sooner had I put the key back in its rightful place than he returned.

"Did you find Morgan?" I asked, disappointed. I already knew the answer. Had he done so, Morgan would have been with him, bound as a prisoner.

"No, lad, sorry to say that I didn't. I thought I might find him lurking in the abandoned tower at Rivington," said the Spook. "He's been there recently, all right—no doubt up to no good. But it seems to me that he never settles in one place for long. Still, don't worry yourself, I'll search again first thing tomorrow.

"Anyway, in the meantime you can do something for me. This afternoon, have a wander down into Adlington and ask that brother of mine if he'd mind coming up to fix the back door," said the Spook. "And tell him I'm sorry that heated words passed between us and that one day he'll understand that I did things for the best."

The afternoon lessons went on later than usual, and it was less than two hours before dark when, carrying my rowan staff, I finally set off for Adlington.

Andrew made me welcome, and his face broke into a smile when I passed on the Spook's apology: he quickly agreed to fix the door within a day or so. Later I spent about fifteen minutes talking to Alice, although she seemed a bit cool. It was probably because she'd been sent to bed the previous night. After saying my good-byes, I set off back toward the Spook's house, eager to return before it was quite dark.

I hadn't been walking more than five minutes when I heard a faint noise behind. I turned around and saw someone following me up the hill. It was Alice, so I waited for her to catch up. She was wearing her woolen coat, and as she approached, her pointy shoes made neat footprints in the snow.

"Up to something, you are," Alice said with a smile. "What was it that they didn't want me to hear last night? You can tell me, can't you, Tom? We don't have any secrets. Been through too much together, we have."

The sun had already set, and it was starting to get dark. "It's very complicated," I said, impatient to be off. "I don't have much time."

Alice leaned forward and gripped my arm. "Come on, Tom, you can tell me!"

"Mr. Gregory doesn't trust you," I told her. "He thinks you got too close to Morgan. Mrs. Hurst told him that you and Morgan spent lots of time together in his downstairs room—"

"Ain't nothing new in Old Gregory not trusting me!" Alice exclaimed with a sneer. "Morgan was planning something big. A ritual, he said, that was going to make him rich and powerful. Wanted my help, he did, and nagged and nagged until I couldn't stand the sight of him. That's all there was to it. So come on, Tom. What's going on. You can tell me. . . ."

Finally, realizing that she was never going to let it go, I gave in, and Alice walked by my side while I reluctantly explained what had been happening. I told her about the grimoire and how Morgan had wanted me to steal it and how he was torturing Dad's spirit. Then I told her we'd been burgled and were now searching for Morgan.

Alice wasn't best pleased with what I told her, to say the least.

"You mean we went into Old Gregory's house together with no mention of what you planned? No mention at all! You meant to go up to the attic, and you didn't tell me. It ain't right, Tom. Risking my life, I was, and deserved better than that. A lot better!"

"Sorry, Alice. I'm really sorry. But all I could think of was Dad and what Morgan was doing to him. I wasn't thinking straight. I should have trusted you, I know."

"Bit late to say that now. Still, I think I know where you could find Morgan tonight. . . ."

I looked at her in astonishment.

"It's Tuesday," Alice said, "and on Tuesday night he

always does the same thing. Been doing it since late summer, he has. There's a chapel on the hillside. Set in a graveyard, it is. People come from miles around and he takes their money. I went there with him once. He makes the dead speak. He ain't a priest, but he's got a congregation to put lots of churches to shame."

I remembered the first time I'd met him—when the news came about Dad and I'd been on my way home. That had been a Tuesday, too. I'd taken a shortcut through the graveyard, and he'd been inside the chapel. He must have been waiting for his congregation to arrive. He'd also asked me to bring the grimoire to him on a Tuesday, just after sunset. I could have kicked myself. Why hadn't I put two and two together?

"Don't you believe me?" Alice asked.

"Course I believe you," I said. "I know where the chapel is. I've been there before."

"Then why don't you go that way on your way home?" suggested Alice. "If I'm right and he is there, you can go and tell Old Gregory. Might just get back in time to catch him! But don't forget to mention that I was the one who told you where he was. Might just make him think better of me. Ain't holding my breath, though."

"Come with me," I suggested. "You could keep watch while I go for the Spook. That way, if we don't get back in time, we'll know where he's headed."

Alice shook her head. "No, Tom. Why should I after what's happened? I don't like not being trusted. It ain't nice. Anyway, you've got your job and I've got mine. The shop's been really busy. Worked hard all day, I have, and now I'm going to warm myself by the fire, not spend my time shivering out here in the cold. You do what you have to do and let Old Gregory sort Morgan out. But leave me out of it."

With that, Alice turned on her heels and set off back down the hill. I was disappointed and a bit sad, but I could hardly blame her. If I kept secrets from her, why should she help?

By now it was almost dark and the sky was starting to glitter with stars. So, wasting no time, I chose a route that took me up the moor and circled back to the drystone wall, at the exact place in the copse where I'd climbed over it that Tuesday night when I was on my way home. I leaned against the low wall and looked at the chapel. Candlelight flickered against the stained-glass window. Then I noticed something far beyond the grave-yard. Scattered points of light were moving up the slope toward me.

Lanterns! The members of Morgan's congregation were approaching. Although I couldn't be sure, he was probably already inside, waiting for them to arrive.

So I turned and set off through the trees, heading in the direction of the Spook's house. I needed to get my master and bring him back in time to catch Morgan. But I hadn't taken more than a dozen paces before somebody stepped out of the shadows ahead of me. A hooded figure in a black cloak. I came to a halt as he strode toward me. It was Morgan.

"You've disappointed me, Tom," he said, his voice cruel and hard. "I asked you to bring me something. You let me down, so I had to go and get it myself. Wasn't much to ask, was it? Not when so much was at stake."

I didn't answer, and he took a step nearer. I turned to run, but before I could move, he caught me by the shoulder. I struggled for a moment and tried to raise my staff to strike him, but suddenly I felt a heavy blow to my right temple. Everything went dark and I felt myself falling.

When I opened my eyes, I found myself in the chapel. My head was hurting, and I felt as if I were going to be sick. I was sitting on the rearmost row of benches with my back resting against the cold stone wall, facing toward the confessional box. On each side of it were two large candles.

Morgan was standing in front of the box, facing directly toward me. "Well, Tom, I've business to attend to first. But we'll talk about this afterward."

"I need to return to the house," I said, finding it hard to form the words. "If I don't, Mr. Gregory will wonder where I am."

"Let him wonder. What does it matter what he thinks?

You won't ever be going back. You're my apprentice now, and I've got a job for you to do tonight."

With a smile of triumph, Morgan walked into the confessional, using the priest's doorway on the left. I could no longer see him. The candles cast their light outward into the chapel, but the two doorways were absolutely dark oblongs.

I tried to stand and make a run for it, but I felt too weak and my legs weren't working properly yet. My head pounded and my vision felt blurred after the blow to my head, so all I could do was sit there, trying to collect my wits and hoping that I wasn't going to be sick.

After a few moments, the first of Morgan's congregation arrived. Two women came in, and as each one crossed the threshold, I heard the clink of metal upon metal. I hadn't noticed it before, but there was a copper collection plate to the left of the door, and each dropped a coin into it before taking a seat. Then, without a glance in my direction, keeping their heads bowed, they sat down in one of the front benches.

The benches began to fill, but I noticed that everyone who came into the chapel left his lantern outside. The congregation was mostly women—the few men present were relatively old. Nobody spoke. We waited in silence but for the clink of coins and the rattle of the plate. At last, when most of the seats were full, the door seemed to close by itself. Either that, or somebody outside had pushed it.

Now the only light came from the candles at either side of the confessional box. There were a few coughs, somebody in front cleared their throat, and then came an expectant hush in which you could have heard a pin drop. It was just as it had been in the darkened room at Moor View Farm. I felt as if my ears were going to pop. Suddenly I shivered. A coldness was creeping toward me from the box. Morgan was drawing upon the power he'd gained by trying to raise Golgoth.

Into the silence Morgan's voice suddenly called out very loudly. "Sister of mine! Sister of mine, are you there?"

In answer came three loud raps on the floor of the chapel, so loud that the whole building seemed to quiver, followed by a long drawn-out shuddering sigh that came from the darkness of the penitent's doorway.

"Leave me be! Let me rest!" came the plaintive plea of a girl. This was hardly more than a whisper, but filled with anguish, the source of the girl's voice again that dark confessional doorway. Morgan's sister was a lingerer and was under his control. She didn't want to be here.

He was making her suffer, but the congregation didn't know that, and I sensed the nervousness, anticipation, and excitement of the people about me as they waited for Morgan to summon family and friends they'd lost to death.

"Obey me first. Then you may rest!" boomed the voice of Morgan.

As if in response to those words, a white shape drifted out of the darkness to be framed in the penitent's doorway. Although Eveline had drowned herself when she was about sixteen, the spirit looked hardly older than

Alice. Her face, legs, and bare arms were as white as the dress she was wearing. It clung to her body as if saturated with water, and her hair was limp and wet. That drew a gasp of astonishment from the congregation, but the thing that attracted my gaze was her eyes. They were large and luminous and utterly sad. I'd never looked upon a face so filled with grief as that of Eveline's ghost.

"I am here. What do you want?"

"Are there others with you? Others who wish to speak to someone in this gathering?"

"There are some. Close at hand is a child spirit who goes by the name Maureen. She would speak with Matilda, her dearest mother. . . ."

At that a woman in the front bench came to her feet and held out her arms in supplication. She seemed to be trying to speak, but her body was shaking with emotion and only a groan escaped her lips. The figure of Eveline faded back into the darkness and something else moved forward.

"Mother? Mother?" cried a new female voice from the

penitent's box. This time, it was that of a very young child. *"Come to me, Mother. Please, please! I miss you so much. . . ."*

At that, the woman left her place and began to stagger in the direction of the confessional box, still holding out her arms. There was a sudden intake of breath from the congregation, and immediately I saw why. A pale shape was just visible in the darkness of the right-hand doorway. It looked like a young girl, no older than four or five, with long hair falling down over her shoulders.

"Hold my hand, Mother! Please hold my hand!" cried the child, and a small white hand came out of the darkness of the doorway. It reached toward the woman, who fell to her knees and seized it, eagerly pulling it to her lips.

"Oh, your little hand is so cold, so bitterly cold!" cried the woman, and she began to weep, her anguished sobs and wails filling the whole chapel. This went on for long minutes, until at last the hand was withdrawn into the doorway and the mother returned unsteadily to her seat.

After that there was more of the same. Sometimes adults, sometimes other children materialized within the darkness of the penitent's doorway. There were glimpses of shadow shapes, pale faces, and, more rarely, a hand outstretched into the candlelight. And almost always there was a strong emotional reaction from the relative or friend who made contact.

After a while I began to feel sickened by the spectacle, wishing for it to end. Morgan was a clever, dangerous man, using the power of Golgoth to bind these poor spirits to his will. As I listened to the anguish of the living and the torment of the dead, in my head I remembered hearing the clink of money as it rattled into the copper collection plate.

At last it came to an end. The congregation filed out of the chapel and the door slammed shut behind them, seemingly as if propelled by an invisible hand.

Morgan didn't come out of the confessional box immediately, but gradually the cold began to fade. When he did walk out and approach me, there were beads of sweat on his brow.

"How's that father of mine after the wild goose chase I sent him on?" Morgan asked with a smirk. "Did the old fool enjoy his walk to Platt Farm?"

"Mr. Gregory *isn't* your father," I said quietly, coming shakily to my feet. "Your real father's name was Edwin Furner, a local tanner. Everybody knows the truth, but you can't face it. You just tell lie after lie. Let's go down to Adlington now and ask a few people. Let's ask your mother's sister—she still lives there. If they all say the same, then I might just start to believe you. But I don't think they will. You're a father yourself—the father of lies! And you've told so many that now you're starting to believe them!"

Livid with rage, Morgan swung a punch in my direction. I tried to get out of the way, but I was still groggy and my reactions were far too slow. His fist caught my temple again, in almost the same place as last time. I fell, cracking the back of my head against the stones.

I didn't quite lose consciousness this time, but I was dragged to my feet and his face came very close to mine.

I could taste blood in my mouth and one of my eyes was almost closed, so swollen that I could hardly see through it. But the expression on Morgan's face was clear enough, and I didn't like what I saw. His mouth was twisted, his eyes bright and wild. It looked more like the face of a savage animal than a man.

CHAPTER XIX
THE ROUND LOAF

"YOU had your chance, but it's gone! I've another use for you now, though. One you won't like! Here, carry these!" Morgan snarled, thrusting something toward me.

It was a spade. No sooner had I gripped it than he handed me a bulging sack, so heavy that he had to help me get it up onto my shoulder.

Then he pushed me toward the door of the chapel and then out into the cold. I stood there shivering, struggling under the weight of the sack, feeling too ill and weak to run. Even if I did, I felt certain that he'd catch me within seconds and another beating would follow. The wind was beginning to gust from the north east, with cloud building to cover the stars. It looked like it was going to snow again.

He gave me another push to start me walking, then followed, carrying a lantern. Soon we were climbing high onto the bleak snow-clad moor, leaving the last of the scattered trees far behind. I didn't have any choice but to keep struggling upward. If I didn't move fast enough, I received a push in the back. Once I slipped and fell flat on my face, losing my grip on the sack. For that he punched me in the ribs, so hard that I was terrified of falling again.

I was ordered to pick up the sack, and we trudged upward through the snow until I lost all track of time. But at last, high up on the moor, he pulled me to a halt. Not too far ahead was a hill too smooth and rounded to be natural, its covering of snow gleaming white in the remaining starlight. Then I recognized it for what it was. It was the Round Loaf, the barrow that the Spook had pointed out to me on our way to deal with the boggart at Owshaw Clough. The mound of earth that Morgan had dug the grimoire out of.

Morgan gestured eastward and pushed me ahead of him. About two hundred or so paces away was a small boulder. When we reached it, he quickly measured out ten paces south of it, while I wondered what my chances were of being able to hit him with the spade and run for it. But I still felt weak, and he was bigger and much stronger than I was.

"Dig there!" he commanded, pointing down at the snow.

I obeyed and was soon through the covering of snow and into the dark earth. The ground underneath the snow was frozen hard, and progress was difficult. I wondered if he was making me dig my own grave, but I wasn't much more than a foot down when my spade suddenly struck stone.

"Fools have dug into that barrow time after time," he said, pointing back toward the Round Loaf. "But they never found what I've found. There's a chamber deep underneath, but the entrance is much farther back than you'd ever suspect. The last time I was down there was the night after my mother died, and I've been trying to get my book back ever since! Now clear the stone — we've a lot of work ahead of us!"

I was terrified, because I now suspected that Morgan intended to raise Golgoth this very night. But I did as he ordered, and when I'd finished, he took the spade from me and, using it as a lever, struggled to pry the stone out of its bed and onto its side. It took him a long time, and by the time he'd managed it the snow was starting to fall, the wind sighing over the moor and gusting even harder. Another blizzard was on its way.

He held the lantern over the hole, and by its light I could see steps leading downward into the darkness. "Right, down you go!" he said, raising his fist threateningly.

I flinched and did as I was told, Morgan holding the lantern while I descended carefully, the weight of the sack making it difficult to keep my balance. There were ten steps in all. At their foot, I found myself in a narrow passageway. At the top of the steps, Morgan had put the lantern down and was struggling with the stone again. At first I thought it would be too difficult for him to manage, but it eventually dropped back into place with a dull thud, shutting us in like a gravestone sealing in the dead. He came down the steps carrying the lantern and spade and told me to lead the way, so I obeyed.

He held the lantern high behind me, and it cast my shadow ahead into the tunnel, which was straight and true. The floor, walls, and roof were of earth, and at intervals timbers had been used to shore up the roof. At one point it had actually collapsed, almost obstructing our way, and I had to remove the sack before squeezing through and dragging it along the narrow gap after me. It made me nervous about the condition of the tunnel. If there was a serious roof fall, we'd be buried alive or trapped underground forever. I had a strong sense of the great weight of earth poised above us.

At last the passage opened out into a large oval chamber. It was massive, with the generous dimensions of a good-sized church, and the walls and ceiling were built of stone. But the floor was the most amazing thing of all. At first glance I thought it was tiled, but then I realized that it was an elaborate mosaic depicting all manner of monstrous creatures by the careful positioning of thousands upon thousands of small colored stones. Some were fabled beings that I'd read about in the Spook's Bestiary, others I'd only glimpsed in nightmares: grotesque hybrids such as the minotaur, half bull, half man; gigantic worms with long serpentine bodies and ravenous jaws; and a basilisk, a snake on legs, with a crested head and murderous piercing eyes. Each of these was in itself enough to compete for my attention, but there was something else that immediately arrested my gaze.

For there, at the very center of the floor, constructed from black stones, were three concentric circles and, within them, a five-pointed star. I knew immediately what it was, and my worst fear was confirmed.

This was a pentacle, a device used by a mage from which to cast spells or summon daemons from the dark. But this had been constructed by the first men who came to Anglezarke in order to summon Golgoth, the most powerful of the old gods. And now Morgan was going to use it.

It seemed that Morgan knew exactly what he intended to do, and he soon set me to work, ordering me to clean the floor until it gleamed, particularly the central section of the mosaic that depicted the pentacle.

"There mustn't be even one tiny speck of dirt, or it could all go wrong!" he said.

I didn't bother to ask what he meant, because I'd worked it out already. He intended to follow the deadliest ritual in the grimoire. He was going to summon Golgoth while we stayed protected at its center. Cleanliness was vital, because dirt could be used to cross its defenses.

There were several large tubs at the far side of the

chamber, and one of them contained salt. In the sack I'd carried, among the other items, including the grimoire, were a large flagon of water and some cloths. Using a damp cloth, I had to scour the mosaic with salt, then swill it clean until he was satisfied.

I seemed to be at it for hours. From time to time I glanced about, trying to see if there was anything in the chamber that might prove useful in helping me to overcome Morgan and escape. He must have dropped the spade in the passageway because there was no sign of it in the chamber; neither was there anything else that I could use as a weapon. I did notice a large iron ring set into the wall, close to the floor, and I wondered what it could be for. It looked like something for tethering an animal.

When I'd finished scouring the floor, to my horror, Morgan suddenly seized me, dragged me to the wall, bound my hands tightly behind my back, and fastened the remainder of the rope to the ring. Then he began his preparations in earnest. I was sick to my stomach as I suddenly realized what was going to happen. Morgan would work from within the pentacle, shielded from anything that appeared within the chamber, whereas I would remain tethered to that ring on the wall without any defense whatsoever. Was I going to be some sort of sacrifice? Was that what the ring had originally been made for? Then I remembered what the Spook had said about the farm dog. When Morgan had tried the ritual in his room, it had died of fright. . . .

From the sack he produced five thick black candles and positioned one of these at the very tip of each of the points of the pentacle star. He then opened the grimoire, and as he lit each candle, he read out a short incantation from the book. That done, he sat down cross-legged at the very center of the pentacle and, holding the book open, looked directly toward me.

"Do you know what day it is?" he demanded.

"It's a Tuesday," I answered.

"And the date?"

I didn't speak, and he answered for me.

"It's the twenty-first of December. The winter solstice. The exact middle of the winter before the days gradually start to lengthen again. So it's going to be a long night. The longest night of the whole year. And when it's over, only one of us will leave this chamber," Morgan said. "My intention is to raise Golgoth, the most powerful of the old gods. And I'm going to do it here, in the very place where it was done by the ancients. This barrow is built at a point of great power where leys converge. Five, no less, intersect at the very center of the pentacle where I'm sitting."

"Won't it be dangerous to wake Golgoth?" I asked. "The winter might last for years."

"What if it does?" Morgan asked. "Winter is my time."

"But crops won't grow. People will starve!"

"What of it? The weak always die," said Morgan. "The strong inherit the earth. The summoning ritual will give Golgoth no choice but to obey. And he'll be bound here, within this chamber, until I release him. Bound until he gives me what I want."

"What do you want?" I asked. "What can possibly make it worth hurting so many people?"

"I want power! What else makes life worthwhile? The power that Golgoth will give me. The ability to freeze the blood within a man's veins. To kill with a glance. All men will fear me. And in the depths of a long cold winter, when I kill, who will know that I've taken a life? And who will be able to prove it? John Gregory will be the second to die, but not the last. And you'll die before him." Morgan laughed softly. "You're part of the bait. Part of the lure to draw Golgoth here. I had to make do with a dog last time, but a human being is so much better. Golgoth will take the little spark of life from your body and add it to his own. Your soul, too. Your body and soul will both be snuffed out in an instant."

"Are you really sure that pentacle will protect you?" I asked, trying not to think about what he'd said, attempting to place a bit of doubt in his mind. "Rituals have to be exact. If you leave something out or mispronounce even one word, it might not work. In that case, neither of us will ever leave this chamber. We'll both be destroyed."

"Who told you that? That old fool Gregory!" Morgan mocked. "He would say that. And do you know why? It's because he lacks the nerve to try anything that's truly ambitious. All he's fit for is making gullible apprentices dig useless pits before filling them in again! For years he's tried to keep me from this. He even made me swear to my mother that I'd never attempt the ritual again. Love for her kept me bound to that promise, until her death freed me at last and finally made it possible for me to seize what's mine! Old Gregory is my enemy."

"Why do you hate him so much?" I demanded. "What's he ever done to hurt you? *Everything* he's done has been for the best. He's a better man than you by far and generous to a fault. He helped your mother when your real father left. He gave you an apprenticeship, and even when you turned to the dark, he spared you what you really deserved. A malevolent witch is no worse than you, and she's bound alive in a pit!"

"He could have done that, it's true," Morgan said, his voice quiet and dangerous. "But now it's too late. You're right. I do hate him. I was born with a splinter of darkness in my soul. It grew and grew until I'm now what you see before you today. Old Gregory is a servant of the light, whereas I belong fully to the dark now. Because of that, he's my natural enemy. The dark hates the light. Always it's been so!"

"No!" I cried. "It doesn't have to be like that. You have a choice. You can be what you want. You loved your mother. You're capable of love. You don't have to belong to the dark, don't you see? It's never too late to change!"

"Save your breath and be silent!" Morgan snapped angrily. "We've talked too much. It's time to begin the ritual."

There was silence for a while, and all I could hear was the beating of my own heart. At last Morgan began to chant from the grimoire, his voice rising and falling in a rhythmic, singsong manner that reminded me very much of the way priests sometimes pray before a congregation. Most of it was Latin, but there were also words from at least one language that I didn't recognize. It went on and on; nothing seemed to be happening. I began to hope that the ritual wouldn't work or he'd make a mistake and Golgoth wouldn't appear. But soon I sensed that something was changing.

It was growing slightly colder in the chamber. The change was very slow and gradual, as if something very big was drawing nearer but had a vast distance to cross. It was that special cold that I'd sensed around Morgan previously; the power that he drew from Golgoth.

I began to wonder what my chances of being rescued were. It didn't take me long to work out that they were very slim. Nobody knew about the entrance to the tunnel. Although I'd dug into the earth and uncovered the stone, the weather had been worsening and a blizzard would soon cover it again. The Spook would miss me, but would he be concerned enough to go out looking for me in a blizzard? If he went to Andrew's shop, Alice might just tell him where I'd gone. But even if he went to the chapel, what were the chances that he'd find my staff? It was in the copse outside the fence; by now it would be covered with snow.

I found that I could move my hands a little. Could I work the rope loose enough to get them free? I began to try, bringing my hands together and apart, twisting my wrists and fingers. At least Morgan wouldn't spot what I was up to. He was too busy chanting the words of the ritual, hardly pausing even when he turned a page of the grimoire. Then, as I looked at him, I noticed something else. There seemed to be new shadows in the room, shadows that couldn't just be explained by the position of the five candles. And most of the shadows were moving. Some were like dark smoke, others gray or white mist, writhing on the outside edge of the pentacle as if trying to get in.

What were they? Were they lingerers, accidentally caught up in the power of the ritual and brought to this

NIGHT *Of* THE SOUL STEALER

place against their will? Or maybe the spirits of those who'd been buried in the barrow and nearby? Either seemed likely, for the ritual was one of compulsion. But what if they noticed me? They couldn't reach Morgan: he was protected. But what if they became aware of me?

No sooner had that thought entered my head than I began to hear faint whispers all around me. It was hard to catch the meaning of what was being uttered, but the occasional word was given emphasis. I heard "blood" twice and also the word "bone" and then, quite clearly, my own surname, "Ward."

I began to tremble uncontrollably. I was afraid, but I struggled hard against it. The Spook had told me many times how the dark could feed upon terror: the first step to defeating it was to face and defeat your own fear. So I tried; I really tried, but it was so difficult because I wasn't facing the dark armed with the skills that I'd learned. I wasn't on my feet, gripping a rowan staff or hurling salt and iron. I was a bound prisoner, totally helpless, while Morgan was performing perhaps the most dangerous ritual that a mage had ever attempted. And I was part of that ritual, a spark of life that was being offered to Golgoth, to compel him to this spot. And according to Morgan, the moment he appeared, he would take not only my life but also my soul. I'd always believed that I'd live on after death. Could that be taken away? Could something kill your very soul?

But then the whispers gradually faded away, the shadows dissolved, and it even seemed to become a little warmer. My trembling eased and I breathed a sigh of relief, but Morgan carried on chanting and turning pages. I started to think that at some point he'd made a mistake and had failed; I was quickly proved wrong.

Soon the coldness came again, and with it the smoke wraiths, contorting and writhing at the boundaries of the pentacle. And this time it was worse, and I recognized one of the wraiths. It had the shape of Eveline, with large, grief-filled eyes.

The whispering intensified and was filled with hate so

fierce that I could almost taste it; invisible things whirled about my head, passing so close that I felt drafts against my face, which lifted the hair upright from my scalp. Soon the threat became more substantial. Unseen fingers tugged at my hair or pinched the skin of my face and neck, and cold, stinky breath wafted against my forehead, nose, and mouth.

Again everything became quiet. But it didn't last long. Once more the coldness grew and the wraiths gathered. And so it went on, minute after minute, hour after hour, through that longest night of the year. But the periods of peace and calm were getting shorter, the times of fear longer. There was a rhythm to what was happening. The ritual was building in power. It was like the waves of an incoming tide crashing onto a steep, stony beach. Each wave was more wild and powerful than the preceding one. Each one drove itself farther up the shore. And at each peak of activity, the tumult intensified. The voices screamed into my ears, and orbs of baleful purple light were now circling the pentacle close to the ceiling of the chamber. And then finally, after what seemed like hours of Morgan chanting from the grimoire, he finally achieved what he'd set out to do.

Golgoth obeyed the summons.

CHAPTER XX
GOLGOTH

FOR long, terrifying minutes I could hear Golgoth approaching. The very ground began to shake, and it sounded as if some angry giant were climbing up toward us from the bowels of the earth; a giant with immense claws that was tearing aside solid rock in his eagerness to force a way up into the chamber.

If I'd been Morgan, I'd have been terrified, simply pet-rified with dread, unable to utter another word. Or I'd have halted the ritual because it was madness to con-tinue. But he didn't. Morgan just carried on reading from the grimoire. He'd surrendered to the dark, seeking the power that he craved, whatever the cost.

Despite the threatening rumbles from below, there was no longer even a breath of wind, but the five black candles began to flicker and almost went out. I wondered how important they were to the ritual. Were they a vital part of the pentacle defenses? It seemed very likely: if they did gutter out, he'd be no safer than I was. The candles flickered again, but there was no sign of fear from Morgan at all. He was totally absorbed by the ritual and just went on chanting from the grimoire, oblivious to the danger.

The ground began to shake more violently, and there were more loud disturbing sounds from far below. By now there were so many wraiths gathered about the pentacle that they were merging into a whirling gray-and-white mist and their individual forms were no longer distinct. A vortex of energy was pressing against the invisible barrier that marked the perimeter of the pentacle, and it threatened to break in at any moment.

A few moments longer and it would have done so—I'm sure of it. But something occurred to blast the wraiths out of the chamber and probably back whence they came. As small stones began to shower down from the roof, there was a roar, together with a grinding, crunching cacophony of sound, and I looked to my right, toward the tunnel that had brought us to the chamber. I saw an avalanche of earth as its roof fell, sealing us in, hurling a mayhem of debris and dust outward. To my dismay, the tunnel was now totally blocked. Whatever happened now, I'd be trapped down here forever.

At that moment I would almost have welcomed death: at least then my soul would survive. For I knew that, very soon, Golgoth would arrive and my body and soul would *both* be snuffed out. I would be obliterated. And the fear I felt at that moment made my whole body shake.

But very suddenly there was a change. Without warning, Morgan ceased chanting and lurched to his feet. His eyes were wide with terror, and he dropped the book. He was making for the edge of the pentacle; he took one step toward me and opened his mouth wide. His eyes were filled with fear.

At first I thought he was trying to speak or scream. Now I know better. On reflection, I realize that he was simply trying to breathe.

Crystals of ice had already formed inside his lungs, and that step was the last he ever took. Opening his mouth was the final conscious movement he ever made. He froze in front of me. Literally froze, dusted from head to foot with a white frost. Then he toppled forward, and the moment that his forehead, arms, and shoulders struck the ground, he shattered like an ice stalactite. It was like brittle glass shivering into splinters. Morgan was broken, pulverized, but no blood flowed because he was frozen to the very core of his being. And now he was dead. Dead and gone.

I suppose that he'd made a costly mistake with the ritual and Golgoth had materialized within the pentacle to slay the necromancer on the spot. For now, within the three concentric circles, there was a brooding presence. Despite the five flickering candles I couldn't see it, but I knew it was there, and I could feel cold, hostile eyes staring out of the pentacle straight toward me.

I sensed Golgoth's desperation to escape. Once beyond the pentacle, he would be free to work his will upon the County; free to plunge it into decades of freezing winter. The candle flames danced again as if they were being wafted with invisible breath, but I could do nothing. I was terrified. What could I do to save the County? Nothing at all: I was tethered to the iron ring awaiting my own fate.

At that moment Golgoth spoke to me from the pentacle. *"A fool lies dead before me. Are you a fool also?"*

His voice filled the chamber, echoing back from its every corner. It was like a harsh wind, blasting the grim heights of Anglezarke with snow.

I didn't answer, and Golgoth's voice rasped again, this time lower but harsher, like a rough file against a metal bucket.

"Have you a tongue, mortal? Speak, or shall I freeze and shatter it as I did the fool?"

"I'm not a fool," I answered, my teeth beginning to chatter with fear and cold.

"It pleases me to hear that. Because if you are indeed blessed with wisdom, then before this night is done, I could raise you up higher than the highest in this land."

"I'm happy just as I am," I replied.

"Without my help you will perish here. Is death what you seek? Will that make you happy?"

I didn't answer.

"All you have to do is dislodge a candle from the circle. Just one candle. Do that and I will be free and you will live."

Bound to the ring, I was several feet short of the nearest candle, so I didn't know how he expected me to reach it. But even if it had been possible, I couldn't have done it. I couldn't save my own life at the expense of the thousands of people who would suffer in the County.

"No!" I said. "I won't do it—"

"Although trapped within the bounds of this circle, I can still reach you. Let me show you . . ."

Cold began to radiate out from the pentacle, the mosaic whitening with frost. A pattern of ice crystals was forming until I could feel the chill rising into my flesh from the floor, starting to numb me to the bone. I remembered Meg's warning when I left for home: *". . . wrap up warm against the cold. Frostbite can make your fingers fall off."*

The most severe cold was at my back, close to my hands where they were bound to the ring, and as the cold bit into my flesh, I imagined my frozen fingers with the blood no longer circulating, becoming blackened and brittle, ready to break off like dead twigs from a dying branch. I felt my mouth opening to scream, the cold air rasping within my throat. I thought of Mam. Now I would never see her again. But suddenly I fell away onto my side, away from the iron ring. I glanced back and saw that it was in pieces at the foot of the wall. Golgoth had frozen and fragmented it in order to free me. He'd done it so that I could do his bidding. He spoke to me again from the pentacle, but this time his voice seemed fainter.

"Dislodge the candle. Do it now, or I'll take more than your life. I'll snuff out your soul, too. . . ."

Those words sent a deeper chill into me than the cold that had shattered the iron ring. Morgan had been right. My very soul was at risk. But to save it, all I had to do was obey. My hands were still tied behind my back and had no feeling in them, but I could have stood, moved toward the nearest candle, and kicked it over. But I thought of those who would suffer because of what I'd done. The severe winter cold itself would kill the old and the young first. Babies would die in their cradles. But the threat would become even greater. Crops wouldn't grow, and there'd be no harvest next year. And for how many years after that? There'd be nothing to feed the livestock. Famine would result. Thousands would perish. And it would all be my fault.

Kicking over the candle would save my own life. It

would save my soul, too. But my first duty was always to the County. I might never see Mam again, but if I freed Golgoth, how could I ever look her in the eye? She would be ashamed of me, and I couldn't stand that. Whatever it cost, I had to do what was right. Better oblivion. Better to be nothing than live to experience that!

"I won't do it," I told Golgoth. "I'd rather die here than set you free."

"Die, then, fool!" Golgoth said, and immediately the cold began to intensify. So I closed my eyes and waited for the end as I felt my body becoming numb. Strangely, I was no longer afraid. I was filled with resignation. I'd accepted what was going to happen.

The cold must have made me pass out, because the next thing I remember is opening my eyes.

It was very still and quiet in the chamber, and the air was much warmer. To my relief, Golgoth had gone. I could no longer sense his presence. But why hadn't he carried out his threat?

The pentacle was intact, and all five candles were still burning. Within it I could see a figure lying facedown. By his cloak I recognized Morgan. I looked away quickly. The white had been replaced by red. The pieces of Morgan were beginning to thaw.

To my astonishment, I was still alive. But for how long? I was trapped. Soon the candles would burn low and go out, and I'd be plunged into darkness forever.

I wanted to live, and suddenly I began to struggle desperately against the rope. I was no longer tied to the iron ring, but my hands were still bound behind my back. I had pins and needles in them, but the circulation was returning. If I could only get them free, I could use the candles one at a time. That would give me hours of candlelight to work by. The passageway was blocked, but I could dig with my bare hands. It was worth a try. The earth would be soft. And the whole tunnel might not be blocked. At some point I might even find the spade!

For a few moments I was filled with hope. But the

rope wouldn't yield, and my attempts to struggle free seemed to be making it tighter. I remembered all those months ago, in spring, when I'd first become the Spook's apprentice. Bony Lizzie had bound me in a pit, intending to kill me and take my bones for her dark magic. I'd struggled then but hadn't been able to escape. It was Alice who had saved me, using a knife to cut me free. How I wished I could call out to Alice now! But I couldn't. I was alone, and nobody even knew where I was.

After a while I stopped my frantic struggle to be free. I lay back and closed my eyes and tried to gather my strength for one final effort. It was then, as I lay perfectly still, my breathing almost back to normal, that I suddenly thought of the pentacle candles. I could use the flame from one of them to burn through the rope that bound me! Why hadn't I thought of that before? I sat up quickly. I now had a real chance of getting myself free. But it was at that moment that I heard a noise from the direction of the blocked tunnel.

What could it be? Had the Spook found out after all

and come to rescue me? But it didn't sound like a spade. It was more like a scratching noise, as if something were scrabbling in the fallen soil. Could it be a rat? The noise was getting louder. Could it be more than one? A pack of rats that lived deep under the barrow? It was said that rats would eat anything. There were even tales of rats snatching newborn babies from their cradles. What if they'd smelled human flesh? Would they want to eat the pieces of Morgan's dead body? What next? Would they turn on me? Attack me while I was still alive?

The noise became louder. Something was burrowing along the blocked tunnel toward the chamber. Something was clawing its way through the earth. What could it be? I watched, fascinated but terrified, as a small hole appeared about halfway between the ceiling and the floor of the chamber and soil crumbled from it, falling onto the edge of the mosaic floor. I felt a draft that caused the candles to flicker. Two hands emerged, but they weren't human. I saw elongated fingers and, instead of fingernails, ten curved talons that had burrowed through the soil into the chamber. So even before the head appeared, I knew exactly who it was.

Somehow the feral lamia had escaped from the Spook's cellar and had sniffed me out. Marcia Skelton had come for my blood.

CHAPTER XXI
THE TRAP

THE feral lamia eased her body out of the hole and scuttled down onto the mosaic floor. I heard her sniff twice, but she wasn't looking at me. Scurrying on all fours with her head down and her long, greasy black hair trailing on the floor, she moved toward the edge of the pentacle, her claws making a sharp scratching noise on the marble. She halted, and I heard her sniff again loudly as she looked at what was left of Morgan.

I kept very still, hardly able to believe that she hadn't attacked me already. Morgan had only just died, but I'd have thought she'd prefer fresh blood from a living person. And then I heard another noise from the tunnel. Something else was approaching. . . .

Once more a pair of hands appeared, but these had human fingers with fingernails rather than sharp claws. As the head came into view, one glance told me who it was. I saw the high cheekbones, the pretty bright eyes, and the silver-gray hair. It was Meg.

She clambered out, dusted herself off, and walked straight toward me. She must have left her pointy shoes outside, but the pad of her bare feet as she approached was terrifying. No wonder the feral lamia had kept her distance. Meg wanted me all to herself, and after all that had happened, I could expect no mercy.

She knelt down within touching distance, and her lips widened in a grim smile. "You're just a heartbeat away from death," Meg said, leaning closer and opening her mouth wide until I could see her white teeth, eager to bite me. I felt her breath on my face and neck and began to tremble. But then she bent low and, to my astonishment, bit right through the rope that was binding my hands.

"Few humans have been *this* close to a lamia witch and lived," she said, before rising to her feet. "Count yourself lucky!"

I just sat there, staring up at her openmouthed. I felt too weak to move.

"Get up, boy!" she commanded. "We haven't got all night. John Gregory's waiting for you. He'll want to know what's been going on down here."

I clambered to my feet unsteadily and stood there for a few moments, feeling weak and nauseous, fearing that I was about to fall. Why should she help me? What had happened between the Spook and Meg? He'd been taking food down to her. They'd been having long talks. Was she doing it because the Spook had asked her to? Were they friends again?

"Go and get the grimoire," Meg said, pointing to the pentacle. "I can't enter that circle and neither can Marcia."

I took a step toward the pentacle but stopped when I saw the book. It was lying in a pool of blood. I couldn't bear to touch it, and it would be ruined anyway. Then I caught a glimpse of Morgan's remains, and my stomach heaved. I bowed my head, trying to blot the image out of my mind. I didn't want to see him again in a nightmare.

"Do as I say, get the grimoire!" Meg commanded, raising her voice slightly. "John Gregory won't thank you for leaving it here for someone else to find one day."

I did as I was told and stepped into the pentacle. I reached down and picked up the book. It was wet and sticky with blood. I could smell it, and my stomach twisted and heaved again. I fought hard not to vomit and left the pentacle, picking up the nearest of the candles. I didn't like the idea of climbing back through a dark tunnel in the company of two lamia witches.

Taking the candle had probably broken the power of the pentacle, and I thought that Marcia would have entered it to feed. But after briefly sniffing toward the body, she turned away. Meg led the way with Marcia somewhere behind me. I just hoped she wasn't too close on my heels.

We emerged into the pale predawn light. The blizzard had blown itself out, but it was still snowing lightly. The Spook was waiting just outside the entrance, and he reached down, offering me his hand. I let the black candle fall into the snow and gripped his left hand with mine; he pulled me up onto my feet. Immediately afterward the feral lamia followed me out, scrambling up onto the snow.

I opened my mouth to speak, but my master put a finger against his lips to signal silence. "All in good time. You can tell me later," he said. "Is Morgan dead?"

I nodded and bowed my head.

"Well, this can be his tomb," said the Spook.

With those words, he moved across and gripped the edge of the stone, maneuvering it into position. He balanced it on the edge of the hole and, when he was satisfied, let it drop back into place. That done, he went down onto his knees and, using his bare hands, began to cover the stone with loose earth and snow. At last, satisfied, he came to his feet.

"Give me the book, lad," the Spook commanded.

I held it out to him, glad to be rid of it. The Spook lifted it up and glanced at the cover. When he transferred it to his other hand, bloodstains remained on his fingers. With a sad, weary shake of his head, he led the way down off the heights of the moor and back toward his winter house. And each time I glanced back over my shoulder, I could see that the two lamia witches were following close behind.

Once back, the Spook led me into the kitchen, fed the fire with coal, and as the flames took a hold, started to cook breakfast. At one point I offered to help, but he waved me back into my chair.

"Gather your strength, lad," he told me. "You've been through a lot."

Once I could smell the eggs cooking and the bread toasting, I felt a lot better. Meg and her sister had gone down into the cellar, but I didn't like to mention them. It was best to let the Spook tell me what had happened in his own time. Soon we were both at the table tucking into big plates of eggs and toast. At last, feeling stronger, I mopped my plate and sat back in my chair.

"Well, lad, do you feel well enough to talk? Or shall we leave it until later?"

"I'd like to get it over with," I replied. I knew that once I'd told him all that had happened, I'd feel a lot better. It would be the first step in putting it all behind me.

"Then start right at the beginning and leave nothing out!" said the Spook.

So I did exactly as he instructed, starting with my talk with Alice on the hillside, when she'd told me where to find Morgan, and finishing with the climax of the ritual — the arrival of Golgoth and how he'd threatened me after Morgan had died.

"So Morgan must have made a mistake," I said.

"Golgoth arrived inside the pentacle—"

"Nay, lad," said the Spook, shaking his head sadly, "He must have recited the ritual word-for-word. You see, I'm to blame. I have Morgan's blood on my hands."

"I don't understand. What do you mean?" I asked.

"I should have sorted him out then, after he tried to summon Golgoth all those years ago," the Spook said. "Morgan was very dangerous and beyond help even then. I knew that and should have put him in a pit, but his mother, Emily, begged and pleaded with me not to do it. He wanted power and was bitter and twisted with anger, but she believed that was because life had treated him unfairly and he lacked a father to stand by him. I felt a bit sorry for the lad and cared for his mother, so I let my heart rule my head. But deep down, I knew that it wasn't a father he lacked. Mr. Hurst and I had both tried to be that to him. No, what he really lacked was the discipline to be a spook, the courage and perseverance to dedicate his life to a craft that carries little in the way of worldly reward. But instead of punishing him for trying to summon Golgoth, I simply terminated his apprenticeship and made him swear to me and his mother that he wouldn't pursue Golgoth or the grimoire.

"Cast out with no trade, Morgan sought power and wealth through necromancy and turned to the dark. I knew that each winter the temptation of Golgoth's power would grow, eventually becoming too much for him. So I set a trap for him, but only if he actually tried to summon the Lord of Winter would that trap be sprung—"

"Trap? What trap? I don't understand."

"He was always lazy when it came to his studies," said the Spook, scratching thoughtfully at his beard. "Language was his weak point, and he never learned his Latin vocabulary thoroughly. He was even worse at some of the other languages. He started to learn the Old Tongue in his third year. It was the language spoken by the first men who came to the County, the ones who built the Round Loaf and worshipped Golgoth. The ones who wrote the grimoire. He didn't get very far. He knew how to pronounce it, how to read the Old Tongue aloud, but there were serious holes in his knowledge.

"You see, lad, I couldn't take any chances. Our first duty is always to the County. So years ago I had the grimoire copied. The original text was destroyed and the new version bound within the original cover. Several words were changed in the book to make the rituals useless. But only one change was made to the Golgoth ritual. The word '*wioutan*,' which means 'without' or 'outside,' was replaced by '*wioinnan*,' which means 'within'—"

"So that's why Golgoth appeared with him inside the pentacle," I said, astonished at the Spook's trap. He'd kept that secret for years.

"I didn't trust Morgan, so I set a snare for him just in case. I went to a lot of trouble having the grimoire copied and changed, but as I said, our duty is to protect the County. Emily knew what I'd done, but she had a lot more faith in him than I did. She thought he'd changed his ways and would never try to raise Golgoth again. He swore that to her, and I was there to witness that oath. I never made any bones about where the grimoire was. That desk was always on view and Morgan knew where to come, and eventually I was proved right. He would have come for it years ago, but the oath to his mother held him fast. As soon as I heard that she'd died, I feared the worst and realized why Morgan had contacted me back in Chipenden. . . ."

There was a long silence, and the Spook scratched at his beard again, very deep in thought.

"What happened at the end?" I asked. "Why didn't Golgoth kill me? Why did he just go away?"

"After being summoned, his time within the pentacle was limited. Every moment he remained there, he'd have been growing weaker. At last he had to go. He had no choice. Of course, had you let him out, things would have been different. He'd have been free to roam the County, which would have been gripped by an endless winter. So you did well, lad. You did your duty, and nobody can ask more than that."

"How did you find me?" I asked.

"For that, your first thanks must be to the girl. When you didn't come back as I expected, I went down to speak to Andrew and find out what time you'd left the shop. It was your friend Alice who told me where you'd gone. She wanted to come and help search for you, but I'd have none of it. I work better alone—I don't need a girl trailing at my heels. We almost had to tie her to the chair to stop her from following me. When I arrived, a blizzard was blowing in from the northeast and the chapel was deserted. I poked around the graveyard for a bit, but I didn't stay long. There was only one person I could turn to then. The only one who could find you in those conditions.

"Meg soon sniffed you out. She found your staff in the copse up on the hill and traced you to the barrow. Didn't take her long to find the entrance, but when I pulled back the stone, the tunnel was blocked. So it was Marcia who dug you out. That's three who deserve your thanks."

"Three witches," I pointed out.

The Spook ignored me. "Anyway, Alice will stay back at Andrew's place, as you'd expect. As for Meg and her sister, from now on they'll be down the cellar steps behind the gate — but it won't be locked."

"So you and Meg are friends again?"

"No, things aren't the way they were when we first met. I'd like to put the clock back, but it just isn't possible. You see, lad, we've come to an agreement. Things can't carry on as they are, but I'll tell you more about it when you've rested."

"What about Dad?" I asked. "Will he be all right now?"

"He was a good man, and now that Morgan's dead and his power broken, your dad should have nothing to fear. Nothing at all. Nobody knows exactly what happens after we die," the Spook said with a sigh. "If we did know, there wouldn't be so many different religions all saying different things and all thinking they're right. To my mind, it doesn't matter which one of them you follow.

Or even if you walk alone and take your own path through life. As long as you live your life right and respect others' beliefs as your dad taught you, then you won't go far wrong. He'll find his way through to the light, all right. There's no need to worry about that. And that's enough talking for now. You've had a long, difficult night, so get yourself off to bed for a few hours."

But it was more than just a few hours that I stayed in bed. I developed a raging fever, and the doctor came up from Adlington three times before he was finally satisfied that I was on the mend. In fact, it was almost a week before I was fit to come downstairs again, with most of the daylight hours spent wrapped in a blanket before the study fire.

The Spook didn't work me too hard at my lessons, either, and it was another full week after that before I was finally fit enough to walk down into Adlington and see Alice. She was minding the shop alone. As no customers called, we had time for a long chat. We talked in the shop, leaning on the bare wooden counter.

While I'd been ill, the Spook had already visited, and she knew most of what had happened. So all I had to do was fill in the details and apologize once more for keeping things from her.

"Anyway, Alice, thanks for telling the Spook I'd gone to the chapel. Otherwise I'd never have been found," I said, reaching the end of my tale at last.

"I still wish you'd trusted me more, Tom. You should have told me a lot earlier what Morgan was doing to your dad."

"I'm sorry," I told her. "I won't hold anything back in the future. . . ."

"Never going to get in Old Gregory's good books, though, am I? He don't trust me one little bit!"

"He thinks a lot better of you than he used to," I said. "Give it time, that's all."

"But in spring, when you go back to Chipenden, I'll have to stay here. Wish I could come with you. . . ."

"I thought you liked working in Andrew's shop."

"Could be worse," Alice said, "but Chipenden's lots better. I like being in that big house with its garden. And I'll miss you, Tom."

"I'll miss you, too, Alice. But at least you're not in Pendle. Anyway, next winter we'll be back, and I'll try and visit you more often."

"Be nice, that would," Alice said.

After a while she cheered up, and finally, just as I was about to go, she asked me to do something.

"The morning you set off for Chipenden, will you ask Old Gregory if he'll take me as well?"

"I'll ask. But I don't think it'll do any good, Alice."

"But you'll ask him, won't you? Ain't going to bite your head off for asking, is he?"

"All right. I'll ask him."

"Promise?"

"I promise," I said with a smile. Making promises to Alice had got me into trouble in the past, but this one couldn't do much harm. At the worst, the Spook could only refuse.

CHAPTER XXII
FOR THE BEST

ALTHOUGH it had been a cold winter, within three weeks of Morgan's death the weather turned much warmer and a thaw set in. That made it possible for Shanks to make his first delivery for ages. As usual, I helped him to unload, but when he left, the Spook followed him for quite a way down the clough

· 455 ·

and they had a long conversation together.

A few days later, just after breakfast, Shanks delivered a coffin to our door, the little pony almost staggering under its weight. After it was untied, we lifted it down carefully. It wasn't quite as heavy as it looked, but it was a bit on the large side, and I'd never seen a coffin so well made. It had two brass carrying handles at each side and was made out of dark polished wood. We didn't carry it into the house but just left it close to the back door.

"What's this for?" I asked the Spook as Shanks disappeared into the distance.

"That's for me to know and you to find out," he said, tapping the side of his nose. "Have a think and get back to me when you've worked it out."

It was lunchtime before my suspicions were confirmed.

"I'll be away for a few days, lad. Think you can manage on your own?"

My mouth was full, so I nodded and carried on tucking into my lamb stew.

"Aren't you going to ask where I'm going?"

"Spook's business?" I suggested.

"Nay, lad. This is family business. Meg and her sister are going home. They'll be sailing from Sunderland Point, and I'm going to see them safely on their way."

Sunderland Point was south of Heysham and the largest port in the County. Boats from all over the world sailed up the River Lune to anchor there. I knew then that I'd guessed right about the coffin.

"So Marcia will be in the box," I said.

"Got it first time, lad," said the Spook with a smile. "An especially large dose of herb tea should keep her quiet. She could hardly board in the usual way. Might upset some of the passengers. As far as the harbormaster is concerned, Meg's sister died and she's taking her home for burial. Anyway, as I said, I'll be going with them as far as the port just to see them safely embarked. We'll be traveling by night, of course. No doubt we'll book into an inn and Meg will spend the daylight hours behind closed curtains. I'll be sad to see her go, but it's for the best."

"I once overheard you talking to Meg about a garden

that you shared together. Was it your garden at Chipenden?" I asked.

"Aye, it was, lad. The western garden, as you might expect. We spent many a happy hour sitting on that very same bench where I often give you lessons now."

"So what happened?" I asked. "Why did you bring Meg to Anglezarke and put her in the cellar? Why did she have to be dosed with herb tea?"

"What went on between Meg and me is our private business!" the Spook snapped, giving me a long, searching look. For a moment he looked really angry, and I realized that my curiosity had made me go too far. But then he sighed and shook his head wearily.

"As you know, Meg is still a good-looking woman, but when she was young she was too pretty by far and turned lots of men's heads. I was jealous to a fault, and we quarreled too many times to count. But that wasn't all. She was willful, too, and made lots of enemies in the County. Those who crossed her learned to fear her. And those who live in fear for too long become dangerous.

She was finally accused of witchcraft, and reports were made to the high sheriff at Caster. It was a very serious business, and they sent a constable to arrest her."

"She'd have been safe in your house at Chipenden, wouldn't she? The boggart would have stopped the constable from getting anywhere near her."

"It would that, lad. It would have stopped him dead! But he was just doing his job, and although I loved Meg, I didn't want the loss of that young constable's life on my conscience. So I had to make sure that Meg disappeared. I went down into the village and met him there and, with the help of the blacksmith as witness, managed to convince him that she'd fled the County.

"As a result, I brought her here, and she spent her summers locked in the room on the cellar steps and her winters confined to the house. It was either that, or she'd swing at the end of a rope—as you know, they hang witches at Caster. At one point, years later, she got out and terrified some of the locals. To keep them quiet, I had to promise that I'd bind her in a pit in the cellar.

That was why Shanks was so upset when he saw her that morning. Anyway, now, at long last, she's going home. It was something I should have done years ago, but I just couldn't let her go."

"So she wants to go home?"

"I think she knows it's for the best. Besides, Meg no longer feels about me the way I still feel about her," he said, looking older and sadder than I'd ever seen him before. "I'm going to miss her, lad. Miss her sorely. Life won't be the same without her. She was the only thing that made the winters here bearable. . . ."

At sunset I watched the Spook seal Meg's sister, Marcia, into her coffin. Then, when the last of the brass screws had been tightened, I helped him carry it down the clough. It was heavy and we staggered a bit under the weight, struggling to keep our feet on the soft, muddy ground, while Meg walked behind, carrying her own bags. As we proceeded in solemn silence down into the gloom of the valley, it reminded me of a real funeral.

The Spook had arranged for a coach to be waiting for us on the road. The four horses became nervous as we approached, their nostrils dilating, breath steaming in the moonlight, and the driver struggled to control them. Once they'd been steadied, he climbed down, looking very nervous himself, came across to the Spook and touched his own cap in deference. His jowls were wobbling, and he looked ready to jump out of his skin.

"There's nothing to fear, and as I promised, I'll pay you well. Now help me lift this up," the Spook said to him, tapping Marcia's coffin. They heaved it up onto the rack at the rear of the coach, and the Spook watched closely as the driver secured it with rope.

While they were busy, Meg approached and smiled at me grimly, showing her teeth.

"You're a dangerous boy, Tom Ward, a very dangerous boy," she said, leaning closer. "Take care not to make too many enemies."

I wasn't sure what to say to that.

"Will you do one thing for me, boy?" she whispered in my ear.

I nodded uneasily.

"He's not as cold as he'd have everyone believe," she said, gesturing to my master. "Look after him for me." So I smiled and nodded.

When the Spook joined us, she gave him a warm, friendly smile that made me think that deep down she still cared something for him. And then she took hold of his hand and gave it a squeeze. He opened his mouth as if to say something, but no words came out. Tears were glistening in his eyes, and he looked choked with emotion.

Embarrassed, I turned my back on them and walked away a few paces. They whispered to each other for a few moments and then walked to the coach together. While the driver held open the door and gave her a little bow, the Spook helped Meg up. Then he walked back over to me.

"Right, lad, we'll be on our way. You get yourself back to the house," said the Spook.

"Would it help if I came with you?" I asked.

"Nay, lad, thanks all the same. There are some things that I need to do on my own. One day, when you're older, I think you'll understand. But I hope you'll never have to go through anything like this."

But I understood already: I remembered seeing him with Meg in the kitchen, tears on his cheeks. I knew how he felt. Also, I could imagine myself being in the Spook's position and having to say good-bye to Alice for the last time. Was this how Alice and I would end up?

A few moments later the Spook got in, and no sooner had he seated himself down next to Meg than the driver flicked his whip above the backs of the four horses. The coach trundled away and began to gather speed. They were on their way north, their destination Sunderland Point, while I made my way slowly back up the clough toward the house.

Once inside, I heated some pea soup for my supper and settled down beside the fire. There was no wind outside, and I could hear every squeak and groan in the old house. The floorboards settled, a stair creaked, a mouse pattered behind the wall. And I even fancied that below in the cellar, far beyond the metal gate, I could hear the whisperings of the dead and the nearly dead, down in their pits.

It was then that I realized just how far I'd come. There I was, alone in a big house with a cellar full of trapped boggarts and witches, and I wasn't scared one little bit. I was the Spook's apprentice, and in the spring I'd have completed my first year of training. Four more years, and I'd be a spook myself!

CHAPTER XXIII
BACK TO CHIPENDEN

LATE one morning at the very end of April, as I went to get water from the stream, the Spook followed me outside. The sun had just risen over the edge of the clough, and he smiled up toward its faint warmth. On the cliff behind the house, the ice stalactites were melting fast, water dripping onto the flags.

"This is the first day of spring, lad," he said, "so we'll go to Chipenden!"

I'd been waiting to hear those words for weeks. Since returning without Meg, the Spook had been very quiet, retreating into himself, and the house had seemed more gloomy and depressing than ever. I was desperate to get away.

So for the next hour I rushed around doing all the necessary jobs: cleaning out the grates and washing all the pots, plates, and cups to make life easier on our return next winter. At last the Spook locked the back door behind us and was striding away down the clough, with me following happily at his heels, carrying two bags, as usual, as well as my rowan staff.

I had remembered my promise to Alice—to ask if she could come with us to Chipenden—but was just waiting for the right moment, when I realized that, rather than taking the most direct route to the north, we were heading straight toward Adlington. Even though he'd visited him the previous day, I supposed that the Spook wanted to say another farewell to his brother. I was still dithering about mentioning Alice when we came in sight of the shop.

To my surprise, both Andrew and Alice came out to meet us on the cobbled street. Alice was carrying a small bundle of belongings and appeared ready for a journey. She was smiling and looked excited.

"Have a good, prosperous summer, Andrew," the Spook called out cheerfully. "See you in November!"

"Same to you, brother!" Andrew replied with a wave.

Next, to my utter astonishment, the Spook turned and led the way, and when I turned to follow, Alice fell into step beside me, grinning from ear to ear.

"Oh, I forgot to tell you, lad," called the Spook over his shoulder, "Alice will be coming to stay with us in Chipenden on the same terms as previously. I arranged it all yesterday with Andrew. She needs to be where I can keep a watchful eye on her!"

"Big surprise, is it, Tom? Glad to see me, are you?" Alice asked.

"Of course I'm glad to see you, and I'm really pleased that you're coming back to Chipenden with us. It's the last thing I expected. Mr. Gregory didn't say a word about it."

"Oh! Didn't he?" Alice laughed. "Well, now you know what it feels like when people keep secrets and don't tell you things you ought to know! Serves you right!"

I laughed as well. I didn't mind Alice's gibe. I deserved it. I should have told her all about my intention to steal the grimoire. If I had, she might have drummed some sense into my head. But it was all over now, and we walked along happily together on our way back to Chipenden at last.

The following day there was another surprise. The route back to Chipenden led us to within about four miles of our farm. I was going to ask if I could call in, but the Spook beat me to it.

"I reckon you should pay a visit home, lad. You might find that mother of yours is back; if so, she'll be expecting to see you. I'll press straight ahead, because I need to visit a surgeon on the way."

"A surgeon? Are you ill?" I asked, starting to worry for him.

"Nay, lad. The man in question does a bit of dentistry as a sideline. He's got a big supply of dead men's teeth, and there's bound to be something that'll fit," he said, giving me a wide smile so that I had a good view of the gap left where the boggart had knocked out his front tooth.

"Where does he get them from?" I asked, appalled. "From grave robbers?"

"Most of them come from old battlefields," the Spook said, with a shake of his head. "He'll make me up a denture, and I'll soon be as good as new. He does a nice line in bone buttons, too. Meg made all her own dresses and was one of his best customers," the Spook said sadly.

I was glad to hear that. At least her buttons hadn't come from her past victims, as I'd first suspected.

"Anyway, off you go now," said the Spook, "and take the girl with you for a bit of company on the way back."

I was happy to obey. No doubt the Spook didn't want Alice following at his heels. But I would have the usual problem. Jack wouldn't want her to take one step across the farm boundary, and as Brewer's Farm belonged to him now, it wasn't worth arguing.

An hour or so later, Alice and I were in sight of the farm when I noticed something very unusual. To the north, just beyond the farm boundary, was Hangman's Hill, where a plume of dark smoke was now rising from the trees at its summit. Someone had lit a fire there. Who would do that? Nobody ever went there because it was haunted by the ghasts of men who'd been hanged during the civil war that had swept through the County generations earlier. Even the farm dogs kept well clear.

Instinctively I knew it was Mam. Why she should be up there I couldn't guess, but who else would dare? So we skirted the farm to the east and, once beyond its northern boundary, headed up the hill through the trees. Of the ghasts there was no sign, and Hangman's Hill was silent and still, the bare branches gleaming in the late afternoon sunlight. The leaf buds were swollen, but it would still be a week or so until they unfolded. Spring had come very late this year.

Immediately we came to its summit, I was proved right. Mam was sitting in front of a fire gazing into the flames. She was sheltering under a refuge of branches, twigs, and dead leaves that shielded her from the sunlight. Her hair was matted with dirt, and it looked as if she hadn't washed for a long time. She'd lost weight, too, and her face was gaunt, her expression sad and weary, perhaps of life itself.

"Mam! Mam!" I said, sitting down beside her on the damp earth. "Are you all right?"

She didn't answer right away, and there was a faraway look in her eyes. At first I thought she hadn't heard me. But then, still staring into the fire, she put her left hand on my shoulder.

"I'm glad you're back, Tom," she said at last. "I've been waiting here for days. . . ."

"Where've you been, Mam?"

She didn't answer, but after a long pause she looked up and met my eyes. "I'll be on my way soon, but we need to talk before I leave."

"No, Mam, you're in no state to go anywhere. Why don't you go down to the farm and get some food inside you? You need a good night's sleep, too. Does Jack know you're here?"

"He knows, son. Jack comes up to see me every day and begs me to do what you've just asked. But it's too painful to go down there now that your dad's not at home. It's hit me hard, Tom, and my heart is broken. But now that you've come at last, I'll force myself to go back down there one last time before I leave the County forever."

"Don't go, Mam! Please don't leave us!" I begged.

Mam didn't reply but just stared into the flames.

"Think of your first grandson, Mam!" I continued desperately. "Don't you want to see him born? Don't you want to see little Mary grow up either? And what about me? I need you! Don't you want me to complete

474

my time and become a spook? You've saved me in the past, and I might need your help again just to get that far. . . ."

Still Mam didn't reply, and Alice suddenly seated herself so that she was facing her directly across the fire. "Not sure, are you?" she said to Mam, her eyes fierce in the firelight. "You don't really know what to do."

Mam looked up, her own eyes glistening with tears. "How old are you, girl? Thirteen, is it?" she asked. "You're just a child. So what can you know about my business?"

"May only be thirteen," Alice retorted defiantly, "but I know things. More things than some who've lived a whole lifetime. Some were taught me. Others I just know. Maybe I was born knowing them. Ain't no idea why. Just is, that's all. And I know about you. Some things anyway. And I know that you're torn between going and staying. Ain't that so? It's true, ain't it?"

Mam bowed her head and then, to my astonishment, nodded.

"The dark is growing in power, that's plain enough, and it's something I've told Tom before," Mam said, turning to face me again, her eyes glittering more fiercely than those of any witch I'd faced. "You see, it's the whole world that's falling under the power of the dark, not just the County. I need to fight it in my own land. If I go back now, I might just be able to do something about it before it's too late! And there are other things there that I've left unresolved."

"What things, Mam?"

"You'll know soon enough. Don't ask me now."

"But you'd be alone, Mam. What can you do alone?"

"No, Tom, I wouldn't be alone. There are others who'd help me—precious few, I must confess."

"Stay here, Mam. Stay here and let it come to us," I begged. "Let's face it together in my land, not yours."

Mam smiled sadly. "This is your land, is it?"

"It is, Mam. This is the County where I was born. The land I was born to defend against the dark. That's what you told me. You said I'd be the Spook's last apprentice, and then it would be up to me to keep everything safe."

"That's true enough, and I won't deny it," Mam said wearily, staring into the flames.

"Then stay and let's face it together. The Spook's training me. Why don't you train me, too? There are things you can do that even he can't. The way you once silenced the ghosts here on Hangman's Hill. He said that nothing could be done about ghosts, that they just faded away in their own time. But you did it. They were silent for months afterward! And then I've inherited other things, too. Intimations of death, that's what you called it. I knew when the Spook was close to death recently. And when I think back, I knew when he was on the mend, too. I'll know next time when somebody turns the corner on the way back to health. Don't go, please. Stay and teach me."

"No, Tom," said Mam, coming to her feet. "I'm sorry, but my mind's made up. I'll stay here one more night, but I'll be on my way tomorrow."

I knew I'd argued enough and it was just selfish to continue. I'd promised my dad that I'd let her go when the time came, and the time was now. Alice was right: Mam was in two minds, but I knew it wasn't up to me to make the decision for her.

Mam turned to face Alice. "You've traveled a long way, girl. Farther than I ever dared hope. But there are bigger tests yet to come. For what's ahead you'll both need all of your combined strengths. John Gregory's star is starting to fade. You two are the future and the hope of the County. He needs you both by his side."

Mam was looking down at me as she finished speaking. I stared into the fire for a moment and shivered. "The fire's nearly out, Mam," I said, giving her a smile.

"You're right," said Mam. "Let's go down to the farm. All three of us."

"Jack won't want to see Alice," I reminded her.

"Well, he'll just have to put up with it," Mam said, in a tone that told me she'd stand no messing from Jack.

And the truth was, in his happiness to see Mam back, Jack hardly seemed to notice Alice at all.

○ ○ ○

After having a bath and changing her clothes, despite Ellie's pleas that she should rest, Mam insisted on making the hot-pot supper. I stayed with her in the kitchen while she cooked and told her most of what had been happening up on Anglezarke. What I didn't tell her was how Morgan had tortured Dad's spirit. Knowing Mam, I wouldn't have been surprised to find out that she knew already. But even if that had been the case, it would still have been too painful for her. So I just didn't mention it. She'd been hurt enough.

When I'd finished, she didn't say much except to draw me close and tell me I'd made her proud. It felt good to be home. Little Mary was upstairs safely asleep, the beeswax candle was in the brass candlestick at the center of the table, a warm fire was blazing in the grate, and Mam's food was on the table.

But beneath the surface, things had changed and were continuing to do so. We all knew that.

Mam sat at the head of the table, in the place that had once been Dad's, and almost looked like her old self.

Alice and I sat opposite Jack and Ellie. Of course, by now Jack had been able to collect his thoughts, and you could tell that he didn't feel comfortable with Alice being there, but there was nothing he could do about it.

Little was said at the table that night, but as we finished our hot-pot, Mam pushed away her plate and came to her feet. She looked at each of us in turn before she spoke.

"This might well be the last supper that we'll ever share together," she said. "Tomorrow night I'll be leaving the County, and I might never return."

"Nay, Mam! Don't say that," Jack begged, but she silenced him by raising her left hand.

"You'll all need to look after one another now," she said sadly. "That's what your dad and I would wish for you. But I've something to say to you, Jack. So listen well. What it says in your dad's will can't be changed, because it reflects my wishes, too. The room under the attic must belong to Tom for the rest of his life. Even if you were to die and your own son inherited, that would still be the case. I can't explain my reasons to you, Jack, because you wouldn't like what I told you. But there are a lot more things at stake than just your feelings. My last wish, before I leave, is that you fully accept what has to be done. Well, son, do you?"

Jack nodded and bowed his head. Ellie looked frightened, and I felt sorry for her.

"Right, Jack, I'm glad that's sorted out. Now bring me the keys to my room."

Jack went into the front and came back almost immediately. There were four keys in all. The three smaller ones were for the trunks inside the room. Jack placed them on the table in front of Mam, who picked them up with her left hand.

"Tom and Alice," said Mam, "both of you come with me." So saying, she turned away from the table, left the kitchen, and started to climb the stairs. She went straight up to her private room; the one she always kept locked.

Mam unlocked the door, and I followed her inside.

Her room was much as I remembered it, full of trunks, boxes, and chests. In the autumn she'd brought me up here and given me the silver chain from the largest trunk, closest to the window. Without that chain I'd now be a prisoner of Meg again or, more likely, have been fed to her sister. But what else was to be found within the three largest trunks? I was starting to feel really curious.

At that moment I glanced behind me. Alice was still standing just outside the room, a nervous, hesitant expression on her face. She was staring down at the threshold.

"Step inside and close the door behind you, Alice," Mam said softly.

When Alice stepped into the room, Mam gave her a broad smile and handed me the keys. "Here, Tom, they're yours now. Don't give them to anyone else. Not even Jack. Keep them by you at all times. This room belongs to you now."

Alice looked about wide-eyed. I knew she'd just love to start rummaging about inside those boxes, discovering all their secrets. I must admit I was feeling the same myself.

"Can I look inside the trunks now, Mam?" I asked.

"Inside you'll find the answers to a lot of things that'll have been puzzling you; things about me that I never even told your dad. My past and my future are inside those boxes. But you'll need a clear head and a sharp mind to work it all out. You've gone through a lot and you're tired and weary, so it's best to wait until I've gone, Tom. Come back late in the spring and do it then, when you're full of hope and the days are getting longer. That would be best."

I was disappointed, but I smiled and nodded. "Whatever you say, Mam," I told her.

"There's one more thing I need to tell you. This room is more than just the sum of its contents. Once locked, nothing evil can ever enter here. If you're brave and your soul is pure and good, this room is a redoubt, a fortress against the dark, better protected than even your master's house in Chipenden. Only use it when something so terrible pursues you that your very life and soul are at risk. It's your last refuge."

"Just for me, Mam?"

Mam looked at Alice and then back at me. "Alice is in here now, so yes, Alice could use it, too. That's why I brought her up here now, just to be sure. But never bring anyone else here. Not Jack, not Ellie, not even your master."

"Why, Mam?" I asked. "Why can't Mr. Gregory use it?"

I couldn't believe that the Spook couldn't use it in time of dire need.

"Because there's a price to pay for using this room. You're both young and strong and your power is waxing. You would survive. But as I told you, John Gregory's power is waning. He's like a guttering candle. To use this room would snuff out the last of his strength. And if the need ever arises, you must tell him exactly that. And tell him that I was the one who said it."

I nodded my agreement, and that was it. Alice and I were given beds for the night, but as soon as the sun rose, after a good breakfast, Mam sent us on our way to Chipenden. Jack was going to arrange for a cart to collect Mam at dusk and take her to Sunderland Point. From there she would set sail for her own land in the wake of Meg and her sister.

Mam said good-bye to Alice and asked her to go ahead and wait for me at the yard gate. With a smile Alice waved and walked away.

As we hugged each other for what I knew could be the very last time, Mam tried to say something, but the words choked in her throat and a tear trickled down her cheek.

"What is it, Mam?" I asked gently.

"I'm sorry, son," she said. "I'm trying to be strong, but it's so hard I can hardly bear it. I don't want to say anything that'll make it worse for you."

"Say it, please say whatever you need to say," I begged, tears in my own eyes now.

"It's just that time rushes by so fast and I've been so happy here. I'd stay if I could, I really would, but it's my duty to go. I was so happy with your dad. There never was a more honest, true, and affectionate man. And my happiness was complete when you and your brothers were born. I'll never know such joy again. But it's over now and I've just got to let go of the past. It's all gone so quickly that now it just seems like a short, happy dream. . . ."

"Why does it have to be like this?" I asked bitterly. "Why does life have to be so short, with all the good things passing quickly. Is it worth living at all?"

Mam looked at me sadly. "If you achieve all that I hope, then others will judge your life to have been worth living, son, even if you don't. You were born to serve the County. And that's what you've got to do."

We held each other tight one final time, and I thought my heart would surely break.

"Good-bye, my son," she whispered, and brushed her lips against my cheek.

It was too much to bear, and I set off walking at once. But after a few paces I turned to wave and saw Mam wave back from the shadows inside the doorway. When I turned again soon afterward, she'd already gone back into the kitchen.

So, with a heavy heart, I walked on to Chipenden with Alice, my mother's last kiss upon my cheek. I was still only thirteen, but I knew my childhood was already over.

WE'RE back in Chipenden now. The blue-bells are finally out, the birds are singing, and the sun's getting warmer with each passing day.

Alice has never been happier, but she's really curious about what could be in the trunks in Mam's room. I can't take her back to the farm with me because it would upset Jack and Ellie too much, but I'm planning to go next month and I've promised to tell her about everything that I find.

The Spook seems to have recovered his health fully now, and he spends hours each day walking on the fells to build up his stamina. I've never seen him leaner and tougher, but something seems to have changed inside his head. Sometimes there are long silences during lessons when he seems to forget I'm there. And he stares into space a lot, with a worried expression on his face. Despite the fact that he seems stronger than ever, he told me that he feels his time on earth is coming to an end.

There are things he wants to do before he dies. Things that he's been putting off for years. First of all, he's talking about going east to Pendle to sort out the three covens of witches there once and for all. That's thirty-nine witches in all! It sounds like a very dangerous thing to attempt, and I can't start to see how he can possibly accomplish it. But I've no choice in the matter, and I'll be following my master wherever he chooses to go. I'm still just the apprentice, and he's the Spook.

Thomas J. Ward

The Journal of
THOMAS J. WARD

GOLGOTH

Golgoth—one of the Old Gods. Name means "The Lord of Winter." Began as powerful elemental force that loved the cold, a spirit of nature that gradually grew in consciousness. Drew power from being worshipped and became willful. Stayed too long after allotted season, so winters became prolonged. Some think this helped to bring about last *Ice Age*. The *Round Loaf* (an ancient barrow high on Anglezarke Moor) became his special altar. Human blood sacrifices made at Winter Solstice (December 21) to appease him. After gorging himself on blood he'd fall into a deep, satisfied sleep and allow summer to return. Men eventually stopped worshipping him, so his power faded. Still stirs in winter so it's dangerous to get close to the Round Loaf.

Ancient deities often have dangerous supernatural powers. Whereas victims of the *Bane* (which lived in catacombs under Priestown Cathedral) suffered the *press* (could be squashed and smeared into the cobbles), victims of Golgoth suffer intense cold. They can be frozen solid in an instant, both flesh and bones becoming brittle and liable to shatter.

ANGLEZARKE

This is a big moor in the south of the County. Word comes from the *Old Tongue*, the language spoken by the first men who came to the County from lands over the sea to the west. Anglezarke is supposed to mean "Pagan Temple," but not everyone agrees. The Spook convinced though. Says it really was a big temple, open to the skies. Men worshipped the Old Gods there—particularly Golgoth.

NECROMANCERS

A *Necromancer* is a type of *Mage* (another word for a
wizard or magician). The word comes from the Greek
word *nekros*, which means "corpse."

    A spook deals with the unquiet dead as a
routine part of the job. Gives them a good talking to
and sends them on their way. Frees the dead.

    Necromancer does the opposite. Binds the dead.
Encourages them to stay trapped on earth to serve his
purposes and help him line his pockets with silver. The
bereaved will pay hard-earned money for a glimpse of
their loved ones or a brief conversation.

    So uses the dead. Either as spies or by preying
on vulnerable, grieving folk. Usually just a case of
trapping graveside lingerers, or those bound to their
bones because they've committed some terrible crime.
Rarely, some powerful necromancers can trap the dead
in *limbo* and stop them from reaching the light and then
summon them, at will, into the presence of the living.

Limbo comes from the Latin word *limbus*, which means the edge or fringe. Souls have to pass through it to reach the light. Some find it harder than others.

ROGUE
STONE~CHUCKERS

Stone-chuckers always evolve from *hall-knockers*, boggarts that rap on walls or doors and cause a nuisance. Often throw pots and pans around, smash cups and saucers and wake up household.

Stone-chuckers move outdoors and throw pebbles or even boulders. Usually invisible and sometimes can cause showers of stones to fall on a house for weeks. Once they kill, Spook reclassifies them as *rogue*, and they must be destroyed rather than just bound. When boggart inflicts terror upon a household, its power grows. Can store energy and this must be bled away first before boggart is dealt with.

Spook says lots of intended County church sites were changed because of boggart interference. Foundations of a church had been dug at Whittle-le-Woods. Stones for building already gathered. Overnight stones mysteriously moved to Leyland. This was done by a stone-chucker based in Whittle. Boggart wanted to keep humans away from one of its favorite places. Rather than bringing in a spook to help, the easy option was taken: church built in Leyland. Stone-chucker got its own way!

GRIMOIRES

Grimoires (sometimes spelled *Grimmores*) are tools of the dark. Ancient books full of spells and rituals. Rituals have to be followed to the letter. One mistake and death can result. Mostly written in the Old Tongue by the first men of the County. Some mages are still writing them now. Spook thinks these are not as dangerous because much of old knowledge lost. Witches have their own grimoires. Alice says that Bony Lizzie had three. Destroyed when her house burned by mob at Chipenden.

INTIMATIONS OF DEATH

This is my first notebook entry not gotten from Spook, Alice, or Spook's library. Taught to me by Mam. Strange smell when Dad was ill. Told us that he was close to death. If patient starts to recover, smell fades and goes away altogether. This is a gift I've inherited from Mam. Could be useful when trying to heal. Could try different potions and intimations could give early guide to which one's working best. As well as a seventh son of a seventh son, I'm Mam's son, too.

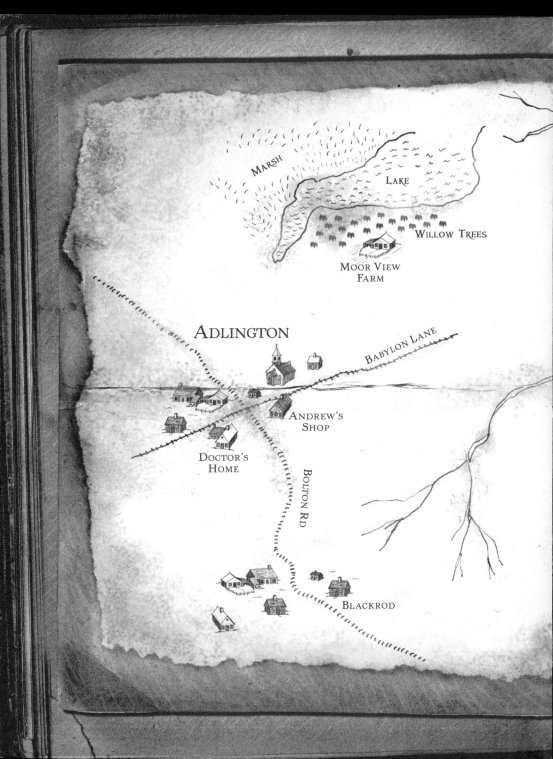

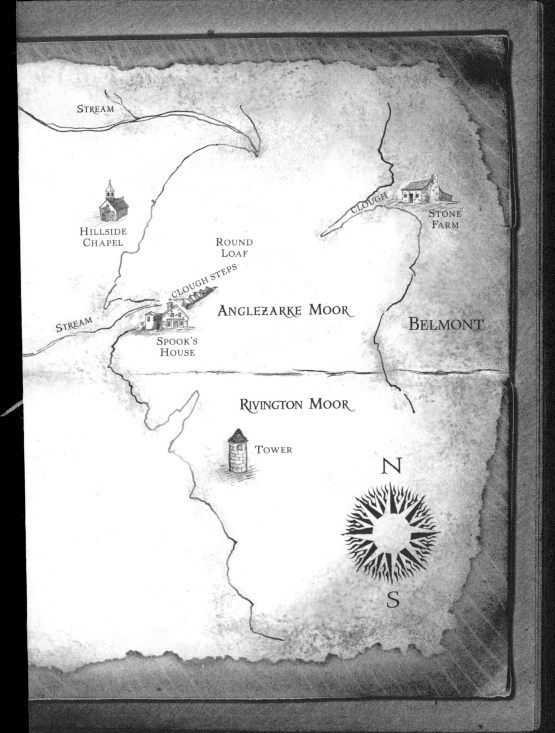

STREAM

HILLSIDE
CHAPEL

ROUND
LOAF

CLOUGH

STONE
FARM

CLOUGH STEPS

STREAM

ANGLEZARKE MOOR

BELMONT

SPOOK'S
HOUSE

RIVINGTON MOOR

TOWER

N

S

Bill Arkwright
Arthur Bleasdale
Billy Br...
Luddock
Stanley Grange
Davy Greenside
Matthew Dempster
Alan Cottam
Dick Carr
Tom
Mark Caster
Paul Wood
Daniel Stone
Graham Cain
Bob Crosby
James Fowler
George Eccles
Jack Farington
Peter Colne
Steven Shaw
Jack Kirk
Henry Burrows
THOMAS WARD
Luke Scorton
Andy Cuerden
Simon Wardick
Judd Brinscal
Paul Preston
Bob Locks
Mark Leland
Peter Dilworth